I0694021

"Just as baby boomers love nostalgia and trivia, they will love *Death in Nostalgia City*. It's a twisty mystery set in a retro theme park in the Arizona desert. The fast-paced story travels to Boston and back as we meet a diverse blend of intriguing characters. Reading this theme park thriller is more fun than winning a trivia contest and riding your favorite wooden coaster on the same day!"

~ *WILSON CASEY,*
SYNDICATED COLUMNIST AND GUINNESS WORLD
RECORD TRIVIA GUY

"Bacon is an excellent storyteller…readers won't be able to put this book down."

~ *KAREN HANCOCK,*
SUSPENSE/THRILLER EDITOR, BELLA ONLINE

Desert Kill Switch

"…straight out of classical detective fiction…told at a fun, engine-revving pace."

~ *ELLERY QUEEN MYSTERY MAGAZINE*

"This is the kind of book where you keep saying 'just one more chapter.'"

~ *ANNE SALLER,*
OWNER, BOOK CARNIVAL MYSTERY BOOKSTORE,
ORANGE, CALIF.

"Mark. S. Bacon serves us a compelling second helping of mystery and mayhem in and around the fictional 1970's theme park, Nostalgia City. The fast-paced plotline is both creative and timely. I'm looking forward to the next installment!"

"Bacon's prose is slick, his dialogue taut, and he makes great use of short chapters to tempt the reader to keep turning those pages. His creation of Nostalgia City, a retro theme park in which nothing older than the 1970s is allowed, is a stroke of genius."

"*Desert Kill Switch* weaves a fascinating mystery around murder, a missing body and a beautiful woman racing against time to clear her name. Antique cars and the threat of death in the desert combine to give readers a thrilling ride."

The Marijuana Murders

"A death at the garage complex of Nostalgia City, an Arizona theme park that simulates an American town in the year 1975, propels Bacon's charming third Nostalgia City mystery (after *Desert Kill Switch*)…readers looking for escapist reading will be satisfied."

~ PUBLISHERS WEEKLY

"Bacon deftly blends nostalgia and crime. If you're looking for a mystery that touches on today's issues while harking back to earlier eras, *The Marijuana Murders* does so in a fast pace with humor and style."

~ DEBBI MACK,
NEW YORK TIMES BESTSELLING AUTHOR OF THE SAM
MCRAE MYSTERY SERIES

"Through finely developed characters and interesting plot twists, this murder mystery, set at Nostalgia City, thoroughly entertains!"

~ BARRY SCOTT,
NATIONALLY SYNDICATED OLDIES DJ

"*The Marijuana Murders* is riddled with action and suspense. It will keep you hooked and make you want more."

~ NANCY ALLEN
THE AVID READER.COM

Dark Ride Deception

"A good mystery can always draw me in and completely captivate me. On top of an expertly crafted mystery, Bacon explores deep into many characters' lives which adds multiple layers to the story."

~ NOVEL NEWS NETWORK

"Two mystery plots tantalize and interweave as chapters and sections alternate.

His previous books in the series give a confidence to the characters and pacing. *Dark Ride Deception* is a mystery thrill ride."

~ KINGS RIVER LIFE

"Bacon's well-told mystery is clever, smooth, and intriguing, with a reluctant detective who has just the right touch of self-deprecating humor. The author's wry wit and engaging voice will keep you turning the pages of *Dark Ride Deception* until the very last satisfying twist."

~ MARY ADLER,
AUTHOR OF THE OLIVER WRIGHT WWII MYSTERY SERIES

"I don't think I was quite prepared to become so addicted and consumed by this story. The writing was smart and witty.... I found the plot to be filled with mystery, drama, and much more."

~ THE INDIE EXPRESS

THE WOKE AND THE DEAD

A NOSTALGIA CITY MYSTERY #5

MARK S. BACON

ARCHER & CLARK PUBLISHING

THE WOKE AND THE DEAD

CHAPTER 1

March 31

The man's T-shirt said, "I'm proud of my—" but the coagulated blood across his torso obliterated the rest of the slogan like the three bullets had obliterated him.

Lyle felt a familiar tightness in his stomach. He took a deep breath and stepped away from the body. He scanned the Nostalgia City parking lot as he reached for his phone. Regulations forbade employees from using cell phones in the park, but he often carried his. Just in case.

Judging by the condition of the victim, the man had been shot some time ago, and whoever did it was not hanging around. Instead of 9-1-1, he dialed the theme park's security office. They had a direct line to the sheriff.

"Howard, it's Lyle. What's the chief of security doing answering the phone?"

"The weekend bash used up overtime. What d' you need?"

"Sheriff's deputies, medical examiner, Rey Martinez if he's on duty, and of course, you. If you can spare yourself." He looked west and shaded his eyes from the sun setting like a slow-motion fireball falling into central Arizona's high desert. "I found a body. Guy's been shot three times."

"Where are you?"

"I'm in the southeast corner of employee lot C. Parking is pretty thinned out. You'll see my car. The body is propped up against one of the low Nostalgia City signs."

Within minutes, Lyle heard the wail of a siren and saw flashing lights. A Nostalgia City security car screeched to a stop. Close behind came a San Navarro County Sheriff's cruiser.

Howard got out of his car and headed toward the body. "What have you been doing, Lyle?"

"Helping our guests enjoy themselves. I was too late for this one."

"You just find the body?"

"Right before I called you."

A young sheriff's deputy walked up, creating a trio standing around staring at the body. The man on the ground might have been resting against the sign, but his fixed stare never altered. The deputy leaned over and felt the man's neck for a pulse. Lyle hadn't checked. His years of experience told him the man before him was beyond help. He chastised himself regardless, remembering a pathologist telling him once he'd received a body that was "not quite dead."

"So you found him?" the deputy asked needlessly.

"I'm Lyle Deming. I drive a cab in the park. I'm sure you know Howard."

"I've seen you around," the deputy said glancing at the security chief.

The deputy moved to touch the dead man's shoulder.

"We should step back," Howard said. "Rey is going to want to set up a perimeter."

Almost on cue, another sheriff's black and white arrived, and San Navarro County Sheriff Jeb Wisniewski stepped out. He wore a tan uniform, his gun belt constraining his slightly bulging gut, his cowboy hat in hand. His long, shiny black hair tied in a ponytail glinted in the sun and hinted at his Native American roots. "Deputy," he growled, "get this area taped off." He motioned with his hat at light poles and sign posts. "String it here and here."

The deputy hustled back to his car, and Wisniewski turned his attention to Lyle. "Deming, what the hell you doing here with a body? Seems like every time there's trouble, you show up." He rested his hat on the back of his head. "Or maybe vice versa."

"Take my word sheriff, I'd rather be anywhere else in the park right now."

Nostalgia City theme park sprawled over many square miles. Streets of Centerville, a meticulous re-creation of an entire small town from the 1970s, crisscrossed what was once open desert. The creation of former Vegas casino owner, Archibald "Max" Maxwell, the park contained the '70s town, plus a cluster of retro hotels, high-tech rides in the Fun Zone—a theme park itself—a golf course, and many other amenities. For Lyle, the park represented his taxi's territory and very much an escape.

"Whatcha doing here, sheriff?" Lyle said. "We expected Rey."

"S'matter, you don't like my company? Your buddy the undersheriff is taking a day off. You'll just have to deal with me." The sheriff offered what passed for a smile then moved his hand in the air as if to wave away any levity. "So what d' we got? How long's the body been here?"

"I dunno sheriff," Lyle said, "I found him like this fifteen to twenty minutes ago."

"Then Lyle called me," Howard said. "The first we'd heard of a body."

As the deputy started stringing yellow tape, the sheriff examined the body and looked at what appeared to be scrape marks in the parking lot dust.

"I noticed that too, sheriff," Lyle said.

"We'll wait until the techs arrive, but I can tell you he wasn't shot here. There's no blood pooled on the ground, and look at the wrinkled pattern of the dried blood. Looks like there could be dust on it, too. That sign behind him would've been broken if at least one of the bullets exited. You didn't pick up any brass, did you?"

Lyle shook his head.

The sheriff bent over, and using a folded portion of a rubber glove, held the victim's right pant cuff and raised his leg exposing dirty and torn fabric on the underside.

"If there was more than one perp," the sheriff said, "he didn't help carry the body. It's been dragged over rough ground."

Lyle pointed to the slogan on the victim's bloody T-shirt. "I wonder what he was proud of."

CHAPTER 2

Kate Sorensen smiled down at her petite friend and Nostalgia City colleague. From her perch on the bar stool, Kate towered over Drenda, but then, barstool or not, at six feet, two and one half inches, Kate towered over many people. "Have a seat. Sauv blanc?"

"I think I'll indulge in a red," Drenda said to the bartender. "Why are you working on Sunday?"

Kate nursed a glass of wine, wondering how she, the queen of special events, could have been caught by surprise.

"I needed to find out more about our unexpected, unofficial celebration today," Kate said. "I wandered the grounds this afternoon, talking to visitors, trying to sort it out. Then I picked up preliminary sales figures."

"And this is your reward?" Drenda said, nodding toward Kate's half empty wine glass.

Kate smiled and lifted her glass in a toast.

Kate and Dr. Drenda Adair constituted the female members of senior management at Nostalgia City.

Maxwell, Drenda's uncle, picked up the idea for the park from an academic paper Drenda wrote when she taught university history. Her paper hypothesized how a small town frozen in time might be an interesting setting for empirical research. Maxwell thought a retro small town might be an interesting setting for making lots of money.

Initially, Maxwell aimed to attract well-heeled seniors but found that his living time machine attracted all ages, provided they could afford it. Drenda became senior VP of 1960s and '70s history and culture, the subject she studied for her PhD.

After the park had been open about six months, he hired Kate, who'd directed public relations for his Vegas hotel, to handle the park's publicity and promotion.

The thirtyish former academic and the fortyish PR director sat at the shiny metal bar in the Boogie Lounge. Open to the public, the tiny, out-of-the-way watering hole was frequented mostly by park employees. Regardless, the lounge was still precisely '70s from the chrome, Naugahyde-upholstered stools to the color, 25-inch, picture-tube TV behind the bar.

Drenda draped her suit coat over the back of her seat and took a sip of her merlot. "So our informal 'gay day at the park' was a success?"

"Yes, a few thousand more guests than average, and hotel bookings were up. Not bad for an almost spontaneous event. I think it happened on short notice—in part—through social media. Took us by surprise."

"How did it get started?"

"Someone in Kingman posted an idea online several

weeks ago, suggesting an LGBTQ day at the park. No date was mentioned and few people responded. We didn't notice follow-up posts on different sites until the middle of the week. According to people I talked to today, texts and old-fashioned phone calls created part of the energy for this."

"You didn't do any promotion?"

"No. I wish I'd thought of the event." Kate tucked strands of her long blonde hair behind one ear. "But planning a park-wide event, even a small one, takes weeks, or more likely months. I think what I would have done—"

Kate paused and she and Drenda looked up as the lounge door opened to admit a middle-aged man in a suit. Kate recognized him as a park employee, so they relaxed. She smiled at the man who took a seat several stools down the bar. She and Drenda were *incognito*, their euphemism for not wearing their name badges, required of all staff when on park grounds.

"So, what's *your* excuse for being here on the weekend?" Kate said.

"I was brainstorming a new history display. It's a welcome break from my usual job as authenticity police telling concessionaires they can't talk on their cell phones or have signs asking customers to give them five stars on Yelp."

"You really need an assistant to handle that."

"You mean *additional* assistants. The park has a lot of transgressors."

Kate stretched her legs to be comfortable. She wore a navy rayon midi skirt and blouse. "So, what's the new display?"

"I would like to expand our history exhibit in the Plaza. The park is primarily history *hardware*. I'd like to explore more of the socio-cultural norms of the 1970s."

"But Max —"

"I know. Max would say—"she frowned, bringing her eyebrows together and adopting an artificially gruff voice—"socio-cultural norms don't bring in paying guests." She smiled. "But I think a focus on these—if not with a new exhibit right away—at least an integration into our staff training programs, would add depth to Nostalgia City's verisimilitude.

"I'm talking about things like women's rights, gay rights, Earth Day. You'd be surprised at the things that happened in 1970 alone. I know Lyle does classes. He could mention a few of these movements."

"He volunteers at the Training Department once in a while. For fun. He enjoys telling the young new hires about the 'good old days,' even though he was just a child back then."

"We could see what he thinks about it. It has to start somewhere. By the way, where *is* Lyle today?"

"His daughter is staying with him this weekend. I'm on my own."

Kate sipped her wine and looked up at the live TV news. Drenda grimaced. Drenda saw to it that park-controlled television consisted of rebroadcasts of 1970s news shows along with westerns, sitcoms, and movies from the period.

"I know," Kate said, "live TV is strictly forbidden. But there's no guests in here now and the bartender is new."

Television sound was low, but it was quiet in the bar. The TV scene showed a field reporter interviewing Arizona Governor Rod Gudgel, a candidate for re-election. His shirt sleeves rolled up, the lanky governor wiped perspiration from his partially bald head and leaned over with a serious expression as he listened to a reporter's question.

"Governor, your proposed legislation about school libraries has been criticized as a form of censorship."

"Jennifer, a concerned mother from Casa Grande actually started the impetus for this bill. She contacted my office when she found books discussing sexual orientation and gender identity in her children's school library. Some of them mentioned perversion of the worst kind. So you see," he leaned over even farther and deep lines appeared in his forehead, "what we're doing is protecting our children. And it's the right thing to do." He made a chopping motion with his left hand.

"Governor, do you think—"

"I've heard enough," Drenda said. "I'm going to tell the bartender to cut the live news and stick with the '70s. Gudgel's an idiot."

CHAPTER 3

April 1

"Time to wake up," a voice said Monday morning. "You're supposed to make waffles."

"Okay, okay," Lyle said. "What about coffee?"

"It's already dripping."

Lyle looked up at Samantha, the young brunette who stood next to his bed already dressed, hair brushed, an impatient expression on her face. "Give me a few minutes," he said. "I need to grab the paper."

"You still getting a printed paper?"

"I know, old-fashioned. This morning I'm looking for something in particular." He sat up on the edge of his bed and ran a hand across his eyes and down his face as if to wipe away the day before. "You got in late last night. After twelve wasn't it, when I heard you come in?"

"I had dinner with Olivia and other friends at her hotel. Then a bunch of us went out clubbing."

"But—"

"It's all right. We were safe. There were several of us. I was never alone, like you taught me."

Lyle adored Sam. She was barely five when he and her mother married. Sam's biological father moved away and saw her less and less. Lyle legally adopted her and helped support her financially and emotionally as she grew up. After her mother left him a few years ago, Lyle remained Sam's backstop.

When she kissed him and called him *Lyle,* not *dad,* in public, he worried people might think this guy in his fifties was a cradle robber, or worse.

"Okay, so get in the kitchen," Lyle said, "and get me a cup of coffee, please."

Lyle ran an electric razor over his face, pulled a brush through his brown hair, and stumbled out the front door of his condo looking for the newspaper. He lived in Timeless Village, a collection of apartments, houses, and townhomes populated mostly by employees of adjacent Nostalgia City.

The condo's landscaped grounds, covered with sand-like decomposed granite, included yucca, mesquite, broom, and other drought-tolerant native plants. Having grown up in the Phoenix area, Lyle learned to appreciate the beauty of the desert flora and fauna. Living things could adapt to an environment many people accurately considered harsh and unforgiving. Lyle had his own ways of adapting to life.

He spotted the newspaper in the seven a.m. shadow of a tall, spiny ocotillo. The local paper from the nearby small town of Polk, the San Navarro County seat, would certainly have a story about the murder.

In the kitchen, Sam had already set the table. She handed her stepfather coffee in his favorite mug.

"Is Olivia coming by this morning?" he asked.

"No, she planned to drive back to the university with Megan. You're off work today. I thought we were going to hang out or go shopping." She gave him a hug, almost spilling his coffee.

Sam was completing her B.S. at Arizona State University in the Phoenix suburb of Tempe and planned to go on to grad school. She'd made the two-hour drive north to Nostalgia City to visit the theme park with friends—and visit Lyle. He didn't know which was her trip's priority, but he was grateful to see her for however long, whatever the reason. She made him smile like no one else.

"So where's the waffle iron?" she asked.

A sudden blast of music from her phone interrupted her. She reached for it.

"Hey, Olivia what's—oh no. Oh my God, how? Uh huh. Okay, of course. We can find it. We'll pick you up at your hotel. You don't have to drive. We'll be right there."

She turned to Lyle.

"Olivia's father died. He lives in Flagstaff. He came down here this weekend to see her. The sheriff wants her to go into Polk and identify him. We have to help her. I told her we'd drive. You probably know where to go. Drive us?"

Sam took emotional jolts with an equanimity Lyle admired. He had a feeling he'd seen Olivia's father the afternoon before, but hoped he was wrong. Maybe it was a heart attack. "Sure love. Let's go. Give me a minute."

Lyle pulled his Mustang up to Olivia's hotel. She stood out front wearing faded jeans and a multi-colored, loose-fitting blouse. She tugged at her lower lip with a thumb and index finger. Sam stepped out of Lyle's convertible and threw her arms around her friend. She held fast for several moments.

"I can't believe it's true. It must be a mistake," Olivia said over and over on the short drive. "I tried calling him, but there was no answer." She alternated between periods of silence and random babbling until they reached Stephens Mortuary which served as Polk's morgue.

Lyle knew Tiffany Smith, the detective who met them at the reception area. He introduced her to Sam and Olivia.

"Are you ready to make the identification?" Smith asked looking at Olivia's blank stare.

Lyle guessed she was in shock, or would be after she identified the body. He wasn't sure he wanted Sam to walk into the room too, but she just glanced at Lyle as she put her arm around her friend and headed down the hallway with the detective on Olivia's other side.

Lyle thought he knew what the victim looked like. If he was right, it was fortunate for Olivia that all his wounds were in his torso, his face unaffected. He loitered for a moment glancing at his watch. A middle-aged man Lyle took for a funeral director strolled past him in the hall. His dark suit—expected—contrasted with a pastel shirt and paisley tie.

"Excuse me," Lyle said. "Is Mr. Lightfoot—"he remembered Olivia's last name—"down the hall, the one who was shot yesterday?"

The funeral director stood staring at Lyle, not a strand of his wavy gray hair out of place.

"I'm Lyle Deming. I work at Nostalgia City and my daughter Samantha is a friend of Olivia, the victim's daughter."

"You found the body, didn't you?" the man said taking a step toward him.

Lyle nodded.

"I remember you. We met once. You're the ex-Phoenix homicide cop aren't you?"

Lyle nodded again remembering Dick Stephens from another death he attended while at Nostalgia City. Years of overarching anxiety and a run-in with two senior officers for whom Lyle would not falsify evidence had led him to willingly leave the police department that labeled him a nut case. He *thought* driving a cab in a theme park would be an ideal escape from the grinding stress of homicide, its victims, and left-behinds. Stress, as his PD-mandated therapist had often reminded him, is internal, not external.

"Yes," Stephens said, "that's the gentleman who was brought in yesterday evening. He was shot several times, but you probably noticed that."

After a few moments the three women returned down the hall, this time at a slower pace. Sam kept a supporting arm around her friend who looked at the floor while she turned the cell phone in her hand over and over.

Lyle wanted to say something to Olivia but fought the habit of saying "sorry for your loss." Instead, he squeezed her shoulder as he glanced at detective Smith.

"Miss Lightfoot, may we talk for a few minutes,"

Smith said. "We have some questions we have to ask. I'm sorry. We can use a room here or sit in the patio in front of our offices. The sheriff's station is just down the block. Your friend can come."

Samantha made eye contact with Lyle then followed her friend and the detective out the door toward the sheriff's department.

Lyle started to follow them, thinking he might talk with his friend Rey Martinez, then he stopped with his hand on the door. He turned around and looked for Stephens.

"Excuse me," Lyle said sticking his head through Stephens's open office doorway. "Can you tell me what Lightfoot's T-shirt said? It was covered in so much blood at the scene I couldn't make it out."

The funeral director looked up. "It was difficult, but I *was* able to read it. The T-shirt said, *I'm proud of my wiseass lesbian daughter.*"

CHAPTER 4

Lyle knew the way to Rey's office. The officer at the front desk smiled as Lyle took a left down the hallway. Rey, on hands and knees in front of a credenza drawer, complained to himself aloud as Lyle walked in.

"Don't worry Rey," Lyle said. "The shrink told me talking to yourself is perfectly normal."

"Ever since we remodeled the offices, I can't find a damn thing around here." The tall undersheriff stood. He wore his tan uniform and blue tie that morning. His gun belt hung on a hook behind his desk.

"Need help?"

"No," Rey said pulling out a slender file, "I think I found it. And wait a minute. *You* talk to yourself all the time. Of course you're going to say it's normal."

"You know, most therapists can't tell you what quote—normal—unquote is. They can just tell you what's *ab*normal."

"Besides giving me a psychology lesson, did you come here for a reason?"

Although they had known each other a relatively short time—since Lyle started at the park—their close friendship was shaped by their responses to a pair of potentially deadly crimes they resolved together, each covering the other's back. Reluctantly, Lyle had accepted a couple of Nostalgia City-related "assignments" from Maxwell in the past that had nothing to do with his taxicab.

Without being asked, Lyle settled into the most comfortable of Rey's guest chairs.

"The Lightfoot murder," Lyle said.

"Yeah, they told me you found the body."

"Why does this happen to me?"

Rey glared. "Correction. *Lightfoot* was *la víctima inocente*."

Usually, Rey used Spanish only when he was joking or mad about something. Lyle knew which occasion this was.

"Time out." Lyle held up his hands forming a T sign. "I *know* he was the victim. The guy's daughter is a friend of Sam's. We just brought her down here to make the ID. Tiffany's interviewing her now."

"Sorry, I didn't know." Rey sat down at his desk. "The sheriff chewed me out this morning over the killing."

"Chewed *you* out? You had the day off. It was Sunday."

"That was part of his problem."

"He gets riled about a murder," Lyle said. "Everyone does. But he seemed like his every-day cranky self yesterday, giving orders and securing the crime scene."

"That was before he knew about the event."

"Event?"

"You had a Gay Pride thing going on."

"News to me. I did see a few same-sex couples—they

were good tippers—but for special events we have banners, advertising. All the staff knows about it."

"Well, whatever you call it, it's the type of event you're supposed to alert us to." Rey clasped his hands on his desk and aimed an index finger at Lyle. "We look at the plans and make decisions about deploying deputies and staff."

"So the sheriff is mad at the *park*?"

"Generally everyone I guess. He's calling Max or your security, or both."

"Considering what the victim wore," Lyle said, "it's possible there's a connection to the pride thing."

"You saw the T-shirt."

Lyle shifted in his chair. He'd dressed so quickly that morning he'd pulled on jeans and a wrinkled Hawaiian shirt. But then that's what he usually wore when he wasn't working. "Yeah, I saw it at the scene, but it was covered in blood. I couldn't read it. Dick Stephens told me what it said."

"Dick told you that? I wish he'd keep quiet. We wanted to withhold that information from the public. I wonder who else knows—besides the shooter."

Lyle uncrossed his legs and leaned forward. "Sam and I were going to have a rare father-daughter day today after she and her friends did the park yesterday."

"A pity."

"All around. Hard to tell how the daughter is reacting. Her name's Olivia. I feel sorry for the kid. Can you tell me anything about her father?"

"We don't know much yet, that's why Tiff is talking to her." Rey tapped computer keys and looked at his screen. "He's co-owner of a Flagstaff catering company.

His business was closed yesterday, and we couldn't contact his wife. Luckily we found a number for his daughter and reached her this morning."

"I wonder if he was a guest at the park."

"Looks like. He had an NC receipt in his pocket," Rey said using the abbreviation for Nostalgia City common with employees and locals. "He bought meals, too."

"Presumably he was visiting his daughter like Sam was visiting me. Olivia goes to the university with Sam. She's a graduating senior, too."

"Is Sam going to want you to stick your nose in this?"

"I don't think she'd ask. She knows your department is thorough. She knows I'm never eager to become a cop again."

"We're damn well gonna be thorough," Rey said. "So, Lyle, is Sam—"

"Gay? No, but she doesn't let that or race or anything influence her choice of friends. What difference would it make if she *were* gay?"

"None. I admire her outlook."

"Me too. Now about Lightfoot. Do we know when he was shot?"

"I thought you didn't want to do cop stuff."

"I don't. Never mind."

"Without an autopsy report I can't tell you anyway. Should get something soon. Our contract ME is supposed to do the postmortem later today or maybe tomorrow."

"Shit, I don't envy you," Lyle said, "especially since the body was dumped and you don't have any evidence from the original crime scene."

"Unless we find it," Rey said.

CHAPTER 5

Although an unknown number of years into his seventh decade on earth, Archibald Maxwell had as much energy as anyone Kate had ever worked for. She and a few members of senior staff had been summoned to his conference room and waited for him to begin. Kate sat next to Howard Chaffee, chief of security, and glanced at the 1970s movie posters that lined the walls. A steely eyed Clint Eastwood glared down from a *Dirty Harry* poster. She did not feel lucky today. Max's sour expression told her he was ready to detonate.

"No matter what we think," he said, "what the sheriff or employees think, the murder is ours. Don't know how it happened, but it ended up on our doorstep."

"Isn't that a little premature?" asked Howard.

"Premature, Howard?" Maxwell took off his glasses and rubbed his eyes with his right hand. "Not our fault, but our murder. He was a guest, apparently killed after he left the park, maybe in our parking lot."

Howard slowly shook his head.

"Okay, we don't know *where* it happened, but it's a fact, and some media are calling it the Nostalgia City murder. Howard, I know you're working with the sheriff. Need to do this. And now it's in the news and being speculated as a hate crime. I want us to be able to respond to the media. The responsible media, not tabloid TV." The sour expression briefly returned to his lined face.

"Let's take this challenge, this murder, one step at a time," he said. "First, Kate, Gabriel, why didn't we *know* we were having a special event?"

"I knew nothing about it," said Gabriel Kovács waving both hands above the table. The voluble director of entertainment traveled in show biz circles, A-list and B-list, to arrange performances, celebrity appearances, and continuing park shows.

"Are you kidding me?" Kovács said. "If I'd known, I certainly wouldn't have okayed booking Danny and the Shifters, Chloe Fargo, and—oh my gawd—barbershop quartet finals. Really? But, you know Mr. Maxwell, we have to think of our key audience. I mean seniors are our bread and butter—whether they're gay or straight."

"So your staff didn't book any LGBT—ah—Q entertainers?"

"What, do we ask them if they're gay or not? We get talent who are good entertainers. People suited to our audience. You know—"

"Kate," Max said quieting the entertainment chief, "what's your take on this?"

"It just happens occasionally. A group decides to come to the park together. Sometimes it's employee groups. And without advance notice, it's a surprise. Larger groups let us know ahead of time. They want to get group rates." Kate pulled her phone from the pocket of her blue blazer and glanced at a note on the screen. "I talked with Germaine in sales, and she said no LGBTQ organization bought group tickets." She noticed Max's intense stare, but she continued unintimidated. "No one even enquired about a group rate for a Gay Pride event."

Kate had worked for Max long enough to know when the billionaire pointed his hawk nose and intense green eyes at you, it just meant you had his full attention.

"But Max, I *did* see our name come up on a few LGBTQ online posts—most of them within the last few days. We monitor social media—as you know. Our name obviously comes up on the internet hundreds of times a day—thousands."

"I'd say even more," Kovács said. "I bet a hundred thousand people posted after we announced Glenn Gura's concert here."

"Could be," Kate said. "We scan for posts telling us which attractions people like and keep an eye out for complaints. We have a lot to look at and analyze. Obviously we didn't attach enough importance to this."

"It slipped by," Max said. "Already done, isn't it? Maybe we can learn from it."

Kate looked down at the tablet computer she'd brought and knew there was more to come. Lyle had told her what he knew about the case. She was prepared to advise Max. As prepared as she could be.

"The sheriff called me today," Max said. "I was in a meeting. I guess he got through to you, Howard."

"As a matter of fact, yes. Sheriff Wisniewski was a

little bent out of shape because we *didn't* alert him to the event we *didn't* know was going to happen."

Max put his arms on the table and nodded slightly.

"We had higher than average attendance," Howard said. "I called in a few more staff. Other than that, a normal day. The crowd was well behaved. We had the usual drunk or stoned teenagers, but that's it. I don't know what we could have done differently."

Howard's gray suit, close-cropped gray hair, and somber tie made him look like the former San Francisco PD commander he was. It must have been the meeting with Max that prompted the suit, Kate thought. In the two years or so he'd been at the park, they'd become friends. Howard had relaxed his everyday wardrobe in keeping with the theme-park ambience and probably to keep from looking like a cop.

"Did your job," Max said. "Not looking to blame. What's the latest with the investigation?"

"We're helping them trace Lightfoot's movements in the park until he left," Howard said. "Detectives are in our Control Center now going over video. We found the victim on our surveillance footage and have a pretty good record of what he did here. We know when he left. That will help pin down the time of death.

"All in all, with Lyle Deming's report on finding the body, we've given the sheriff everything he's asked for—maybe a little more."

"Are they calling it a hate crime?" Max asked.

"It's looking that way," Kate said. "You've all seen the news story about Lightfoot's company catering same-sex weddings."

"And the victim wore a T-shirt that said he was proud of his lesbian daughter," Howard said.

"Where'd you get that?" Kate blurted. Lyle had told her about the shirt slogan, but she'd kept the confidence.

"I heard it on the radio this morning," he said.

"Hate crime," Max mumbled. He slid back his chair, got up, and wandered to one of the floor-to-ceiling windows. Staring out, he said something Kate couldn't hear. Then he turned. "Thank you all. Howard please keep me posted on developments. I'd like to hear from you *before* I see it on TV, OK? Kate, stick around for a moment will you?"

When the others left, Max stood next to Kate at the table.

"So, you heard the governor's comments?" she said.

"Just a sound bite. I think it's shit. What's his problem?"

"I wish I knew. I brought clips from the interview. Here, sit."

She flipped open her tablet case and turned it on as Max sat down next to her.

"The governor," Kate said, "gave a stump speech in Tucson earlier today. Afterwards, reporters asked about the shooting here."

Kate clicked on the video, and the narrow face of the governor appeared. Gudgel stood behind a lectern decorated with campaign signs. His eyes became slits as he looked into the camera. He either had vision problems or his natural expression was a squint. His shirt sleeves were rolled up almost to his elbow.

"What do I think about the shooting?" the governor

told a reporter. "I think there's been too much overreaction. Your paper is calling it a hate crime. It looked just like a random shooting. Every murder or assault isn't a hate crime. The woke media are making too much out of this. Just a random shooting," he said drawing out the last four words. "A woke response is irrelevant. There's far too much of that. Woke is not welcome in Arizona."

He stood straight and tall on a platform flanked by stern-faced men in camouflage uniforms.

"But governor," said another reporter, "the victim, Mr. Lightfoot, catered gay weddings, and the shooting happened at an LGBTQ gathering at Nostalgia City."

"I know." Gudgel leaned back from the podium and paused to offer an expression between a thin-lipped smile and a sneer before he continued. "I was surprised. I didn't think they wanted to attract those kinds of people at the amusement park.

"They probably came from California and spent a lot of money. That amusement park is incredibly expensive." He slapped a hand on top of the lectern as if he'd concluded the whole issue, then added, "Maybe the shooter was from California, too."

Max grunted as he pushed himself away from the table and stood up. "That bastard. He castigates *woke* all the time. Makes it a dirty word. *That's* going to get him votes? We're *woke* if we recognize a hate crime for what it is? Yet our governor dismisses it as an everyday shooting, talks about *those people,* and wants to ban discussion of gender in schools. What's the opposite of woke, bigotry? And why in hell does he need a military guard? Looks like a dictator."

Kate had rarely seen her boss as heated. He stalked the length of the room. "We have to respond."

"That's why I'm here." Minimizing the death of a loving father without mention of his family, denigrating gay Americans, and slamming one of the largest employers in the state? Damned right he deserved a response.

"You want me to release a statement about the shooting? You want to challenge the governor's comments, express sympathy for Lightfoot's family?"

"Want you to get me an interview. I'd like to tell the governor he's a reckless son of—"

"Now Max." Kate pressed a hand to the table.

"Last year," he said, "a woman in Los Angeles was murdered just because she had a rainbow flag outside her store. She wasn't even gay. The killer shouted insults, then fired."

"Okay Max. I understand. But what would it get us if the media quoted you swearing at the governor? Gudgel's comments are so snide and insensitive people will understand the kind of person he is. And you know how you can get when you talk with the media. You don't want to start something."

"But Kate."

"I agree with you, but let's consider this before we respond. Why don't I draft a statement from you that is supportive of the family, calm, and reasonable?"

CHAPTER 6

"Can I interest you in fish in the air fryer? You look hungry," Lyle said as he and Kate sat on stools at his condo's kitchen counter.

"That sounds fine. I burned up a lot of energy with Max today."

Did she look tired? He got up. "Let me get dinner started and you can tell me all about it."

"What time did Sam leave?" Kate asked. "Must've been tough for her. She's a good kid. I'm sure she helped her friend deal with it all."

"Sam left about an hour ago. Look at this, she even cleaned up the kitchen. She *is* a great kid. I was looking forward to having her here for the weekend, but of course—" Lyle glanced at the rubber band on his wrist, one of his anxiety crutches. Pluck it and the sting breaks the chain of negative, self-defeating thoughts and brings you back to the present. But he didn't need it now. Just thinking, not stewing.

Kate stepped off the bar stool, pulled off her suit coat,

and plopped it on the back of a family room chair. She pulled one of the artistic knots out of her hair and let a blonde wave flow down her shoulders.

Lyle paused to take in her curves. She reminded him of a taller, younger Julia Roberts with her slender nose, wide smile and, well, everything. She'd stayed at her apartment while Sam visited so he could have as much father-daughter time as possible. He and Kate spent most nights at either his condo or her apartment.

Slipping off her shoes, Kate padded back to the kitchen bar. "You should have seen Max today. You know how stirred up he gets sometimes. But *today*."

"More than normal?"

"Did you hear Governor Gudgel's comments about the shooting?"

"Do I want to know?"

"He was interviewed after a speech in Tucson and said he didn't think the shooting here was a hate crime. He made a disgusting remark about the people at the LGBTQ event. And he even called NC an *amusement* park."

"Maybe he didn't know about the catering company or Lightfoot's daughter."

"He knew. That's what made Max so mad. I'm mad, too, but Max was volatile."

"Good for him. Max is becoming more empathetic in his old age. Or maybe we're getting a glimpse beyond his crusty exterior."

Kate stared blankly for a moment. "He wanted me to get him an interview so he could call the governor a son of a bitch."

"You talked him out of it?"

"I did. I wrote a statement we released from the office of the NC CEO."

Lyle stirred a saucepan of noodles on the stove while looking over his shoulder at the timer on the air fryer.

"What I wrote," Kate said, "is that the park is designed for families. Not just certain families the governor seems to recognize by sexual orientation, race, or other factors. I expressed sympathy for the Lightfoot family and said that Nostalgia City *theme* park has open arms for *everyone*."

"You made Max sound thoughtful, especially omitting four-letter words."

"However," she said, "he made me add that Gudgel's anti-gay school bill represents the opposite of Nostalgia City's inclusive policies and is a reversion to the ignorance of the past."

"Take that, Rod Gudgel."

"I agree with Max," Kate said, "and that's how it went out. I wonder if he has a close gay friend or relative?"

Lyle spun around, pulled something out of the microwave, and turned off the fryer while Kate grabbed plates and utensils and set them on the counter.

"I could ask Drenda, see how well she knows her uncle."

"Why don't we put it down to Max being a caring individual."

Before he started serving food, Lyle came around to the other side of the counter and slipped an arm around Kate's waist. After a long day's work, she still smelled like a woman, like Kate, like someone he wanted to devour. He put his mouth on hers for long seconds.

"It's been at least ten minutes since we did that," he said, inhaling her aroma again then heading for the stove.

Kate helped him serve up tilapia, angel hair pasta, and mixed vegetables. She pulled off a crispy corner of the fish and popped it in her mouth.

"Speaking of Drenda, she's putting together an exhibit for our history corner about the dawning of gay rights and other social movements in the '70s. She wondered if you could integrate socio-cultural events in your orientation talk. Women's rights, climate change."

"I'd be happy to. It's been quite a while since I've done one of my talks. I kind of miss them."

"That's how we met, remember?"

"Of course." He touched her shoulder. "I love it when I have to explain to the young new-hires that telephones used to have wires attached, and you made a call by spinning a dial around with your finger." He mimicked dialing a rotary phone. "A kid once asked me, 'Is that why they say *dial* a number?'

"I tell them that back in the NC years you did research using an encyclopedia."

"Do they know what that is?"

"If they don't, I tell them to look it up in Google."

"Google it?"

Lyle frowned.

"I know you majored in English, and turning nouns into verbs upsets you."

"Among too many other things."

"Oh," Kate said, "Did you know the information about Lightfoot's T-shirt was on the news? I didn't tell anyone at the meeting, but Howard mentioned hearing it."

"Rey will be pissed. They wanted to keep that out of the news—in case they needed to use it when questioning a suspect."

"Howard also said they used the surveillance camera system to see what Lightfoot did at the park and what time he left."

"I wanted a peek at that myself, but Sam was still here and I treasure every minute with her these days. She's going to grad school in the fall. I'm hoping it will be a local school or maybe one close by in California."

After dinner, they stood up and embraced. Even in bare feet, Kate still stood nearly three inches taller than Lyle. It made her even more alluring.

"I have to dash over to my apartment to feed Trixie, see if she's okay," she said, referring to her cat, "but I'll come back and help you with the dishes."

"Just the dishes?"

CHAPTER 7

April 2

Lyle saw Rey's cruiser parked in front of the NC security office that morning. He wanted to talk to Howard and find out details on Lightfoot's day at the park without asking Rey and having to put up with his razzing. He could hear Rey say, "I thought you said you weren't getting involved in this one."

With black ceiling fans, a watercooler, typewriters, and an assortment of desks, the security office looked like a fifty-year-old police station. It was supposed to. NC designers, and of course the park's historian, insisted on accuracy everywhere. A laptop computer might be slightly visible behind a low partition, but then guests rarely made it to the security office. And for those who did—especially involuntarily—historical authenticity was the least of their concerns.

The uniformed security officer at the front counter directed Lyle to the conference room. He knocked once and opened the door. Howard and Rey stood before a computer monitor.

"Hey," Howard said. "You looking to figure out how the body you found got there?"

"You know the answer?"

"As a matter of fact, no. But we're closer than we were when you found Lightfoot's body."

Lyle walked to the end of the room to see the computer screen. "Morning," he said to Rey, dressed in a suit rather than his uniform.

"This is the video we assembled tracking Lightfoot around the park that afternoon," Howard said, glancing at the screen.

Rey looked at Lyle. "I thought you said you weren't getting involved in this one."

"You need to practice your I-told-you-so look," Lyle said.

"No, I'm just curious," Rey said, followed by a tight-lipped smile. "Did Max talk to you about it?"

"No. And Sam didn't say anything. You can put my presence here down to idle curiosity. It's not every day a simple cabbie stumbles on a body."

"Simple?" Howard said.

"Figure of speech," Lyle said. "Let's see your pictures." He stepped toward the almost living-room-TV-size monitor, the screen divided into four video segments.

"Lightfoot's daughter said she and her friends spent the morning with her dad," Howard said. "In the bottom corner you can see Lightfoot and the young ladies going into a ride. You can read his T-shirt and see he has a camera strap over his shoulder."

Lyle looked closely and could see Sam wearing shorts and sandals walking with the group.

"Your surveillance system is amazing," Rey said. "You can follow anyone anywhere in the park."

"Thanks to an AI upgrade," Howard said. He pointed to another segment of the screen. "Nowhere do we see Lightfoot or his daughter and friends having a confrontation with anyone or having *any* kind of problem."

"You looked for somebody following him, too," Rey said. "Didn't you?"

"As far as we can tell, he wasn't followed. Of course, every time you're in line for a ride, you often get followed by the same people for a half hour or so."

"They reached the center of town shortly after noon," Howard said. "You can see them hugging and saying goodbye."

He scrolled to bring up a view of NC's downtown Centerville. Cars of 1960s and '70s vintage cruised the streets. Although rental rates were steep and guests were limited to driving only within the park's confines, one of the park's attractions was the opportunity to rent a fully restored classic car from the period.

"You can see Lightfoot getting in the back seat of this Oldsmobile," Howard said, pointing at the screen. "They drove around for a while, circled the hotel area and later went inside."

"So, who rented the car," Lyle asked.

"Pretty sharp for a simple cab driver," Rey said. "Way ahead of you though. The car was rented by a guy from Flagstaff. He's still here. He and his wife are staying at an NC hotel. Detectives talked to him. He was a friend of

Lightfoot's. Has a clean record and no motive we could find. Our guys said he was pretty shaken up."

"So, a couple of hours later," Howard said, "Lightfoot took a shuttle bus back to the Fun Zone. He took lots of pictures of rides and scenery."

"His daughter told us he was an amateur photographer," Rey said.

"After he finished these shots," said Howard, "he walked out to his car and drove off. That was about two hours before you found him."

"The detectives told me you didn't see how his body got back to the park." Rey said.

"The cameras don't extend beyond the park. That corner of the lot is far away from the nearest camera and shielded by landscaping. All we could capture was a fuzzy picture of a light-colored pickup truck. The truck passed out of view when presumably the person or persons dumped the body."

"So that gives you an idea of the time of death," Lyle said.

"And it jibes with the autopsy," said Howard.

"The sheriff thought one person might have done this because the body was dragged, not lifted." Lyle said.

Rey shrugged, then looked at Howard. "Thanks for the recap." He turned toward the door. Lyle followed.

Outside, Rey headed for his car. Lyle stepped ahead and leaned back on the car, blocking the driver's-side door. "You find Lightfoot's car?"

"Still looking."

"So, this is a hate crime, right?"

"Detectives talked to Lightfoot's family and friends.

I talked to his wife, daughter, and employees, too. The guy had a clean record, well-liked in the community. His company made money, no business disputes. He didn't owe anyone."

"What about gay weddings?"

"Yeah, his wife and business partner both said they occasionally received dirty looks or crude comments from people about gay weddings."

"So this *was* a hate crime."

"You ever get involved in hate crimes?"

"Not often."

"We call this a hate crime," Rey said, "then we have to report it to the FBI."

"Then they take jurisdiction, come in and tell you what to do, etc."

"Maybe not," Rey said. "There's so many hate crimes these days. They may come in and take a look at it, maybe not. We could ask for help."

"And of course the governor is saying it *wasn't* a hate crime."

Rey took a breath, stepped back a foot, and put his hands on his hips, pushing his coat aside exposing his 9mm. "I'm going to manage this investigation wherever it takes us. I'm dodging the damn reporters' calls about what the governor said, and is this really a hate crime? Politics is Sheriff Wisniewski's territory. He's a pretty secure elected official. Popular in the county. I'm just a hired hand. There's no upside to getting in a pissing contest with the governor."

"Right on all counts." Lyle stepped aside to let Rey leave if he wanted to. "You asked me about hate crimes

I worked on. One I remember involved a paramilitary organization. I don't think that group is around anymore, but there are lots of others, aren't there?"

"Now you're really getting your nose into the investigation. You sure you want to go there?" Rey opened his car door and sat down.

Lyle put a hand on the top of Rey's cruiser and leaned over. "You mean there are hate groups active around here?"

Rey started the engine. A frown appeared as he nodded his head.

"Then they're all yours," Lyle said.

CHAPTER 8

"That looks like an Egyptian sarcophagus," Kate said as she walked into Drenda's cluttered office.

"It's King Tut," Drenda said. "He was born in 1331 BC and became a rock star in 1978."

For Kate, every visit to the office of the senior vice president of history and culture brought surprises. Part workspace, part 1960s and '70s museum, Drenda's roomy office was made small by display cases, shelves, and tables filled with assorted period artifacts. Stacks of eight-track tapes and an Atari game console shared space with academic journals and stacks of period commercial magazines.

At a table near the door Kate looked at a series of drawings on poster board including one of the late Egyptian ruler's coffin. "What is all this?"

"One of our graphic artists put together drawings for a proposed expansion of our history exhibit to include more social issues. I'm also going to throw in tidbits from the '70s that might brighten up the exhibit a little." She pointed to the sarcophagus.

"Something for our Egyptologist guests?"

"Not exactly." She led Kate around a table laden with albums of yellow newspaper clippings and they sat at Drenda's desk.

"I don't want this to be viewed as esoteric twentieth century history. Many events in the 1970s changed our society and some are still being debated today. But working at the park taught me about making history interesting." She reached over and patted the top of one of her office's period touchstones, a nine-inch statue of Elvis Presley at the corner of her desk.

"Where does King Tut fit in?"

"An exhibit of Egyptian artifacts, including King Tut's gold death mask, toured the US in the '70s and drew millions of people. It renewed interest in ancient Egypt and inspired movies and books."

"And a novelty song by someone."

"Steve Martin," Drenda said.

"I wonder if Max remembers."

"I hope so. I thought this might help sell him on the social issues." The petite NC executive with black-framed glasses looked young enough to be mistaken for a college student. When she became involved in an issue, however, her erudition overshadowed her youthful looks. "The 1970s saw the passage of the Equal Rights Amendment, Satchel Paige's induction in the Baseball Hall of Fame, and the first Gay Pride parade."

"I'm thinking about an LGBTQ day at the park soon," Kate said.

"I like it. My exhibits will take months to construct—if and when I get Max's approval to spend the money. It's a good symbiosis anyway. A history park commemorating history. Are you considering this because of—"

"The shooting? Partly. We had a good turnout over the weekend and we've never done an official event for the gay community. Obviously, I need to run it by Max, but first I wanted to talk to you and a few other departments. This will be well into our busy season, so we should be staffed up with temps. I'll have to check with Gabriel about entertainment, security about their staffing, and allow enough time for merchandising to load up on rainbow clothes, hats, and other items."

"You've generated myriad tasks for yourself. Let me know if I can help."

Kate glanced at Elvis. "I think Max will approve. He was crazy mad at the governor for his statements about the shooting not being a hate crime and referring to the gay community as *those people*."

"I wonder what he thinks of Gudgel's comment today."

"I haven't heard. What'd he say now?"

"At a press conference, Gudgel announced the opening of a campaign office in Polk—right in our backyard. He was asked about Max's comments and he said NC was a great attraction for the state, but he thought our new rides were untried and untested. Something like that." Then he said, 'We hope they're safe. Maybe someone should look into it.'"

"We hope they're safe? Oh my God, the governor is questioning the safety of our rides? I better get back to my office to field reporters' calls on this. There'll be an explosion in the president's office as soon as Max hears about it."

■ ■ ■

"We've been getting lots of calls," Joann, Kate's secretary, said when she walked into the office.

"Don't tell me. Are our rides really safe?"

"Yes."

"Well, everyone knows the drill on that question. Have the calls been mostly local?"

"Local yes, but also the *LA Times, San Francisco Chronicle, The Washington Post,* the AP, and NBC. To name a few."

That scumbag governor. Okay, take a breath. Stay calm. "Maybe we should have a quick department staff meeting so we're all on the same page."

"That may be tough," Joann said, "everyone's on the phone and we have calls waiting."

When Kate joined the park, she inherited Joann Nye. Kate's predecessor, the park's first PR VP, lasted only months after the park opened. Max could be demanding. Joann quickly earned Kate's respect, and she had no thought of replacing her. Among other tasks she performed, Joann helped prioritize the demands on the department and on Kate.

She relaxed a little. Joann understood this was an all-hands-on-deck moment.

"We're not only getting calls from the news media. People who want to visit the park are asking if we've had problems with our rides. A few calls are going to safety engineering, but their number is not on our website so people call *public information*."

"That's us." *Dammit*. "I'll help take calls, too. I imagine guest relations is also getting calls. Can you check with them? Make sure they have our safety fact sheet. And would you call upstairs and see if Max is in? If he's heard the news, he's boiling."

"Will do. I've just been scanning news online." She pointed to her computer screen displaying the website of the *Phoenix Standard*, the largest newspaper in Arizona. The headline read:

Governor says Nostalgia City rides

should be inspected for safety problems

CHAPTER 9

April 3

Elton John's "Daniel" played on the radio as Lyle drove his silver Mustang into employee parking. He regularly listened to his friend, Big Earl Williams, the popular disc jockey on K-BOP, the oldies radio station of Nostalgia City. Ready for work, Lyle wore his yellow cabbie hat, white shirt, and bow tie. He turned off the car but didn't get out. Before he found his cab, he wanted to check in with Sam. He pulled out his phone.

"How are you doing m' love?"

"Okay. Prepping for a test."

"Have you heard from Olivia?"

"Just texts. She and her mom are dealing with it. It still doesn't seem real, even though I saw, you know, Mr. Lightfoot's body."

A burden for a 21-year-old, Lyle thought. But then she'd grown up hearing about Lyle's cases, as much as he tried to shelter her from the grim business. "You sound okay."

"I've been looking through the pictures that Olivia's father posted during our time at the park. He really liked to take pictures of all of us."

"Where are the pictures?"

"Social media, of course. Have you looked at them?"

"You know me and social media. I don't spend a lot of time tweeting."

"*Lyle.*"

"I'm kidding. Can you tell me how to find the pictures?"

"Okay, put me on speaker, and I'll tell you what to do."

In thirty seconds, Lyle had a website open. He moved his phone to avoid sunlight glaring through the windshield and paged through photo after photo taken during the tragic weekend. Lightfoot liked to take selfies with his daughter and her friends. His T-shirt slogan was as visible in the pictures as his broad smile when he had his arm around his daughter. Sam and two other girls were in many of the pictures posed in front of a Fun Zone ride or a retro storefront.

Lightfoot's captions with the photos read like an amateur's travel log. He described the rides and attractions they entered and explained, with a happy father's exuberance, what they planned to do next. In two pictures, he named the four young women, identifying them as seniors at Arizona State.

"Do you see the picture of us in front of the record store?" Sam said. "I asked a clerk about Taylor Swift albums and he said, 'who's that?' I know. It's all realistic."

Lyle stopped scrolling and stared at a picture of Sam

and two of the others arm-in-arm. Sam's name appeared under this picture, too.

As he stared at the photo, one of Lyle's coworkers walked by his car and waved. Lyle barely noticed.

"We have to erase these," he said, trying to keep his voice level.

"Only Olivia or her mom can do that—if they know the pass—wait a minute. What—"

"I just think there may be figures in the background, stuff the sheriff would like to see. But no one else."

"These are the last pictures Olivia has of her dad. Why would she delete them?"

"She could download and save them for herself," Lyle said. "Maybe she has."

Sam sounded as if she might be thinking what Lyle was thinking—and he didn't want that.

"He's part of an investigation. It just maybe makes sense. I dunno." He tried to sound offhand. "But I don't know social media either."

He paused and Sam didn't speak so he jumped in to fill the silence. "I'd better get going to work. I'm sitting in my car right now. You do sound good. Talk soon? Love you."

After he hung up, Lyle continued to scroll through the photos until the end. Obviously, Lightfoot was a photo expert. Many of his "snapshots" were well composed, including several he'd obviously taken after he'd left the park Sunday.

Lyle muttered several obscenities, then reached for another of his anxiety remedies, the plastic orange pharmacy container in his glove box. The rubber band wouldn't be enough. Not today.

On the way to the San Navarro County Sheriff's Department, Lyle called Rey to see that he was in the office, then called his boss with a lame excuse why he would be a little late for his shift.

■ ■ ■

"I know where Lightfoot's car is," Lyle said without preface as he rushed into Rey's office.

Rey looked up from his desk. "So do we. Our techs are going over it now in the garage."

"Oh." In the time it took him to drop into one of Rey's chairs, Lyle knew. "You figured it out the same way I did, except I just now saw his online photos."

"There ya go. Detective Smith studied the victim's social media pages. After he left the park, he took scenic shots out at Mexicali Canyon. There's that skinny hoodoo rock formation near the road. It took us a while, but we found his car shoved into a ravine. Unfortunately, his phone and camera were missing. No unexpected prints in the car so far, but we recovered one 9mm casing, probably from the shooter."

Lyle lowered his brows. "Yesterday, why didn't you—"

"We only found the car this morning."

"So the shooter killed him out in the desert, then dumped his body in front of an NC sign as a kind of message."

"And we don't know what that is," Rey said.

"I'll tell you what message it sends *me*." He fumbled in his back pocket for his phone. "Have you seen the pictures of the girls?"

"Yes, I know," Rey said lowering his voice. He shoved

the paperwork on his desk aside. "Lightfoot identified Sam and the others."

Lyle leaned forward. "We've got to delete those posts, those pictures."

"I thought we already did. I'll check. But—"

Lyle pushed back in his seat and rubbed his hands over the tops of his thighs. "But it's too late."

"That's not what I was going to say. Millions of people post billions of pictures on the web every day. They are not all related to crime or result in a crime."

Lyle took a breath before he spoke. "I don't know if you're trying to protect or respect my feelings, but it's pretty obvious that the shooter followed Lightfoot by his internet posts. That's why the surveillance footage didn't tell you much. The shooter didn't need to be right behind Lightfoot to know where he was going."

"The shooter would have to know Lightfoot's name in order to find his internet pages."

"There's plenty of ways he could've found out. Lightfoot's catering company advertises in Flagstaff. Maybe the shooter lives in Flag. Or maybe he spotted the T-shirt and decided to kill him just because he's a fucking crazy bigot."

"But Lyle."

"So how else could he get the guy's name? He could have heard him make a reservation, stolen a credit card receipt, many ways."

"You really thought this out. But it's just—"

"Yeah, bullshit supposition. But I know *this*. That bastard knows Sam's name, knows what she looks like, and knows she goes to Arizona State. And for all he knows, she's gay, too."

CHAPTER 10

April 4

Austen Danvers, NC's chief legal counsel, wore a charcoal three-piece suit, a subdued tie, and a composed expression that helped calm Kate's misgivings. He sat next to her in the back seat of an electric cart carrying them across the park. She matched his professional look with a navy suit, off-white blouse, and three-inch heels.

Danvers had called Kate late the previous afternoon, telling her the governor was sending a state attorney to talk about Arizona inspecting all NC rides for reported safety issues.

Kate watched as the cart driver took them to a behind-the-scenes section of Nostalgia City. "This is ridiculous, isn't it?" she said. "Any statements about our rides being unsafe came out of the governor's mouth and nowhere else."

The attorney nodded.

"I hope we can do something about it. We've been swamped with calls from the public and the media," Kate said. "We have routine answers to safety questions, but they rarely come up. Only now it's *the governor* raising the question." She knew the governor's widely circulated comments had caused their attendance dip.

They arrived at the safety engineering building early, ready for the meeting. Kate had chosen her three-inch heels because they guaranteed she would be taller than anyone she was likely to meet—possibly without the heels. From her height, she could glare down if necessary. Or she could sit down, smile, and engage. Whatever style worked.

"We're meeting with someone from the attorney general's office?" she asked in the elevator to the second floor.

"No. Charles Ramey is general counsel to the governor. One of his primary jobs is to keep the governor out of trouble. And with Gudgel, I think he has his hands full."

"Max is not going to be here," Kate said. "He doesn't want to give Ramey the status of meeting with the CEO. I like it."

"Yes, and he thought you and I might be less apt to say what we really think of the governor than he would."

Kate and Danvers reached the meeting space ahead of their guests. He'd chosen a loft overlooking the park's safety lab. Below, employees bent over workbenches while others peered at the underside of a sleek, stream-lined, multiple-wheeled car elevated on a lift. The room extended for what looked like seventy-five or one-hun-dred yards of metal workbenches, test equipment, and computer screens.

A long, polished wood table in the loft above

supported a large video screen at one end. Danvers set down his case and opened it just as the guests arrived.

Kate pegged the 40ish guy in the expensive blue suit as Ramey, the attorney, the young man with him, his assistant. Ramey introduced himself, showing a determined business-like mien. His assistant, introduced only as Bailey, gave Kate the once-over, perhaps deciding it wouldn't be another boring meeting after all.

"I'm sorry Mr. Maxwell couldn't be here today," soft-spoken Danvers began. "He had another engagement. But we're here to talk about our ride safety and inspection programs."

"Is this part of your testing facility?" Ramey asked.

"Yes," Kate said. "Of course, we examine and test all rides and attractions on site, but here we perform a variety of scientific tests. In the facility next door we monitor rides every minute the park is open."

Ramey and Bailey sat facing the lab opposite Kate and Danvers. Bailey pulled out a yellow pad, ready to take notes.

"You're chief legal counsel," Ramey said. "And you're public affairs VP. I hoped to talk to someone involved in safety testing."

"You will," Danvers said with a reassuring nod at Ramey. "Terence Dewitt is our chief safety engineer. He's a corporate vice president, so safety is represented at all senior staff meetings. Terry has his master's in engineering from MIT, and we've attracted top people in ride safety from other major theme parks. Oh, here's Terry."

Kate thought if you could create a person to look like an engineer, Terrance Dewitt would be it. Slender and tall, with dark hair flecked with gray, he looked studious and athletic at the same time. He wore a light blue dress shirt and tie.

"Gentlemen," he began after introductions, "Austen asked me to give you an overview of our inspection protocols. We have videos that show, up close, the concepts I'll be talking about."

He picked up a remote, clicked, and the Nostalgia City NC logo appeared over a moving aerial view of the park showing the '70s town, Centerville, then swooping down to the park's Fun Zone.

"Let me begin by saying that all our rides are inspected *every day* and monitored continuously through a network of thousands of sensors and cameras. Here's a view of our computer room. These technicians work in tandem with our Control Center staffed by security personnel, who also watch over the safety of our guests.

"Have you been to the park before?" Dewitt asked. Both guests said *yes*, and Bailey nodded his head enthusiastically.

"Then you know that unlike a lot of theme parks, NC doesn't rely on speed-crazy rides. Yes, we have a rollercoaster, considered tame by comparison to other parks, a Ferris wheel, and a form of auto racetrack. But the majority of our rides are based on entertainment, with optical illusions, misdirection, and forms of AI special effects. We call these *dark rides* simply because they take place indoors. Speed is often simulated."

The TV video changed to show men and women in hard hats and work clothes harnessed to the superstructure of the rollercoaster.

"In addition to the computerized monitoring, inspectors climb all over every ride watching for any minor obstruction, looking at bolts and supports."

"Terry," said Kate, "could you mention training?"

"Of course. We conduct rigorous in-house training, and require all safety engineers and inspectors to take NAARSO courses and most of our staff are NAARSO certified."

Kate noticed Bailey had been taking occasional notes, and occasional glances at her across the table, but now he started writing faster and looked up at Dewitt.

"NAARSO stands for the National Association of Amusement Ride Safety Officials."

Bailey kept writing. Ramey glowered.

"We perform a variety of safety examinations," Dewitt said, "and I won't dump all the technical details on you, but they include magnetic particle and liquid penetration tests, acoustic emissions tests, radiographic and ultrasonic tests, and others. And we comply—in fact exceed—ASTM standards for amusement rides and devices."

Dewitt glanced at Bailey writing furiously. "I have a summary of the relevant tests and standards I can give you."

Ramey tapped fingers on the table and glared at Dewitt. "Impressive," he said, "but you have accidents. People are injured."

"That's true," Dewitt said.

CHAPTER 11

Kate had heard Dewitt's response to the injury question before. She relaxed.

"All parks have accidents," he said, "but the vast majority of injuries here are caused by people acting recklessly, like trying to stand up on a ride or actually trying to get out of a vehicle or boat while it's moving.

"We engineer our rides to protect people from their own dangerous behavior. One example. On our rides—especially the faster moving ones—we build in safe zones. People like to stick their hands out and touch things as they go by. But even though it may seem like you can slap the side of a building or other set, they are actually far enough away that even a gorilla couldn't reach out and break an arm."

Danvers thanked Dewitt, who clicked off the monitor display and sat down.

"Next," said Danvers, "I presume you'd like to talk about government oversight, inspections."

"Yes." Ramey opened a folder and pulled out a stack of legal-size papers.

"I assume," Danvers said, "you're familiar with Arizona Revised Statutes regarding amusement rides, especially section 44-1799.63.

"Section sixty-three requires amusement ride operators to have rides inspected once a year by qualified outside inspectors. And note the preceding code section grants the power to administer and enforce the inspection requirements to counties, not the state."

"That may be," Ramey said, looking up from his papers and adopting what Kate thought was a courtroom stare. "But the governor wants state inspectors to ensure the safety of Nostalgia City rides."

"Clearly you don't have jurisdiction," Danvers said. "We follow the law by working closely with the San Navarro County Board of Supervisors and file the required inspection reports with the county. Regardless, since Nostalgia City is the only theme park in Arizona, I'm sure the state has no qualified inspectors."

Kate looked over at Ramey, who flipped through the papers in front of him. His blank expression didn't betray whether he'd done his homework. With his files collected, he said, "we haven't mentioned *federal* oversight. Although Governor Gudgel opposes government overreach—especially at the federal level—he has asked me to contact the Federal Consumer Product Safety Commission."

"Fine, fine," said Danvers.

Ramey started to stand.

"One last item," Danvers said. "You now know how

we comply with state laws and work closely with the county and also exceed industry safety standards." He paused and Kate could imagine him speaking to a jury. "Therefore, when the governor questions the safety of this park, it becomes trade disparagement."

"That's a form of defamation," Ramey said, his voice level.

"Correct, but of a business or corporate nature. Several recent cases clearly identify what a plaintiff needs in order to prevail including an Arizona State Supreme Court case of trade disparagement involving a *state agency*. If you like, I can send you the citations."

Kate had a sense the general counsel would deliver the message—the park's undisguised threat—to the governor and they would not hear from them again. She hoped.

As Ramey walked out, Bailey lingered. He looked up at Kate. "Did you play basketball?"

"Yes. That was a while ago. I played forward at USC. Nineteen points per game paid my tuition." It was her stock answer, but didn't mean she wasn't still proud of her athletic accomplishments, even though she now played in the corporate world.

"I bet you get that question often," Danvers said after the governor's men left.

"Yes, of course. People also want to know how tall I am. So, Ramey's contact with the Consumer Product Safety Commission in Washington also will get him nowhere."

"Oh, you know about that."

"Yes, the CPSC might be the appropriate agency were it not for the continued success of theme park and trade association lobbying."

"Stationary theme parks—rather than traveling carnivals—are exempt from federal oversight," Danvers said. "It's left to the states. And regulation-adverse Arizona has placed supervision at the lowest governmental level."

CHAPTER 12

April 5

Kate heard popping sounds and almost simultaneous screams. Bullets crashed through picket signs, crashed through windows, crashed through flesh.

Seconds before, she'd passed a line of gay rights demonstrators marching in front of Governor Gudgel's new Polk campaign headquarters. When Kate walked into the office, the shooting began.

She dropped to the floor as the storefront picture window shattered and a coffee machine at the back of the room exploded. Somewhere in Kate's mind, terror mixed with split-second knowledge that the prospect of being shot by a lunatic with an assault weapon had become part of American life. Would this be her final thought?

The shots continued rapidly, pop, pop, pop, one after another. Then stopped.

Kate stayed glued to the floor, along with the half dozen office workers. She listened. Sounds eerily similar to moans from the park's zombie ride drifted in through the broken window. More than a minute without gunfire passed before she dared to raise up on hands and knees, keeping her head low. A man in the corner held his arm, attempting to staunch the blood that soaked his sleeve. Kate's first impulse was to crawl over to him, but two other people, crouching low, inched to him with towels to stop the bleeding. After another frozen minute, a siren.

When a chorus of sirens sounded, Kate raised up enough to peer through the splintered window out to the street. A sheriff's car skidded to a stop. Its doors flew open. Two deputies, one armed with a semi-automatic rifle, jumped out and scanned the surrounding buildings. Across the street more black and whites arrived. Uniformed officers dashed up and down the opposite sidewalk.

An ambulance braked to a stop. EMTs leaped out carrying gear. Kate stood up and took tentative steps to the door, her senses on hair-trigger alert.

She stepped outside, gagged, and turned away. Three of the LGBTQ picketers and a sheriff's deputy lay on the ground, surrounded by blood. The blood ran from the narrow sidewalk into the gutter. Kate knew immediately two of the four were dead, organs horribly ripped apart by the barrage. The injured demonstrator and deputy appeared to be conscious.

The protester held her head and groaned as two of the unhurt demonstrators knelt next to her. One uninjured protestor pulled off his shirt and used it to stop the bleeding wound in the deputy's chest. Another, overwhelmed by the carnage, threw up into the street, his vomit mixing with the flowing blood.

After two more ambulances and other emergency vehicles arrived, Kate reasoned she could relax—a little—without putting her life in danger.

"Did you catch him, the shooter?" she asked a deputy.

He just shook his head and trotted into the campaign office while EMTs attended to the injured woman and deputy.

Another woman stood against the building, quivering as she sobbed in shock and despair. Kate stepped over and held her, sharing her fright. "Are you hurt?"

The woman could only shake her head and cry. An EMT approached. Kate released the woman to the medic's care and backed away. Was she trying to put space between herself and the catastrophe? She avoided sight of the mangled dead, but looked for something to do, someone to help.

She saw Rey Martinez pull up and get out of his car. "Rey, what's going on? Did you get the shooter?"

"Kate, are you okay? Were you here when this happened?"

"I came here to check out the campaign office, but I barely got through the door when the shooting started."

"Did you see anything, where the shots came from?"

"I saw the floor up close, Rey. That's all. This was a mass shooting. Did you *catch* the person?"

"Apparently we're still *looking*," he said through gritted teeth. He glanced down the street and waved to a deputy. "I have to go."

If she were still a reporter—her first job out of college—she would be interviewing and taking pictures. Now she felt purposeless. Was this shooting connected to the Lightfoot murder? It must be. She'd decided to visit the newly opened campaign headquarters when she heard there would be an anti-Gudgel protest. Joann told her that park employees had planned to take part. She shuddered when she realized the casualties could be from NC.

How many people did the sheriff assign to the political demonstration? Had to be more than the one injured deputy. Did any marchers display a connection to the park? Although shootings such as this happened all too frequently, it would make the national news, especially as a hate crime—and this looked just like it.

Soon law enforcement vehicles and ambulances clogged the streets, dozens of red and blue lights flashing calamity. Armed deputies searched door to door like soldiers at war clearing buildings. Back inside the headquarters, upended tables and chairs created an obstacle course for emergency personnel. Campaign flyers littered the floor as if marking a celebration. Water from a toppled vase of red, white, and blue flowers pooled in a corner.

Kate saw that the injured man in the office had been taken away. Tiffany Smith, who Kate knew, and another detective took statements from the shaken campaign volunteers. Smith acknowledged Kate and soon she recorded what little Kate could report about the shooting.

Knowing she was suffering a form of shock, Kate still looked for a way to help, something to do. She bent over and picked up two Gudgel brochures. The first contained a list of his legislative goals that included reducing early voting, banning the teaching of critical race theory, and permitting police to detain anyone suspected of being an "illegal."

On the cover of the second brochure, an idealized white family, mother, father, three beaming children posed in front of a home. It proclaimed Gudgel wanted to "protect the nuclear family of Arizona." Inside, boldface headings highlighted the governor's unyielding support of second amendment gun rights.

A picture showed a smiling Governor Gudgel in jeans and a faded green shirt cradling a rifle.

CHAPTER 13

Lyle had almost stopped fretting over Sam. He called her three times in the past week. He stopped calling when she asked if he was worried about something. Maybe he'd been overreacting about Sam's potential danger. But she was the one person he loved more than anything in the world.

He did a little random online research on hate groups. Most of the information concerned a few nationally known events, and he learned little.

He poured himself a gin and tonic and flipped on the TV news.

"The two people killed were protesting in front of Governor Gudgel's campaign headquarters in Polk," the reporter said. She stood in next to a sheriff's tape barrier lit by the surreal glow of flashing red and blue lights.

"Holy shit," Lyle said and gulped his drink.

"Three people including a San Navarro County Sheriff's deputy were injured in the shooting," the reporter said, her eyebrows narrowed. "Authorities say an assault rifle was used in the attack on the LGBTQ demonstration."

Lyle had stepped to the kitchen counter to refresh his drink when Kate walked in.

"Have you seen the news?" he said. "As I left work, someone in the garage mentioned another mass shooting, but I didn't know it happened in Polk."

"I was there."

"What do you mean?" He set his drink down with a clunk.

"I just walked into the campaign office and the shooting started."

Lyle grabbed Kate around the shoulders and stared at her. His grasp turned into a hug. She said she needed to sit, so he reluctantly released her. "Tell me," he said.

He poured her a drink. She set down her purse and told the story as they sat on Lyle's couch. "I wanted to check out the campaign headquarters, and I'd heard about the protest."

He held her hand. Kate described a scene Lyle had never witnessed in nearly 20 years in law enforcement. She finished by saying, for the third time, "I can't believe it happened. It was so quick." Her hand shook as she sipped her drink, and the glass rattled as she set it on the table.

"It was the most horrifying thing I've ever seen. I want to forget what I saw." She stared off, her eyes unfocused. Lyle squeezed her hand, and she came back to him.

"I stuck around and gave a useless statement to detectives, then I went back to the office. We received calls that my staff handled. The media wanted to know if this was related to the Lightfoot shooting. There was nothing we could say because we had no information. Nothing we could do."

She held fast to his right hand and placed her other hand on top of his. "One or more of the victims could be park employees. I knew some planned to be at the demonstration."

"I wonder if it's anyone we know," he said, and his mind drifted back to shootings he'd visited. "Did you recognize anyone at the scene?"

Kate shook her head and shivered.

"Brutal, sorry," Lyle said. "Names won't be released until they notify kin." He let go of Kate and reached for his drink. "I don't understand. It's a hate crime, right?"

"I don't understand either. I only gave a bare bones description of the event back in the office, then I walked around the park for an hour feeling numb and hoping it didn't really happen. This is so much bigger than the park, than the governor's race. It just can't be—"

Kate's phone chime interrupted her.

"Hello? Yes, I did. I was actually in the area. Yes, I'm okay. Horrible. No, I don't think we have heard from the national news. Probably tomorrow."

She held her hand over her phone. "It's Max."

Lyle nodded. *What kind of PR miracle does Max expect Kate to pull off now? She's right about this being bigger than any one thing.*

When she spoke to Max, Lyle heard her succinct business voice. A job to do, follow-up events to anticipate. She would be okay. Not unfamiliar with guns, Kate had used a pistol in self defense the year before and come through the shock, denial, and anger. She'd have anger to dissipate now, too; work would help.

Lyle wanted to hear Kate's conversation, one side of it anyway, but found himself too absorbed in the consequences of the day's catastrophe. He wandered into his den-office and turned on the TV. News footage revealed the front of Gudgel's campaign office surrounded by yellow tape. Crime scene technicians walked in and around the building. The camera panned to show the entry to another building roped off and two sheriff's cars as sentries at each end of the block. Lyle clicked it off. He wondered if Sam had heard the news. "Maybe she'll call," he said aloud.

After ten minutes, Kate walked in. "You forgot this." She put his drink on the desk next to him and sat on a saloon-style chair below a baseball poster.

"Max was in Scottsdale all day. He heard the news."

"What does he want you to do?"

"He's shaken up. I could hear it. I think he's fighting his natural reaction to start ordering everyone to solve this right away. But he knows it can't be done, and the murders can't be undone. He's taking it personally."

"Don't you do the same thing. It didn't happen at the park and we don't know—"

"Max told me the two people who died worked for the park and the injured demonstrator I saw is also a park employee."

"How did Max find out? The news said law enforcement would have an announcement about the victims' identities tomorrow morning."

"He has contacts. Maybe the sheriff, maybe employees who were there."

"Names?"

"He didn't say. One man, one woman died, one woman injured."

"What's he going to do?"

"He's going to treat it delicately, help the families, and try not to blow up."

"That's what you advised?"

"Yes," Kate said, "and he's already started our response. He called HR to supply relatives with information on insurance claims, social security, grief counseling, anything they need."

"And you?"

"I'll have to be ready with a statement of condolences for the family, write words for Max to say." She leaned over and put her head in her hands. "Gives me something to do."

Lyle thought about Sam again and about any possible links to Lightfoot's murder that might—however loosely—connect to his daughter or put her in the sights of hate-blinded killers. He'd call her, maybe drive down. There just wasn't enough to go on, and he wondered if the sheriff and the FBI would work together, discover unshakable evidence, and find the bastards. He snapped his rubber band and reached for his drink.

Kate sat up then and walked back to the family room. Lyle followed.

"Max said he wanted to put resources into the case," Kate said. "Into the search for the killer or killers. And I don't know what to tell him about how this is going to impact the park, future guests—and employees."

"Did he say anything else?"

"He said, 'What's Lyle doing?'"

CHAPTER 14

April 6

Lyle's brain sifted the facts, alternating as ex-cop, father, and theme park cab driver. Crazy people killed NC employees because they were gay. Max wanted him to do *something*, but neither he nor Lyle knew exactly what. In the past, when crime threatened the relaxed atmosphere of Nostalgia City, Max called on Lyle to apply his detective skills if the CEO thought protecting the park's future might not be a high priority for law enforcement.

Things weren't different now. While the sheriff's department and FBI, under the glare of the news media, searched for the killers, how would the park be affected? Kate could deal with the media; Lyle *could* look into multiple connections the killings could have to the park. Were the campaign office shooting victims connected to the Lightfoot murder?

Maxwell told Lyle the transportation department would allow him a flexible schedule and the cab-driver detective told the boss he would "look into things."

What he definitely didn't want to do, but what he knew was a mandatory first step, was talk with spouses or other family members of the murder victims. He'd done it plenty of times. Emotional detachment, that's what you needed, and Lyle found it. At times.

Fortunately, he would not be delivering the bad news and trying to collect information from distraught spouses at the same time—like he'd occasionally had to do as a cop. Natalie Lawson was first on his list.

She and her spouse, Sue, had a condo in the NC employee enclave, Timeless Village. Both worked at the park. Lyle had called Lawson, told her he worked for the park, and explained, vaguely, why he wanted to talk to her. He wanted to help the victims however he could, in addition to gathering information relevant to the murders. He bypassed his usual off-duty outfit in favor of a sport coat and slacks.

Lawson, a slender brunette with short hair, opened the door with a stick vacuum cleaner in her hand. Lyle introduced himself and offered condolences. He noticed a tub of rags and spray bottles on a coffee table.

"Sorry," Lawson said, "I'm in the middle of cleaning. Sue likes the place to be spotless."

Textbooks explain that losing a spouse produces five levels of grief, from denial to acceptance. Lyle had seen outbursts of anger and other initial reactions, too. Denial was common.

He asked her if they could talk for a few minutes and he indicated a sofa and chairs in what looked like the family room. Lawson set the vacuum against a wall and took off lightweight work gloves. She sat across from him.

"Did you receive information from the park about survivor benefits, social security, and other services the park can help you with?"

"I think so. My cousin wrote it down when they called."

"The park can help you find whatever you need."

"Okay." She looked at him with an expression she might have used if he were complimenting her on her choice of vacuum cleaner.

"Does your cousin live here?"

"She lives in town, but she said she would be back this afternoon."

Lawson sounded chatty, almost light as if she were gossiping with a neighbor. Her light hazel eyes looked clear when she spoke; she frequently glanced toward the front door.

"We're trying to figure out how all this happened," Lyle said, trying to get to the subject without jarring Lawson. "Was Sue active in politics or campaigning? Had she demonstrated anywhere before?"

"Not really. Several days ago, she heard from friends at work that a bunch of people wanted to protest the governor and so she said she'd go. She even made a sign."

"Do you know who told her about the demonstration?"

Lawson shook her head.

"She went voluntarily? She wanted to go?"

"Oh yeah."

"Did she drive down by herself?"

"No, they carpooled." She'd been holding her gloves; now she set them on a knee.

"Do you know who she drove down with?"

"Yeah, two friends. Why are you asking? Are you from the park? You ask the same questions the sheriff's detectives did."

"Yes, I'm from the park. I wanted to be sure you received the support you need from Nostalgia City. I'm also investigating the crime for the president. We're troubled and angry when something like this happens to our employees—especially when it's done because of hate."

"Hate," she repeated. She must have realized what the killings were. Would she have watched or read the news? She clutched her gloves.

"Did Sue get along well at work?"

"Sure."

"Arguments with anyone? Did she see any LGBTQ discrimination?" For some reason, he couldn't bring himself to use the word *lesbian*.

"You mean because we're girls, and we're married? Sometimes, yeah. Sue gets upset. I try not to let it bother me."

Being gay in Arizona, or anywhere in the US for that matter, still posed challenges. Even though conditions improved—Arizona legalized same-sex marriage more than ten years before—Lyle knew prejudice, expressed in subtle or direct, spiteful ways, existed. "Anybody in particular dislike Sue? Anyone who would want to hurt her?"

"No one would hurt Sue. She works in the group vacations office. She's a problem solver and often leads tours. Her boss says she's the best with people."

Lyle had another question for himself. What could he gain by annoying this young woman who was obviously having trouble grasping the reality of death, not to mention what it would mean for her life.

"Ms. Lawson, the HR department at the park can refer you to a counselor if you'd like to talk to someone."

"The police talked about a therapist."

"It can help. You can also find grief therapy with a group of people who are going through just what you are. Please consider it. I had a therapist myself once and it, it's helped."

He pulled out his business card. It showed his name and the words "Nostalgia City Transportation." The phone number was the cab dispatcher, but he wrote his cell phone number on the back.

"Please keep this. This is my personal cell number. If you can think of anything that might help the park's or the sheriff's investigations, call. If you need help getting any social services, call me."

With reservations, he got up and ambled to the door. Lawson put on her gloves and reclaimed the vacuum.

"I'll check back to see how you're doing," he said.

Walking to his car, he glanced back at the building. He recognized it. He drove by every day going to work. Now when he passed, he would remember the confusion in Lawson's hazel eyes.

CHAPTER 15

"Governor Rod Gudgel first called the shooting a politically motivated attack on his headquarters," the TV newscaster said. "A Gudgel spokesperson today said everyone in the governor's office grieves for the victims and their families. She said the governor would make all necessary state resources available to law enforcement."

"We don't want his help," Kate said, freezing the news broadcast on her computer. She threw a pencil at the screen. It missed and hit her desk and bounced across her empty office.

That son of a bitch. I bet his press person had a heart attack over that one.

She'd come into the office dressed in a business suit. It was Saturday, the day after the shooting, and an NBC reporter had called for an interview. Staring out her window to calm herself, she reviewed what she'd told the reporter and thought she'd touched the necessary points. She knew how a PR person deals with tragedy. But when she turned from the window and clicked on the computer to Gudgel talking about the tragedy as a political inconvenience, she lost all composure.

She dialed Max's private cell number.

"Max, I just did an interview with NBC, and I wish we could talk."

"Are you here, in your office?"

"Yes."

"Then just come up."

Not surprised at Max's presence, Kate grabbed her laptop and headed for the elevator. During the short ride, she paced back and forth, despair mixed with anger.

"Max," she said, entering his office, "we need to—to hammer that bastard."

Max stood up and walked around his desk. "Gudgel, huh? What do you want to do?"

Clutching her laptop, Kate made a fist with her other hand. "He thinks the shooting was aimed at his office. He should be impeached. If he was *there* yesterday…" Kate let out a quick sob. She let Max point her to a chair. *How can cops deal with such horror day after day?* She forced herself to focus on the present. Max stood next to her.

"Talking to NBC was one of the hardest things I've had to do." *Except stand on that sidewalk after the shooting.* "Yesterday was a nightmare. Talking about it, I had to stick to notes I wrote. I needed something prepared or I might have cried or sworn. I recognized our three employees who were hate crime victims. I gave them a statement from you—the one you agreed on—and said the park was helping families of the victims."

"Should have done that. We *are* helping."

"But I didn't mention Gudgel. I hadn't heard his

response at the time. Now I think we should call him what he is."

"Aren't you supposed to be restraining *me*?" Max said.

Kate smiled and at looked up at him. "You're right Max. I'm upset."

"But you're damn right. We need to respond. I heard about those comments today and wanted to do something."

"Without talking with me?" She managed another smile.

"Okay then, let's get going. I see you came prepared." He pointed to her laptop.

For the next half hour, as they talked Kate typed and edited. They revised the statement several times. The news release expressed Max's distress over the governor's ignorance, insensitivity, and disregard for the NC employees who lost their lives, and the others who were injured. They quoted Max saying Gudgel should be ashamed for blindly—or intentionally—failing to condemn the homophobic hate crime. Kate read the final draft and felt better.

"I'll go downstairs and send this out, if I can remember how. If I have a problem, I'll call Joann. I'll send it to all Arizona media, selected national and regional outlets. And," she said, "the NBC reporter I talked to."

When she had sent the release out to all her target audiences, she slumped in her desk chair. She wanted to talk to Lyle, to tell him she understood his struggle with the effects of regular exposure to murder, to violent death. She wanted to tell him she could function—with focus— for a few hours, but she could also feel life as purposeless. She needed to talk, but Lyle was in Polk looking for Rey.

She called Drenda. "I know it's not five o'clock yet, but I want a glass of wine. Are you busy, thinking about work or anything?"

"You want to talk?"

Obviously, her friend heard the misery in her voice. "Yeah. Can you meet me at Gilligan's Island?"

"That Timeless Village bar next to the Chinese restaurant?"

"It's not bad. See you in a half hour?"

CHAPTER 16

Drenda arrived first and stood at the bar. Gilligan's modeled itself after the 1960s TV show, with reedy wallpaper, faux palm trees, and the bow of a boat sticking out from a corner. Tropical fish swam in a lighted blue tank. Not bad, she thought, and the boat in the corner was correctly named the S.S. Minnow. She listened to the background music. Was that Don Ho? Only a few patrons sat at the bar, mostly NC employees, Drenda guessed.

"Did you get dressed up for this?" Drenda asked Kate when she came in wearing a business suit.

"An NBC news crew came out to talk about the shooting."

"Oh." She couldn't imagine what her friend must have gone through and then to have to talk about it for the news the next day. "How are you holding up?" She touched Kate's shoulder.

"Day by day. You look dressed up too."

Drenda wore a light blue floral dress with Peter Pan

collar. "It's late '70s, but I'm afraid it makes me look about 14 years old. It doesn't make me stand out too much, however."

"You're cute. You'd stand out in anything."

"Tell that to my ex-husband."

"You made a joke," Kate said.

Did Kate think she was *that* staid? "Academics have senses of humor too, Ms. Vice President."

The bartender walked over. "Kate, right?" he said.

"That's right, Skipper. And this is Drenda. We work together."

"Welcome aboard."

After they ordered, the Skipper offered to serve them at a booth.

"He calls himself Skipper?" Drenda asked as they sat down.

"It's a character from the show."

"I know, but he's skinny and has bushy hair. He looks nothing like Alan Hale, Jr., the actor from the program."

Drenda gave the Skipper a smile as he delivered the drinks. *Really, the Skipper?*

"Thanks for coming out to lend a shoulder," Kate said.

"Of course," she sighed. "If I went through what you did, I'd be unable to talk, let alone to a TV reporter. What did you say?"

"The reporter knew I had been at the shooting, so she asked me about it." Kate took a sip of wine. "I said it was the worst day of my life. Just mentioning it made me break down." She paused and looked as if she might break up again.

Drenda put a hand on her arm. "Will you be on TV?"

"Maybe. Or they might just use my voice and show B roll of park rides." Kate stared at her wine glass. "Gudgel said the shooting was an attack *on his office*."

"What?"

"That's what he said."

"That's inconceivable. Is he so dense? Incredibly self-centered that he thinks everything is about *him*?"

"It made me furious. Max was in the office so we put together a statement saying what an insensitive jerk the governor is."

"You got it off your chest. Did it help?"

"Yes, but it still makes me so angry he can dismiss a hate crime."

Drenda looked at her friend and squeezed her arm.

"I'm focusing on my work and other things. If I just sit, yesterday comes back." Kate swallowed more wine and put her hand over Drenda's that rested on her arm.

"I can't tell you what it was like. I want to go back to a time before it happened—and have it *not* happen. That doesn't make sense. How could it happen? Did it happen?"

They sat in silence for minutes. Drenda held Kate's arm, wanting to take Kate's pain away. "Finish your last sip and I'll wave to *the Skipper* to bring us another round."

"The good news," Kate said, "is that it's been a few days since Austen Danvers and I had a come-to-Jesus meeting with the governor's counsel about our ride safety. And there hasn't been a word about it since." She paused for a minute, then her phone chimed. "It's NBC."

"Hello Claudia," Kate said, "you have a follow-up question?"

Drenda caught the Skipper's eye and held up two fingers.

"Where did you hear this?" Kate said into her phone. "Or can you tell me?"

Drenda saw distress on Kate's face as she turned from weepy to angry in seconds.

"What did he say about it?" Kate said. "Well, there's nothing planned. We've talked about this as well as other special events for the summer. I can tell you, if and when we decide. So do look at the release I just sent out. It may be helpful." She turned off her phone.

"Kate?" Drenda said.

"Apparently, Gudgel said on the news that we're having a Gay Pride event. That's why the reporter called."

"Where'd he get that?" Drenda said. "Didn't you—"

"Of course. I told Germaine and the other department heads this was tentative and to please *not* mention it to anyone."

Drenda put a hand to her mouth. "But people talk."

"Yes, apparently they did."

"Is there a likelihood that the governor has—to use the vernacular—a snitch in Nostalgia City?" Drenda said.

"I dunno. It put me in the position to either confirm or deny. I think I wriggled out of it by telling the truth."

"I can imagine what Uncle Max's reaction to this will be, especially if an employee is leaking information to the governor."

"We'll have to be careful who we share information with, especially if it has to do with Gudgel. Max will want us to either find the snitch or, what I don't know."

"Respond in a like manner?"

Kate frowned. "You mean recruit a spy in the governor's office?"

"Or plant one."

"This sounds like we'd be asking for," Kate said, "or actually *causing* more trouble."

Drenda shook her head. She looked around. The Skipper was pouring, and other customers sat out of earshot. "I disagree. I think this could be strictly *defensive*. Wouldn't it be advantageous to know—ahead of time—what the governor's next insanity is going to be? Is part of this a personal vendetta against the park or Max? Is it simply based on Gudgel's homophobia and bigotry? I'd like to know."

And she had an idea who would be ideal for the job.

CHAPTER 17

Where was Rey? Lyle drove down Escondido Drive, a major Polk thoroughfare lined with commercial buildings. Rey was supposed to be around here somewhere. He turned left on Silver Strike Avenue, then slowed as he made a right turn at a drugstore. Up ahead he saw Rey in a suit, walking away, straddling the gutter with an odd up-and-down stride. He took one step on the sidewalk, then put his other foot in the street. He looked at the gutter as he walked.

Lyle parked and caught up with his friend down the block. He walked next to him as Rey continued his up-and-down steps. It took Lyle a moment to realize Rey was studying the crime scene.

"Hey, Lyle, stay with me for a few minutes."

"Sure."

After about fifty feet more, Rey stopped and looked up. "Okay, hang on." He dashed across the street to where his cruiser sat heading west, leaving Lyle staring after him from the sidewalk. Rey jumped in the car, started up and hit his red and blue flashers. He swerved out from the curb, did a U-turn, accelerated briefly, then turned left.

Lyle trotted across the street and followed Rey's path. He spotted the patrol car idling where an alley emptied into a parking lot. Looking from side to side, Rey walked down the alley then turned and got back in his car just before Lyle reached him. Rey then sped down the alley, slammed on his brakes, and threw open the door. He got out holding a handful of papers and glanced at them as he stalked further down the alley. Lyle watched him crumple the papers, then kick a concrete wall with a cowboy boot.

"Another minute," Rey said when Lyle caught up with him again. He moved up the alley twenty feet, looking on both sides before trudging back to his car.

"Sorry to make you come down here," Rey said, not sounding like Rey, "but this was the only free time I had to talk. This has all been gone over, but I needed another look." He pointed with his handful of papers down the alley.

"Appreciate the time," Lyle said. "Understood."

"Really?" Rey grunted. "Two people dead, three injured, including a deputy, and we don't have shit on the damn shooter. Why in hell," he said, his voice trailing off. He flung the papers onto the hood of his car then swore in Spanish.

Lyle always saw his friend as unshakable, especially at times when his own outlook cast a dark shadow. Would Rey's manic behavior mean *he* would have to anchor reality?

Rey swore again and leaned over with his hands on the car hood. "I gave the sheriff my resignation."

Lyle put a hand on his shoulder and took a deep breath. Rey remained silent for what seemed like five minutes.

"I should have been there," Rey said, his head still down. "We should have assigned more men. I should have known." Rey threw his head back, looking at the narrow rectangle of sky above the alley.

Lyle started his own useless, should-have thinking. He should have known the mass shooting would have landed hard on Rey. He should have realized Rey's position and not just call him up because he wanted details on the park employees killed.

"Can't be your fault, Rey. No one could have known."

"Thanks, amigo. But there were mistakes," he said, still leaning on the hood. "We weren't prepared. Not enough men in the right places."

"Who would expect this in Polk? You can't predict the future."

"That's what I'm supposed to do," he said, turning to Lyle. "I came down here early in the morning when the first demonstrators arrived. I met with the sergeant in charge of deploying the deputies. A handful of protesters milled around in front of the office. Peaceful. I talked to a couple of them. They said they just wanted to send a message to the governor and then go home. They weren't threatening. They drank coffee and talked. If I'd only known."

Rey picked up the crumpled papers from his hood. "Here's the Gudgel headquarters on Saddlehorn Street," Rey said, pointing to a hand-drawn map of the area. "There's an intersection in each direction. Here's a T where Silver Strike dead ends. We had two deputies just up that street. The other intersection is here. We were supposed to have a car and two deputies near that corner, too—but we didn't."

"What happened?"

"I don't know exactly. A mix-up in assignments late in the morning. One deputy took a break for coffee. His partner, deputy Lamont, was supposed to cover but we think he was down the street watching some crap on his phone, but of course he's not saying now. That's the corner where the shooter crouched beside a dumpster and fired off 18 rounds. Another deputy was right here," he pointed to the map, "next to the demonstrators and, of course, he got hit too. He's in serious condition.

"I suggested putting someone on the headquarters building roof, but the front edge slopes steeply and HVAC units take up a lot of room. Was just not feasible. We had someone on an adjoining roof, but his view was partially obstructed.

"When the shooting started, the deputies up Silver Strike Avenue couldn't see where the shots came from. They parked too far up the block. They didn't notice it until one of them saw the victims fall."

"The sergeant was somewhere close, too, right?"

"That's the way it was *supposed* to work. The sergeant and deputy Lamont are both suspended." Rey sagged against the fender of his car, his eyes directed downward.

"Bad timing and dereliction of duty. Not your burden," Lyle said. "Not yours."

■　■　■

He persuaded Rey to walk down the block for coffee, and they sat at an outdoor table. Lyle insisted they buy a huge, deep-fried apple fritter. Rey needed the energy.

"I told Melissa last night," Rey said.

"That you resigned?"

"That I planned to."

"And you told her this was all your fault."

"She told me to think about it. Not to talk to the sheriff until, well, until all the facts were known."

"But you quit anyway?" Lyle said.

Rey looked up from his coffee. "Yeah, but the sheriff refused to accept my resignation. Said he needed me to help find the shooter."

Lyle gripped Rey's arm. "You'll do it."

Rey responded with a smile of the condemned. "Thanks." He pulled the plastic cover off his coffee cup and blew on the contents. "But we screwed up. The bastard got away, and we're left with little evidence." He sipped his coffee and set it down.

"What have you got?" Lyle tore open the paper bag holding the fritter.

"It's easier to tell you what we *don't* have. Virtually no useful video, except from doorbell cams in adjoining residential neighborhoods. Assault rifle casings are clean of prints. We put the casings' ejector marks and the recovered slugs through the databases but got squat. The FBI did it. That rifle has never been used in a crime—that we know of."

"Witnesses?"

"The shooter was kneeling, *possibly* in a marksman's position. The deputy in front of the office saw him for just a split second before he hit the ground. The suspect wore dark clothes and maybe a dark knit watch cap. He was close enough to be accurate, but far enough away to make identification tough. White male, medium height to tall. That's about it."

Talking to Lyle seemed to ease Rey's pall, and he reached over and tore a large lump off the fritter.

"Vehicle?" Lyle said.

Rey shook his head as he chewed a mouthful of the sugary confection. "No one, including the responding deputies, saw one. The guy ran down the alley we were just in. Must have had a car or ride waiting."

Lyle bit into a chunk of fritter and wiped sugar from his mouth. "Was any media there for the event? Any photos?"

"The protesters sent out a news release to the local paper and beyond. But no media was present at the time. The official opening ceremony wasn't scheduled until two o'clock. And of course, when the guy fired, no one was using their phone cameras."

"What's the FBI doing?"

"Trying to make this fit a profile. Going over similar shootings, especially anti-gay ones."

Lyle wanted to keep Rey focused on details, not hopelessness.

"We're both looking for connections to the Lightfoot murder," Rey said. "Different weapons, but targeting gay people and a supporter, plus we can't overlook a possible link to the park."

"The shooting was in Polk, not at the park."

"But park employees were killed."

"Hmm." Lyle paused. "The other connection was simply *hate*."

"Uh huh. And the FBI is also looking into Arizona hate groups, digging deep online."

"You told me we have hate groups here. I thought about that after the shooting."

With his coffee apparently cooling, Rey took a gulp. "Yes, hate groups have arrived in San Navarro County, but they haven't been a big problem. We monitor them as much as we can. Now the Cadre Brave, for example, has had clusters of followers in different parts of the state—including here—for a number of years."

"That group I've heard of," Lyle said. "One of them got busted for assault just before I left the PD. Who exactly do they hate?"

"They're a white supremacy type like most of them, so anyone who looks like me, plus Blacks and Muslims, are the enemy of America. They have a crazy manifesto on their website."

"Are they anti-gay?"

"Homophobic? Yeah. They're anti-everyone except white males, *straight* white males. Many of them believe in conspiracy theories, too."

"So you're familiar with these swell guys."

"Not enough. I wish we had more time to keep up on internet hate, especially these local crazies."

"I don't need to ask if they have guns."

"Does a cholla have spines?"

CHAPTER 18

April 8

Smiles and cheerful dispositions were de rigueur for all who worked at Nostalgia City, from ride attendants to shopkeepers. It says so in the employee manual. But Kate felt a change this morning. Employees slaughtered, whether or not it happened at the park, casts a shadow, triggers fear. Nostalgia City's usual bustle, revs from retro muscle cars, the lively chatter of tourists, became a low hum.

Her typical morning route from the nearest employee parking lot to her office took her past a snack shop specializing in 1970s treats such as Ding Dongs, Ho Hos, and Twinkies. The store had a window counter so guests could get Twinkies to go as they strolled the Centerville streets. Marie, the outgoing window clerk, always gave Kate a cheery greeting, this morning a wan smile. It was the same with other employees she passed. She recognized the signs brought on by the disaster while she still struggled to accept it had happened.

As she walked by her secretary's desk, she noticed Joann's glum expression and sensed she wanted to talk. Kate paused. "What's up Joann?"

Joann nodded toward Kate's office.

Average height and tending to the heavy side, Joann wore her highlighted brown hair just above her shoulders. She looked to Kate like a person you might see at the supermarket and pass by with little notice, probably the reason she could unobtrusively pick up park rumors.

In the seclusion of Kate's office, Joann took a seat opposite her boss's desk. "You look as serious as everybody here today," Kate said.

"It's tough. I see details on the news every night now. Sue had a lot of friends here. And poor Brooke," she said, referring to the injured employee who survived the attack.

"This atmosphere is self-reinforcing," Kate said. "Perhaps employees can focus on guests enjoying themselves and lift their own spirits a little."

"Well Kate, not everyone, I mean," she lowered her voice, "not everyone here is happy we are supporting gay rights."

"Sadly, a small percentage of the population is still prejudiced. What have you heard?"

Joanne was one of Kate's best sources for employee information, gossip. She was a longtime resident of the area and, equally important, circumspect.

"I heard a bunch of people talking about the park and gay rights. Every once in a while someone used a slang term." Joanne made a face.

"Where was this?"

"The parking lot. Then yesterday I heard someone

else in the cafeteria say he wondered if a local group had planned the shooting. And would there be more? I couldn't hear all of what he said, and then the people with him told him to shut up."

Kate thanked her for the intelligence. She hoped her concerns represented a tiny segment of park employees and was based on ill-informed office chatter, but she filed the information away.

Before Joann left, Kate's phone chimed. Max wanted to see her.

■   ■   ■

"Our brain-dead governor is at it again."

Max spoke before Kate had even settled into a guest chair in the president's sprawling office.

"Max," Kate said, standing before him. "I don't know *how* he found out about the Gay Pride day."

"Gay Pride?" he said. "Oh yeah, that too."

What else? Kate dropped into a chair, landing hard. She took a breath and stared at her boss.

"They're trying to cancel our lease at the Phoenix airport, ban our busses."

"What? Our welcome center?"

"Gudgel is pushing it with help from a couple of his Phoenix cronies. I heard it this morning from a friend in city hall."

Why can't he leave us alone to grieve? "Our busses carry thousands of guests a week to the park. We can't strand them at the airport. The city can't do this."

"You think our little news release set him off?"

"Could be, but he reacted quickly. How can they cancel our lease?"

"Maybe this has been in the works. Talk to Austen. He's looking into it."

"Gudgel hasn't responded *publicly* to our news release," Kate said. "But the media is now focused on our disputes with the governor. Reporters have been asking his office for a reaction and he's been strangely silent."

Kate hated the 'let's you and she fight' mentality that often ruled newsrooms. Public feuds, lawsuits, and the like, especially those filled with rancor, made good stories. She knew, however, she'd stoked the fires by lambasting Gudgel, but couldn't let his wild, uncaring public notions go unchallenged.

She realized she was staring blankly at the Campbell's soup can painting hanging on the wall behind Max. Her concentration still lagged at times.

"So what do you think, Kate?" Max said.

"Sorry. About what?"

"The Gay Pride thing. Gudgel knew about it."

"I don't know how he found out," she said. "Maybe he just invented that to bait us."

"Or?"

"Or the word got out somehow. I talked about it with department heads, but I told them to keep it to themselves."

"So somebody talked. Who was it?"

Kate didn't want to feed his resentment. "I'm looking into it, Max. But as you would say, 'It's done.'"

"Okay. Keep on it."

Kate nodded. Could it have been one of the

department heads or someone who worked for them? Should she hunt for the snitch? Or should she take Drenda's advice and figure out a way to infiltrate Gudgel's Phoenix organization?

Did their secrets get passed through a chain of command, or did an NC employee report directly to the governor?

CHAPTER 19

Hudson Ragsdill's spouse, Jordan, an NC employee, died in the Polk attack. Lyle found their apartment in an older section of town. Their second-floor unit in the L-shaped High Desert Apartments faced the cracked concrete parking lot and street beyond.

On the phone, Ragsdill told Lyle he would be home that afternoon. When Lyle knocked, Ragsdill opened the door and stood there for moments after Lyle identified himself.

"Okay, c'mon in," he said finally and ushered Lyle into a living room tastefully furnished in what Lyle thought of as fall colors, reds and deep golds. Ragsdill, in black jeans and an open-neck shirt, looked like a visitor, not a resident. His thick, curly black hair had not seen a barber in a while, and he needed a shave. Lyle guessed him to be in his mid- to late-forties.

"So you're offering park services, but you want to talk about Jordan?" Ragsdill stood in the middle of the room, one hand thrust in a pocket.

"That's right. First, I want to say—"

Before Lyle could finish the sentence, Ragsdill turned and walked through an archway to the kitchen. Lyle saw him reach for a coffee pot.

"Want coffee?" he said, not looking at Lyle.

"No thanks." Lyle noticed a ragged six-inch diameter hole in the kitchen wall partially obscured by a toaster. Something had punched through it.

Ragsdill poured himself a cup and walked back to the center of the living room.

Lyle pointed to an upholstered chair. "May I?"

The man responded by sitting opposite Lyle's chair. He placed his coffee on a side table and sat on the edge of the seat as if telling Lyle their conversation would be brief.

Lyle began with condolences he hoped didn't sound perfunctory. "I'm here for a couple of reasons," he continued. "The first is that the park wants to help you find any resources you may need."

"Really, a gay dead guy counts for something?" Ragsdill's dark eyebrows hung over his pale blue eyes. "Jordan always said we needed to stand up for our rights. That's what he was doing out there, wasn't he? He wanted me to go with him."

"Count for something?" Lyle said. "That's why I'm here. The park president is upset over what happened. No, not upset, outraged. Among the things the park is eager to provide is extended insurance coverage. If you're on the park's health plan, when COBRA ends, we can try to help you find insurance if you can't get it through work."

"Maybe. We've been using the park's health plan. They don't have nothing like it at Superior Hardware."

"That where you work?"

"Yeah."

Ragsdill eased a few inches back in his chair. He took a sip of coffee and held his cup. Around the room, a collection of snapshots, plaques, and other memorabilia decorated one wall. Lyle noticed the glass on an eight-by-ten framed group photo was broken, one sliver of glass missing.

"You should receive a package of materials from HR," he said, looking back at Ragsdill, "It will explain additional employee benefits."

Lyle looked at a framed military patch with Ragsdill's name on it. "You were in the Army like me. Is that an MP insignia?"

"Yeah I fought in Afghanistan. And I was an MP in Germany."

"I was an MP, too. It can be a thankless job."

"Yeah. What's your point?"

"As a vet you probably already have VA medical benefits."

"VA benefits? Ha." He set his coffee down, got up, and walked toward the kitchen. "*You* were in the service?" he said as he turned back to look at Lyle. "When did you get out?"

"Long time ago."

"Well I got out in oh-eight. And I didn't get an honorable discharge. So what kind of VA benefits you figure I got, huh?"

He paced to the front picture window then turned.

"Know why? Not because of anything I did, just because of who I am. Remember 'don't ask don't tell?' That helped a lot, didn't it? But I didn't get hassled as much when I was an MP. I fought the Taliban and Al Qaeda, but in the Army if you were gay, you were a pervert."

"And now this happens to your partner," Lyle said shaking his head.

"Jordan's answer was to fight for your rights. Demand rights. Force society to face it. I wanted to stay home and watch baseball. Not picket for rights." His scowl matched his tone of voice.

"I get it, Mr. Ragsdill."

"Do you? Sometimes Jordan would drag me to events like that demonstration in Mesa last year. What did it get us? Well that wasn't enough, so he started a website. Wanted to rally support, plan protests. Vent."

"A Gay Pride website?"

"Yeah."

"What kind of responses did he get?"

"He was just starting to get noticed. He got threats, but most people supported the site. See for yourself."

Survivors often responded in remarkably similar patterns. Others, not so much.

"Did Jordan ever have conflicts with other employees?"

"You mean because he was gay, or what?"

"Anything."

"Damn right."

"Did he make complaints?"

"What do you think? Why don't you look at the records."

"Nostalgia City administration is taking this seriously.

That's why I'm here. One of our guests, the father of a lesbian daughter, was murdered. And now the shooting here. We're trying to figure out what's going on and what we can do."

"I'll tell ya what's going on. It's the anti-gay movement and the crazy motherfuckers with guns everywhere. Why you asking? Sheriff's detectives were already here."

"It could be a waste of time. If so, I'm sorry."

"You said you worked for the park. What is this?"

"Please Mr. Ragsdill. I *do* work at Nostalgia City. But because of my background the president asked me to talk to survivors and family members, to tell them we're in their corner, *and* see if they know of anything that might have prompted the shooting."

Ragsdill looked at Lyle, then looked from side to side. Was he deciding between throwing him out or punching him out? He rose and stood in front of Lyle, arms crossed on his chest. "Look, I just lost my partner, my life partner. Where you coming from?" He took a step back and sat on the arm of his chair. "You want to know how society treats Jordan and me? Really? Go to hell." He forced his lips tightly together.

Obviously anger, in addition to denial, was a reaction. And Ragsdill had plenty to spare.

As Lyle walked out, Ragsdill held the door and grunted, "have a nice day."

CHAPTER 20

April 9

A long drive through stop-and-go Phoenix traffic on a warm spring morning brought Kate to the meeting of the Phoenix Aviation Advisory Board. Gudgel had struck again, and Austen Danvers had asked her to back him up at the meeting.

"Kate, the board's proposal would end the lease on our Welcome Center at Sky Harbor International," Danvers had explained on the phone. "It would restrict our coaches from picking up our guests at the terminal. They say the busses cause too much congestion. Airport passenger counts have increased, and they have an offer from another company to occupy our exhibit booth space."

The Welcome Center was a joint project of the PR and marketing departments. Kate had a hand in setting it up. Located where arriving passengers sought bags and transportation, the center attracted tourists' attention with a fully restored 1971 American Motors Rambler

Ambassador in shining emerald, its door open to display its lime green interior. Guests with reservations could check into their NC hotel, book park admission, and a table for dining. But the main function of the center was to direct thousands of guests to NC busses for a ride to the park.

Kate met Danvers outside the board meeting room in a structure adjacent to the airport that looked like an abandoned hangar turned into an office building. "Austen," Kate said, "here we are less than a week after the *last* time we had to persuade a government body not to meddle with the park."

Danvers, decked out in a lawyer suit—a different color this time—whispered, "It *is* Gudgel again. My paralegal dug into this, and it smells. But we have resources and options, so let's go at them. Thanks for coming." He handed Kate a copy of the meeting agenda and lease proposal.

Inside, fluorescent ceiling fixtures labored to light the cavernous room. Six people, two women and four men sat at a broad wooden counter on a foot-high riser at the front of the room. To the left sat representatives of airport staff. Only a handful of people occupied the five rows of guest seats facing the dais. Kate and Danvers sat in the first row. Kate had a sense of a courtroom scene in a bucolic southern town.

A suntanned man in his fifties introduced himself as chairman of the advisory board. He noted that two of their members were absent.

"We still have a quorum today, so we can conduct the business before us. We will dispense with the reading of the minutes and move ahead. Mr. Symington, county director of aviation services, has the first order of business."

"We have a two-part proposal before us today," said the overweight man in aviator-style glasses. "The first part limits the number of daily theme park bus trips to the airport. Passenger arrivals at Sky Harbor have increased nine percent in the last year alone and this step is necessary to clear congestion.

"Second, we have a request from Leslie's Travel Town that would like to rent space to sell travel gear and bottled drinks in an area convenient for arriving passengers. Board member Francine Williamson has suggested the Nostalgia City site. Their contract is up for renewal. Is there a representative from Leslie's here?"

Kate wondered if the aviation services director wanted to be a pilot but had to settle for bureaucrat. The representative of Leslie's spoke briefly outlining its need for space to broaden its reach in the Phoenix area. He said he didn't realize it would involve Nostalgia City.

The board chair asked for comments from Nostalgia City. Danvers tugged at the bottom of his vest and stepped forward.

"Mr. chairman, I'm Austen Danvers, chief legal counsel for Nostalgia City. This suggestion to limit our passenger bus access to the airport and cancelling our Welcome Center is more than troubling. We have been a partner with the airport since the park was built. It has been a successful relationship and while Leslie's may wish to open a location at the airport, it should not come at the expense of one of the largest employers in the state of Arizona.

"Nostalgia City is one reason people *come* through this airport. This is why traffic has increased. The written proposal in front of us cites no traffic studies, no engineering surveys to support the idea that restricting us to *one bus per day* is going to ease traffic. In fact, our efficient transportation service actually eases congestion."

Danvers told the board Nostalgia City would sign a renewal agreement for any reasonable term for bus access and the exhibit booth but that he would favor a long-term lease. He finished and introduced Kate, who stood and faced the board.

"Mr. chairman and board members. As vice president for public relations at the park, I'm responsible for managing our Welcome Center and we've been a good partner with the airport. In addition to representing Nostalgia City, our employees routinely assist lost travelers. One of our representatives once helped a lost little girl find her parents, and as we have discovered, we are relied upon to direct arriving passengers to the restrooms."

Two of the board members chuckled, one glared.

"Our most important function at the airport is to assist passengers—guests—to find our coaches that take them to Nostalgia City. Guests can book the transportation here if they didn't do it ahead of time.

"But we provide other services, too. Our bright booth allows passengers to rest if they like and learn more about one of the largest theme parks in the world. And," she paused for emphasis, "we promote not only Nostalgia City but everything this area has to offer from the Phoenix

Art Museum to Scottsdale, the Grand Canyon, and the Botanical Garden right here near the airport.

"I'm curious why the proposal restricts only *theme park* busses. Nostalgia City is the only theme park in the state. That should lead to obvious conclusions. And one bus per day is worthless. We transport thousands of people.

"So, let us stay," she said, "and do our job for Phoenix and Arizona." She ended with a smile.

Board members' discussion centered on income from lease agreements and the advisability of essentially "kicking Nostalgia City out of our airport," as the chairman phrased it. Regardless, the board voted three to two to do just that.

"Beautifully spoken," Danvers said outside the meeting room. "Thanks for pointing out the *theme park* restriction. It's obvious who prompted this proposal."

"We still lost."

"We have options. First, I'd like to hear from the two absent members."

"We might also want to find out *why* they were absent," Kate said. "Maybe they were kidnapped and held by Gudgel goons."

"Remember," Danvers said, "the board's action is only a *recommendation* to the City Council, which has the final say, and Max has contacts."

■　■　■

Danvers headed off, and Kate paused to put the meeting papers in her leather tote. As she walked to the exit, a man in the hallway spoke.

"That was a fine presentation, Ms. Sorensen," he said. Kate had noticed him seated behind her at the meeting. "Too bad the fix was in."

"Excuse me?" Kate said. The guy wore a herringbone sport coat and striped tie. She noticed his look was less admiring than appraising. In his 40s, he stood just an inch or two shorter than Kate and carried more weight than he needed.

"You know who wanted to kick you out of the airport, right?"

"I have a good idea, but why do you ask?"

"I'm an investigator, and I've come across information that may be valuable to you."

"Yes?"

The man looked over his shoulder at people walking into the building. "Could we talk someplace else? Coffee?"

"Could you give me an idea of what you're talking about?"

"Involves the governor, but I think you know that."

Where did this guy come from? She would talk to him— in a public place. She gave him directions to a coffee shop in an office building not far away.

When she drove up, the investigator stood outside smoking. He dropped his cigarette on the walkway and crushed it as she approached. They bought coffee and sat at a table apart from other customers.

"I hope I didn't startle you back there," he said. "Thanks for the get-together. My name is Gregory Hurt. Here's my PI license."

He pulled out a small wallet and showed Kate the

documentation. She'd never seen an Arizona private investigator's license before—or any PI license, for that matter—so she nodded and said, "Okay, tell me what you want. What's going on?"

"Let's be frank. The governor's office is harassing you. Harassing Nostalgia City. It's been in the news, but I wonder if other things have happened, too. You're head of PR, so this is in your wheelhouse."

"It's been a concern, yes, especially the murders. So how did you know I would be at the meeting today? Do you subscribe to the airport board's meeting notices?"

Hurt's square face was handsome despite his large pores. "Just part of my investigation."

"And is this going to help us?"

"Possibly. The governor is a petty tyrant and crook. I'm collecting information. I suspect his trail of monkey business and general fraud is a long road. I've already discovered incriminating details." He sipped coffee.

"Did you want to *share* some of that information with *me*?" Kate stretched out the last word.

"I believe we have common interests, so we could work together."

"And what are *your* interests?"

"I represent a client." His head down, he looked into his coffee cup and mumbled. Kate took in his thick dark hair, combed straight back. "A client that would like to see the governor…"

"Lose the election?" Kate said after Hurt paused for an irritatingly long time.

"Go to prison."

"Do you have proof that he broke the law? Is that what you're offering?"

"I can't say specifically now, but that's the general idea."

"Does this involve the hate-crime murders?"

Hurt looked over his shoulder. "My client is willing to share my findings on *everything* if we agree to work together."

Was it Hurt's mumble or his habit of turning his head a few degrees, then looking at her at an angle that made him look shifty? "What do you mean by work together? Why does your client want to see him in prison?"

"Of course I can't betray my client, but I will tell you about the governor's sneaky-ass schemes—aimed at opponents—*if* you'd like to work together."

What have I got to lose? I'll hear what he has to say first. "Okay. Let's do that." She expected Hurt to provide more details, but he just finished his coffee in a gulp and stood up.

"Thank you for your time, Ms. Sorensen. I will be in touch."

"That's it? How can I contact you? Do you have a card?"

He briefly patted one of his jacket pockets. "All out. Sorry." He recited his phone number.

She typed it into her phone, and when she looked up, he was gone.

CHAPTER 21

Brooke Powell, a secretary in NC's restoration garage, survived the Polk shooting with a minor injury. Lyle knew her only casually. Always fascinated by classic cars, Lyle saw her when he visited friends in the garage or brought his cab in for service. They exchanged jokes occasionally. Rather than make a production out of interviewing her, he caught up with Powell late in the morning in the restoration break room.

"Brooke, is the coffee any better this morning?" Lyle said to her back.

"Can't be. I didn't make it." Powell's straight auburn hair reminded Lyle of a girl he knew in college. She turned around with a cup in her hand to see who had spoken. "Lyle, haven't seen you in a while."

"I'm so sorry you got hit."

"I'm lucky to be alive. See what the bullet did?" She tilted her head down and pointed to a row of stitches stretching from the top of her forehead into a swath of shaved scalp. "A little higher and the guy would've missed me. A little lower and—" She made a face and drew a finger across her throat.

Lyle smiled at her gallows humor. Plucky. "You said the word *guy*. Was it a man? Did you see him?"

"I've been thinking about that since I talked to the sheriff's detectives. I think now I may have seen him for a split second, a guy in dark clothes. He looked like he was squatting."

She took a few steps to a table, placed her cup down, and pulled out a chair. Seated, she placed her hands around her cup. "Someone spoke to me just before the shots, and I turned my head. That's when I got hit. I blacked out for a second. Maybe that's what happened to the memory."

Lyle took the chair next to her but sat sideways to face her. "Can you think of what he looked like?"

She thought for a moment, then said, "That was it. A dark figure kneeling or squatting. I think he was wearing a ski mask."

"A *man* in a ski mask."

Powell moved her head up and down slowly. "But the sum bitch missed me, didn't he? Well almost." She touched her stitches and made a noise that could have been a stifled laugh or a groan of pain.

"Brooke, the administration wanted me to talk to the victims or their families and see if there's anything else the park can do for them. I'm also trying to find out what happened."

"You talked to others?" She pursed her lips. "How are they doing?"

"Like you'd expect. I talked to Jordan Nichols' partner—"

"Hudson? How is he?"

"Upset, angry. It's not an uncommon reaction." Lyle's voice trailed off.

"Hudson was angry before this."

"Yeah?"

"Issues at work, home, resentful over homophobia. You know, the usual."

"You know him?"

"Well, some of us at the park occasionally hang out together."

Lyle looked up from his coffee. "Then you're…"

"Gay? You didn't know? C' mon, I was at the protest."

"You could be in support. People should help advocate—"

"Yeah? Where were you?" She locked eyes with Lyle. "You and I don't know each other very well."

He instantly regretted misjudging her emotional state. "I'm sorry Brooke. I know it was horrifying." He let his words die out and he said nothing for minutes. Then he tried, "is there an LGBTQ organization at the park?"

"Not that I know of. Maybe I should start one. Let me think. How about L-S-W-A-R? Lesbians shot with an assault rifle."

Lyle shut up. Should he mention counseling?

After a minute of silence, Powell said, "Are you going to ask me if there's anyone who would want to harm me? That's what the detective wanted to know."

"What did you tell him?"

"No one in particular, except maybe the Cadre Brave."

"The hate group? You know about them?"

"I try not to. Jason wrote about them on his blog."

"Sorry to bother, Brooke. I'm not normally insensitive.

The HR department talked to you about all the services available?"

"Yeah."

He touched her shoulder briefly as he eased out of the room, leaving her to stare into her coffee.

"You did a great job of consoling, didn't you Deming?" he said aloud as he walked out of the garage.

■　■　■

Before going to the transportation office, he'd called Rey and found out the undersheriff was going to be at the park around lunchtime. Lyle wanted to see how he was faring after trying to resign and trying to carry the full responsibility for the screw-up *and* for the investigation. Lyle suggested lunch at one of his favorite NC restaurants, Chili Dog Kennel, hoping the odd-ball eatery might distract Rey, if only for a few minutes.

"You and your chili dogs," Rey said when they picked up their food at the counter. "Why did you get only two?"

They settled into a booth in the narrow restaurant that looked like an architect's afterthought at the end of a block. "This is just what you need before a high-level meeting here," Lyle said.

"I bet you haven't had a chili dog in at least a week."

Lyle took a breath. "Actually, two weeks. I've been busy." He squirted mustard from a plastic bottle onto the first dog then dumped on onions from a paper cup. Should he try to pick it, up or use the plastic utensils?

Ray opted for a bowl of chili and bag of chips. He wasn't in uniform today. "So, you've been talking to victims. Find out anything?"

"That I have the sensitivity of a chilidog." He held up his dripping bun, then shoved it into his mouth.

"What?" Rey said.

Lyle mumbled, then had to chew and swallow soda before he could talk.

"Brooke Powell," he managed to say.

"The woman hit in the head?"

"Yeah. I just talked to her. She joked about almost getting killed if the shooter had better aim. It was a nervous reaction, but I thought she shrugged it all off. I said the wrong thing."

"People react differently."

"Tell me. I should know." He took another bite, not caring that chili dripped on the plastic-coated table.

"Brooke said she remembered seeing a figure just a second before the bullet hit her head. Thought he was wearing a ski mask."

"That's not in the report. Sounds important."

Lyle swallowed a gulp of soda to clear his mouth. "You doing okay, Rey?"

Rey stirred his chili. "Focusing on the job. That's what we're all doing in the department. Have to. And pressure from the media and elected officials isn't helping. The FBI's pushing, too."

Lyle knew the feeling and was glad his job and his psyche were no longer on the line. Working hard would get Rey through it. And finding the killers would be a partial release.

"Listen," Rey said, "I appreciate your help the other day. I was a little crazy."

"Overworked, stressed. Trying to do it all yourself."

"There ya go. I'm not back to normal yet, but you got me going in the right direction."

Lyle gave a slight nod, finished another bite. "Do you think Jordan Nichols could have been the target? He went to all the rallies and he ran a Gay Pride website. Maybe the shooter aimed for him and kept firing because there were more targets?"

"We're checking comments and reactions to his website," Rey said, "however, the shooter would have to know what Nichols looked like. *And* know he was going to be there. Is that likely?"

Lyle took another bite and dribbled more chili. This time on his plate.

"So far Nichols's personnel file hasn't helped either," Rey said. "He made a formal discrimination report. The issue was resolved. Still, we talked to the other guy and there's no way he was the shooter. But, we hadn't heard about the ski mask. If you remind me where Powell works, I'll talk to her this afternoon."

"How about Sue Lawson? Her spouse told me everyone at the park liked her."

"Almost everyone. Lawson got rave reviews from her boss when detectives talked to him. But she earned a promotion about a year ago and two coworkers didn't like it. Someone vandalized Lawson's computer and cancelled a group tour she was scheduled to lead, making the guests think she flaked out on them."

"Would they shoot up the demonstration because they were jealous over a promotion?"

"What do you think? The info's in the file, for what it's worth."

Lyle used three paper napkins to clean up the table-top. "How is the injured deputy doing?"

"Deputy Beard. He has another surgery ahead in Flagstaff."

"Sorry. Anyone taking responsibility for the shooting?"

"Online, you mean? Not yet." Rey finished his chili and pushed the bowl aside. "So, what are you going to do now?"

"I dunno. Possibly nothing."

"Really? I thought Max gave you time off."

"Maybe I'll visit Sam and check out the security at her place."

"Again?"

"Shut up, Rey."

CHAPTER 22

April 10

"Lyle, are you awake? Sit up."

Kate sat up in bed with her knees up, propping her tablet computer on her legs. She'd wanted a slow, casual morning, reading, maybe dozing. But the morning paper startled her. Lyle didn't move, so she nudged him awake. He looked up, smiled, and reached for her.

"Sit up. You've got to read this ad in the *Phoenix Standard*."

He leaned over to the nightstand and grabbed his reading glasses. They balanced the tablet between them and read the full-page ad.

WHY WE ARE NOT SUPPORTING ROD GUDGEL FOR RE-ELECTION

We're his family. We know him.

When Rod Gudgel ran for governor four years ago, we were skeptical. We are familiar with his background and didn't think he was a promising candidate. But his platform sounded realistic and necessary. We gave him benefit of the doubt.

We cannot do that again.

His opponent in the upcoming election has insight, integrity, and an interest in the future of Arizona and its citizens. Rod Gudgel does not. He's working for himself. As he always has.

The balance of the ad said Gudgel had used his family name to get into law school where he did not distinguish himself. It implied he was a carpetbagger, saying he moved to Arizona after a few terms in the Montana legislature. He moved, the ad said, when his trustworthiness became an issue and polls showed he would not win re-election.

Gudgel relatives said the governor spent too much time on divisive social issues while ignoring the genuine problems of Arizona including education funding, water, affordable housing, and immigration. The twelve signatories of the ad said they endorsed Gudgel's opponent. They identified themselves as either a cousin, aunt or uncle of Gudgel.

"Holy kinfolk," Lyle said looking at the names on the bottom of the ad. "If his good old aunt Angie says he's a crook, maybe everyone will believe it."

"The election is a long way off. People forget."

"Now and then, you're as cynical as I am, Kate."

"Politics. I'm afraid there's a lot to worry about." Slipping out of bed she pulled on her robe then sat on the edge of the mattress, the tablet in her lap. Trixie jumped up and rubbed against her arm. "Good morning, Trixie.

But you have to get down just now." The cat protested, but Kate set her on the floor.

Lyle reached over to touch Kate where the cat had been, his left arm next to her thigh. She put her hand on his. "Nice, but pay attention for a minute. You're right. I *have* been feeling cynical, and it doesn't help. I read an op-ed the other day about political despots. They want you to be cynical and fatalistic because you think nothing can be done. And if everybody thinks that way, the bastards in power keep on going. They win."

"They often do," Lyle said.

"But that's my point. Look at this." Kate tapped her tablet. "After the airport fiasco yesterday, I asked our media monitoring service to start recording Gudgel speeches. I need to know what he's up to. This is a clip from a speech late yesterday." She tapped her tablet again and Gudgel's face appeared on the screen.

"And in conclusion," the governor said, "let me reiterate that the bizarre ideology that permeates *other* states and purports to act in the name of justice for the violent illegals and other so-called *marginalized* people, ignores our sacred American institutions, and will *not* survive in Arizona. Why do teachers discuss race in the classroom? They're spreading lies about racial inequality. *All* this is wokeness, a form of cultural Marxism. The goal is to destroy our society and poison our American blood. It will *not* happen in Arizona." Gudgel made a fist and brought it down hard.

"Does that mean we're cultural Marxists?" Lyle said. "What exactly does that mean?"

"His hate speech is telling followers it's okay to divide

society." She clicked the video ahead to questions and answers. "Here's another clip."

"Governor," said a reporter standing close to the platform, "Did you say that the shooting at the Polk demonstration was the work of LGBTQ activists?"

Gudgel glared at the reporter, shook his head, and scrunched his shoulders. "Totally misquoted. I did not blame the gays for the shooting. That's stupid."

He cocked his head. "And some people are saying it could have been an idea started by enemies who don't want me reelected. Maybe they should look into that."

"*The gays?*" Lyle said. "*Cultural Marxism, poisoned blood.* This guy is—hell, I don't know what he is."

"Dangerous?" Kate said, folding up her tablet. "And why does he always have a military guard?" She crossed the room and leaned against the dresser, facing Lyle.

"He makes insensitive, horrid comments after people are killed. He calls Hispanic Americans dangerous illegals and his opponents Marxists. And when we speak out, he attacks us and makes up lies about our rides. I can't just decry we have a vicious governor and throw my hands in the air."

"What are you planning to do?"

CHAPTER 23

"Joann, here's a little research work for you," Kate said when she walked into the office.

Joann looked up from her desk. "Oh good, detective work?"

"You could say that. It's detective work about a detective."

Joann leaned forward and flashed a smile.

"I met a private investigator yesterday after the airport board meeting. I'd like you to check him out for me. He said his name was Gregory Hurt. He insinuated he was investigating governor Gudgel but didn't say more than that. Can you find out if he's legit?"

"Did you ask Lyle? That's his specialty, isn't it?"

"I completely forgot," Kate said. "I was so bothered by the airport meeting I didn't ask him. But it can't be too difficult. See if there's a state directory. This guy showed me what he said was his state license, so he must be registered—if he's on the level. Here's his phone number. See if you can get additional contact information. I haven't even looked him up on the web yet."

Kate sat at her desk. The memory of innocents being slaughtered still invaded her thoughts. She could do little to help law enforcement, but she could take on the vicious governor who just might be involved—at least by encouraging the cancer of hate.

She looked at a printout of the anti-Gudgel newspaper advertisement. "Hmm." She scanned the list of Gudgel's relatives. None of the names looked familiar. She needed help. Reluctant to let anyone know she wanted to contact Gudgel relatives, Kate turned to an AI-assisted search engine and entered all the names from the advertisement. Since Gudgel came from Montana, she searched for the names in that state and in Arizona.

Two sites offered ancestral searches for the Gudgel surname. She had no interest in great-great-grandfather Gudgel. She did, however, receive individual responses about a number of people named Gudgel, many of whom lived in Montana, but a few were closer.

Refining her parameters, she ultimately found contact information for three Arizona Gudgels. She first called Leo Gudgel at his business number in Phoenix. Mr. Gudgel was in.

"My name is Kate Sorensen and I'm a vice president at Nostalgia City. I read the ad that your family ran in the *Standard* today, and I wonder if I could talk to you about it."

"What did you want to know?"

"Could I come by and talk with you for a few minutes?"

"Today I'm quite busy. If you want to call me back in a few days, maybe…"

"I won't say this is urgent, but the governor has not been kind to Nostalgia City."

"Yes, I know."

"Then you can understand why I'd like to know more about the governor's—oh—*dis*qualifications for office."

"You mean being a self-centered dodo?"

"Uh huh."

"Listen, why don't you talk to my cousin Mila? I'm sure she'd be happy to give you anything you'd like to know about the dear governor."

Leo Gudgel gave Kate a phone number and in a few minutes she had an invitation to visit Mila Edwards.

■　■　■

Sun City Grand offered the largest homes in a cluster of three Del Webb senior communities northwest of Phoenix. Kate knew the area because Del Webb towns represented one of Nostalgia City's prime markets. Busses regularly took seniors on day trips and often longer outings to visit the 1970s in NC.

Mila Edwards lived in a broad adobe-colored home with a red Spanish tile roof at the end of a cul-de-sac. Two large mesquite trees shaded the front entrance. Mrs. Edwards met Kate at the door wearing a polo shirt and green golf shorts the color of the fairway in the distance. She led Kate into a family room with casual southwest furniture and Native American rugs on the wall. She offered coffee or scotch, or a little of both. Kate opted for plain coffee.

"You're right," Edwards said. "It's too early for me, too. But I like guests to be comfortable."

They sat in front of a window with a view of a tiny lake and the fairway beyond. "I appreciate the chance to find out a little about Governor Gudgel," she said. "He's your cousin?"

"Second cousin. He's the son of my late cousin Billy."

Edwards, who Kate placed in her eighties, looked fit. "Your ad got my attention. It's not often that so many members of a candidate's family advertise he's not qualified for office."

"I can imagine you were surprised and…pleased, right?"

"You probably know that he's been taking swipes at us in the media, and he made insane comments after the horrible shootings."

"Yeah, Rod Gudgel is a real douchebag." She stared at Kate. "I say what I think. Hope you don't mind."

Kate waved a hand. "Go right ahead." She was going to like Mrs. Edwards. "I'm eager to learn a little about his background, maybe figure out what makes him tick."

"Mostly adding to his bottom line is what makes him tick. You've heard of the *me* generation, right? Well, he's the *me* governor."

"I'm relatively new to Arizona. How did he go from Montana to being governor here?"

Edwards set her coffee cup down. "By ass-kissing and becoming the most extreme person in the party. Leo, who you talked to, had political connections and made introductions. I'm sure he regrets that now.

"Rod found a vacant seat in the Arizona State House

of Representatives when a member retired. He became the loudest primary candidate—most deranged I really think—and got the nomination. In the general election, he moderated himself to look like cookies and milk, right? So he won. He goes through stages like that, being moderate when it suits him."

"A lot of politicians do."

"Yeah, but Rod can do it the same day."

"So what did he do in the legislature here?" Kate said.

"Ass-kissing again got him on the appropriations committee. That's where the money is."

"Graft?"

"He moved on to richer pastures after he did what he could to line his pockets in Montana."

"So he was getting kickbacks or something in Montana?"

"Oh yeah." She tossed her head back and chuckled to herself. "Everyone in the family knew. My husband and I moved here more than twenty years ago. We had some Gudgel family here."

"What brought you to Arizona?"

"Montana winters."

Edwards explained Gudgel became widely known in Arizona after being elected to the State Senate. Inflammatory rhetoric gave him a statewide name, and when the party fractured, looking for someone to run for governor, Gudgel became the compromise candidate.

"We used to have a few family gatherings here. Rod invited us to his home in Wickenburg once or twice. I wondered how he could afford the place. Lavish I'll tell you. And he also has a condo near downtown since

Wickenburg is such a drive. There's no governor's mansion in Arizona, and he doesn't make that much. We figured he was back to his old scams, and I couldn't stand it. My late husband and I avoided him. Leo keeps me up to date if there's anything big."

"He sometimes talks about God in his speeches. Is he devout?"

"Ha. That's just pandering to voters. I doubt he's seen the inside of a church since he got married. His idea of contributing to a worthy cause is paying his country club dues. Oh, and he's also a philanderer. There's an old word for you. I don't know if that's a secret. Maybe it's just family."

Kate let it all sink in. Nothing truly surprised her, but she wanted more substantial details. "What types of—can you call them crimes?—was he committing in Montana?'

"I don't know all the specifics. He'd brag at family gatherings that he controlled millions of state dollars from his chair on the appropriations committee. You know, a wink and a nod. We knew he was getting a cut. And he liked to collect dirt on people as insurance."

Not surprising. "What did he do to 'get a cut?'"

"The usual, accept bribes. He was always open to that. Oh yeah, then he had the crazy idea to make a gambling mecca in Great Falls. What a crazy idea that was, but it died."

"Gambling, like Las Vegas?"

"It was on TV news for a while before it fizzled. Crazy idea," she said again. "You should talk to Betty and Jay in Billings. I'll give you their number. They were more involved in it."

She picked up her coffee without sipping. "What're you gonna do with the lowdown on Rod? Just curious."

"I'm not sure," Kate said. Ideally, she wanted information that could shut him up for good.

Edwards glanced at the view outside. "So, if you want more details about his dirty history in Montana, talk to Betty and Jay. I can give you a couple more names, too. Tell 'em I told you to call."

CHAPTER 24

Lyle had taken a few shifts driving his cab while he tried to find what else he could do to sort out the murders. He'd just dropped off his last fare of the day when a stalled NC shuttle bus and tow truck blocked the road ahead. The bus driver, arms folded across his chest, stood in the street next to two unsmiling tourists. The tow truck inched backward toward the front of the bus. Lyle squeezed around, drove his cab to the end of the block, and pulled a U-turn.

He drove up next to the pedestrians as the wrecker driver started rattling cables and chains. "What's going on?" Lyle asked the bus driver.

"Bus broke down and they sent a small van to pick up my passengers." The man, dressed in the white shirt and tie *uniform* of NC drivers, lowered his voice and leaned down to Lyle's cab window. "But the van was too damn small. The van driver told me to radio for another. That sucks. These folks have a dinner reservation, too."

"I'm done for the day," Lyle said. "I can take them wherever they need to go."

"That's great. Can I come? I'm supposed to be off duty, too."

"More the merrier."

The driver, at least fifteen years younger than Lyle, introduced himself as Cody. He sat in the front, and the middle-aged couple climbed in back.

"My name's Lyle," he said to the couple, "and we're on the way. Don't worry, the meter is turned off. I'll have you at your hotel in a few minutes."

Centerville sat—not coincidentally—in the park's center. Adjacent, in a semicircle, were the other themed areas, including the Fun Zone and hotels all connected by roads that radiated out from Centerville like spokes on a wheel. Lyle took the shortest route and delivered the guests in time for dinner.

"Thanks so much," Cody said after Lyle pulled his cab into the Transportation Center. "Can I buy you a beer?"

Why not? Kate was going to be late, having to drive back from Sun City Grand. But then he and Kate didn't *always* spend the nights together. Usually they'd spend a few days at his condo, then her apartment. Alone time was important. He thought Kate understood when having a meal at her place, he'd say he wanted to "go home."

He'd say he needed to clean up his place or wash clothes. What he needed was solitude. Time by himself told him he was an individual—besides being part of a couple. He pondered relationships—not obsessively, he told himself. When he struggled over his future at the Phoenix PD, when he faced bogus accusations and felt the crushing burdens of his job, his wife left him for someone else. But he had Sam.

And now, Kate.

"Yeah, I'll go for a beer. Where d' you want to go?"

"I'm meeting friends at West's Bar and Grill in Polk. Why don't you come along?"

■　■　■

Lyle followed Cody's late model bronze pickup through town. Unlike many establishments in Polk, West's had not adopted a '70s retro, rock 'n' roll décor inside or out. The heads of dead deer, javelina, and mountain lion kept watch from above the bar, along with two rattlesnakes for good measure. A Confederate battle flag hung above the door. Customers at the bar favored ball caps or cowboy hats, denim vests, and western boots. Several of the patrons looked as if they'd been born on their barstools.

Cody scanned the darkened room. He nudged Lyle and pointed to his friends. They joined two other men in a booth. Cody introduced Andrew, a fiftyish guy with muscular, tattooed arms and a gray moustache, and Jake, a fortyish guy in a dress shirt and loosened tie.

"Lyle drives a cab in the park," Cody said. "He saved my bacon today. The bus broke down."

"All those Nostalgia City cars look so real," Jake said. "Do they spend a fortune for reproductions or what?"

"Everything's authentic," Lyle said. "I know some of the mechanics. Yes, they look for well-maintained cars in good condition, but most of the old cars they get are junkers, found in barns or in the back of used car lots. Hundreds of man hours go into them. So, you've been to the park?"

"Of course. Never rented a car though."

"You been to the park?" Lyle asked Andrew, who sat across from him.

He nodded, but his expression said a theme park was not his idea of a good time.

"Is that cute brunette barmaid still working here?" Cody asked his buddies. "The one with the, you-know."

"Here she comes," Andrew said, turning his attention to a server.

They all ordered beer, refills for Cody's two friends. Cody criticized Jake's choice as cow piss. The young server gave Lyle an endearing smile. When she'd gone, Andrew made crude suggestions, smirked, and elbowed Cody. Perhaps this would not be the guy's *second* beer. Lyle studied Andrew's tats. In addition to many old and blurred designs, several new ones decorated his lower arm and wrist.

Lyle turned to Jake. "What do you do, Jake?"

"I'm senior planner with the county planning department. I review plans and specs for subdivisions and commercial development."

"I've always wondered how a city plans for growth, to make it orderly. You don't want a store selling adult novelties in a residential neighborhood, or next to a school. Must be a challenging job."

"Zoning provides guidelines, but there's more to it. We have to balance the rights of developers with the views of homeowners who are also stakeholders."

Lyle glanced at Andrew, and without being asked, he explained he worked for an HVAC company.

"Andrew makes sure that your AC is always working," Cody said.

The beer arrived. "Thanks darlin'," Andrew said.

"Is this on the same tab?" she asked.

"I'll cover ours," Cody said, pointing to Lyle's beer.

"I'd love to buy," Jake said, "but I'm saving up for a new toy."

Cody hoisted his beer. "What is it this time?"

"I've had my eye on an Old West style revolver."

"A Ruger Single Six?" Lyle asked.

"True story," Jake said. "It's a cowboy gun, fun for plinking, and it's a .22lr so the ammo's cheap."

Andrew pointed a finger like a gun barrel at Jake. "Okay, Wyatt Earp,"

Jake took a sip of beer, then looked at Lyle. "You like to shoot?"

Lyle shrugged. "I haven't been to a range in a long time. I oil my handguns regularly, but that's about it. Is there a range in Polk?"

"We just go out in the desert," Cody said.

"Yeah," added Andrew. "Saturdays about twice a month. A bunch of us shoot up things."

"What kind of things do you shoot up?" Lyle asked.

"Old boxes, trees, anything we can find," Andrew said. "And sometimes we put up targets."

"Hey, stop that, you asshole." The shout came from the bar, silencing Lyle's group and the rest of the room. A six-foot-plus guy stood up and loomed over the guy on the stool next to him. When the seated man got up, Andrew put his arm under the table, and Lyle recognized the reaching-for-your-gun motion.

The taller man at the bar slugged the other in the stomach with quick one-two jabs. Immediately, two other men, almost as tall as the first, grabbed the shorter man, who appeared to be Hispanic. They held his arms, shook him, then dragged him out of the bar.

Lyle told himself he could have helped, but the tussle lasted about a minute. What he did was watch to see if Andrew was going to pull out a gun. When he was a cop, he always reminded himself that anyone in Arizona could be carrying.

"We don't usually have fights like that here," Andrew said.

"Usually?" said Lyle.

Andrew lifted his beer. "Usually *white* folks in here, but now and then an illegal comes in. What can I say? Sometimes there's beefs."

With the excitement over, the hum of voices returned to the bar. Lyle and the others talked about baseball and movies for fifteen minutes, and Lyle was ready to leave. He stood.

"I'm going, too," said Jake. They walked out of the bar together.

"If you'd like to come shooting sometime," Jake said when they reached his car, "I can give you a call."

"Where do you go?"

"The national forest east of Polk is one of the places. I've only been there once. They say park rangers and San Navarro County deputies can be a problem. They also go to an area north of Cottonwood. It's outside San Navarro County. That's where I've been the most."

Lyle hesitated before he gave Jake his number.

CHAPTER 25

April 11

The day after her trip to Sun City Grand Kate sat with Lyle at her kitchen table over coffee. Trixie sat purring on her lap as Kate stroked her. The executive apartment in Timeless Village, near Lyle, was originally going to be temporary when Kate accepted NC employment. But plans changed. None she regretted.

"My plane leaves for Billings tomorrow at nine in the morning," Kate said. "Max approved the trip, as long as I don't break the law."

"That gives you a lot of leeway," Lyle said. "I'll sleep here if you like and look after Trixie."

Kate nodded. She rubbed under Trixie's chin and looked at her. "You going to miss me, little one?"

"You want a ride to the airport in the morning?"

"No. I found a flight from Flagstaff, not Phoenix, so it's an easy drive. The plane has one stop in Denver. A long flight."

"Any trouble persuading Max to let you go?"

"No. I told him what Mila Edwards said about the governor's crooked deals in Montana. He smiled and rubbed his hands together. He would love for me to dig up anything I can on Gudgel. I'm eager too, but Mila didn't have enough specific information we could count on. So, I need to go to Montana.

"I called the Gudgel relatives Mila put me in touch with. The family is in Billings, and a few agreed to talk to me."

"I hope you can find something useful. While you're gone, I'll spend more time online trying to figure out hate groups. I started researching them this morning. Rey says that's what the FBI is focusing on, and I don't know where else to go."

We have to fight hate every way we can. Kate got up and put her coffee cup in the sink.

"Kate, do you think it's possible that—"

"—Gudgel was involved in the shootings?"

"Yeah. Is he *that* wicked?"

"I don't know. Maybe I'll find out in Montana. Someone else is investigating him, too. I forgot to tell you about Gregory Hurt."

"Hurt?"

"He's a private investigator. He talked to me after the airport hearing. I don't know how he knew I would be there."

"Sounds fishy already."

"Wait, listen. We had coffee. He says he's investigating the governor for a client—a client who would like to see Gudgel in prison. He asked if we'd like to share information."

"About Gudgel?"

"Right. I went along with him to see what he'd tell me, but he didn't give me any details before he left. I asked Joann to check his background."

"Who else," Lyle said, "besides us, would want to dig into Gudgel's wretched life?"

"No idea. Have you had experience with PIs?"

"A little." Lyle got up to refill his cup. "Many do corporate work, like for insurance companies, and background checks for employment. Then there's always divorce cases. Sounds puzzling in connection with the governor. Not surprising he has enemies."

Lyle walked over and stood next to Kate. "This trip to Billings. What kind of schemes was Gudgel involved in up there? It's not dangerous, is it?"

"He was a minor cheat. Sounds like most people were happy to see him go. I'll be fine."

She looked into his eyes. "Lyle, I've been thinking."

"About what?

"About life, the future, you know, serious stuff."

"About?"

"Propinquity."

Before Lyle could respond, Kate's phone chimed.

"Hey Joann. What's—Where? That's horrible. Didn't the manager take over? What about security? Okay, when?" She looked at the time. "All right Joann, call the main gate and have them block off a parking space for me right up front. Tell them it's an emergency. Then call transportation and have an NC cab waiting for me at the gate in 10 minutes. I'm leaving now. If there's a problem, call me."

Kate put her phone down. "That's what I get for taking time off this afternoon to pack. Trouble at the park. Discrimination. Sounds like homophobia."

She pulled on her suit coat, kissed Lyle, and rushed out the door.

Twenty minutes later, she was looking at two young women holding hands near the counter in one of the park's fast-food restaurants. One stared at the floor, the other held a tissue in her free hand.

"Are you Alicia and Madison? I'm so sorry about this." Kate introduced herself as an NC vice president and said she would straighten things out. At the other side of the room, a young man in a paper hat—likely the clerk—stood talking with another man in a restaurant uniform and a security officer. The tallest one in the room, Kate took strides over to the group.

"Are you the person who refused to serve these two guests?" she said to the clerk.

"Yeah. I can't serve lesbos." He looked down for a moment, then back up at Kate. "It's against scripture. It's not normal." The clerk clenched his teeth and put his hands in his pockets.

Kate identified herself to the short, balding man in the yellow and blue uniform, as retro as the costume department could create. "Are you the manager? Why didn't *you* just give them their order? You know the park rules. I can't believe you'd let this happen to those two young ladies." She glared down at him. Her voice carried a note of violence she was nearly prepared to administer.

"I called security," the man stammered, glancing over at the two female customers who still clung to each other.

"I mean…" He held out both hands, palms up, as if the situation stymied his ability to think.

Kate looked at the security officer. His uniform insignia said he was the deputy security chief. "Do I know you?" she said.

"I don't think so, ma'am. I recognize you."

She motioned for him to follow her behind the counter and into a storage area. "You'll excuse me if I'm a little upset," she said. "I'm just wondering why you didn't straighten this out the minute you arrived."

"One of them was shouting, saying she was going to call TV news. I guess someone called your office."

"Maybe I would call the news media, too. This is the twenty-first century. Not the dark ages."

"Do you think, ma'am, the clerk has to be forced to serve someone?"

"Why don't I let *you* find out the answer? I want you to call your boss, Howard Chafee, and ask him if discrimination is a feature of Nostalgia City. Ask him to explain our policies to you."

The man's eyes cut to the side. He pursed his lips when he looked back at Kate.

"Or," she said, pulling out her phone, "I can call Max Maxwell and have *him* explain our tolerance of homophobia, just before he fires you." She lowered her voice for the last few words, but not so low he couldn't hear.

"Let me apologize again for the park," she told the young women when she was back out in front of the counter. "I'd like you to be our guests at the Ranch House Restaurant. It's just a couple of blocks from here. I'll call and tell them to give you anything you'd like, on us. Also, if you give me contact information, I will see that we refund your admission today and send you a year-long pass."

One of the women offered something close to a smile, the other scowled, defiant. "We were going to call the news media."

"That's absolutely your right. You can still do it, and it won't change anything I've told you. I'm not doing this to buy you off. I'm doing it because I'm disgusted that a park employee treated you this way. I will do everything I can to make sure this never happens again, to anyone."

CHAPTER 26

Lyle felt relieved when Kate dashed off to put out the PR fire. Was it time for a serious talk? Their relationship warmed and comforted him, occasionally confusing him. Sam liked Kate, and he wanted the best, whatever that was.

Rey and dozens of law enforcement people struggled to find answers to the recent evil, and he pondered imponderables. *C'mon Deming, people were killed. People you worked with. What can you* do?"

He pulled out Kate's laptop and logged into an anti-government hate group site he hadn't seen before. At first glance, it looked like Facebook for Nazis. Random racist rants mixed with general complaints about government regulations, bad weather—caused by science experiments—discussions about individual hate organizations, and the occasional cat video.

He noticed posts about one local hate group and saw stylized letters, *CBA,* for Cadre Brave Arizona. He stared at it for a moment, then remembered where he had seen it before: on the forearm of Andrew, who he'd met at the bar. Continuing through the site, he saw another design he'd seen on Andrews's arm: an iron cross. *How can hate be a venerated commodity?*

Lyle filled up his coffee to search further, but soon feelings of shock and revulsion from the racist screeds and insane conspiracy theories were too much. *Is it okay to* hate *hate?* Time to change the subject, momentarily. Kate was still at work, so he called Howard to see if he had time to talk.

When Lyle started at Nostalgia City, an ex-FBI agent ran park security with a heavy hand, one that came down indiscriminately on Lyle, even while he was doing Maxwell's bidding.

Howard brought stability, consistency, and common sense to the job that required law enforcement experience at managerial levels, and perhaps above all, cognizance that everyone at the park was a paying *guest*, not a suspicious perp—even though they might be. He and Lyle had worked on a few NC *issues* together and understood each other.

When Lyle stepped into Howard's open office door he saw an assortment of papers on his desk and the security chief staring with wrinkled brow into his computer screen.

"You said you weren't busy," Lyle said as he took a hesitant step into the office.

"I'm usually busy these days," Howard said. "The shootings are having a cascading effect at the park. But I could use a break. C'mon in."

"Bet you didn't expect to be in the middle of hate crimes when you signed on here."

Howard had jettisoned his sport coat and loosened his tie. "It's not like we didn't have them in San Francisco, but these days they can appear anywhere. The sheriff and the Fibbies are looking for a hate group to take credit, or give them hints on the dark web, or elsewhere."

Lyle sat in a wooden chair several feet from a corner of Howard's desk. "I think I had a beer with members of a local bunch of crazies yesterday."

He explained his meeting Cody, Jake, and Andrew.

"West's Bar and Grill?" Howard said. "My wife and I wandered in there a few months ago. We didn't stay."

"I know what you mean. We arrived in time for the bar fight du jour. The place makes a biker bar look like Applebee's. Has a racist atmosphere. One guy in our group had a Cadre Brave tat on his arm."

"That would be right."

"I don't understand the attraction of hate groups. You get together to celebrate your anger?" Lyle scrunched up his mouth in a crooked, quizzical expression.

"They blame others for their problems and the country's. Everything is someone else's fault," Howard said. "Everybody else gets the breaks."

"So they band together to blame Asians, Hispanics, Blacks, gay people?"

"I didn't say it was logical."

"Why don't they blame Democrats, too?"

"They do, but they call them socialists or Marxists."

"Is there an anti-Bernie Sanders hate group?"

Howard raised his coffee mug in a toast. "Speaking of politics, what's the latest with the governor? I heard about the airport thing."

"Max wants to go on the offensive. We'll see what develops." Lyle trusted Howard but figured anything that Kate, Max, and possibly he did to derail the governor should be handled need-to-know.

"I have a question for *you* Howard, what's with the guys in camo uniforms who are always around Gudgel? Is it the National Guard?"

"No. *State* Guard, Arizona State Guard."

"Okay, that was formed after I left the PD, but from what I read at the time, I thought it was volunteers who help out during local disasters. Supplement the National Guard maybe."

"Funny you should ask. I heard about the State Guard recently. It goes back to an organization formed during World War II set up to provide domestic disaster assistance. It was also seen as a last line of defense if the US had been invaded. A few years after the war, it was disbanded. But Gudgel had it reinstated."

"To help with floods? In Arizona?"

"Any kind of disaster, I guess. A bunch of other states have state guards too, remnants from World War II. But about ten months ago the guard here in Arizona morphed into a militia. I have no idea what its responsibilities are. All in all, it looks like a small private army under control of the governor."

"Holy Paul Revere," Lyle said, "how come I didn't read about this?"

"It's been a low-key transformation. I learned the details from one of the managers in the park's surveillance center. He used to be with the State Guard, but quit. He told me he thought it was becoming a band of undisciplined storm troopers. Guys who report only to Gudgel."

I need to find out more about this. *I wonder if Max knows.* "You see these guys on TV when the governor makes an appearance. Makes it look like Gudgel is protected by the U.S. Army."

"You ought to talk with this guy in the Control Center. I'll give you his phone extension. He's not afraid to talk about it. Says he was glad to get out."

A bigoted, spiteful governor with his own army? And at NC we create make-believe adventures and try to make people happy. This sounds like an even contest.

Lyle's phone buzzed, signaling a text:

This is Jake. We're going shooting
Saturday. Interested?

CHAPTER 27

April 12

Why am I going to Montana? Kate asked herself at 35,000 feet.

What am I looking for? Evidence of Gudgel's soiled political career? A witness willing to admit Gudgel accepted a bribe? A person materially harmed by his actions?

She squirmed in her seat and stretched out one leg in the aisle. Even though she had booked a coach-plus seat, realistic legroom, especially for someone over six feet, was a myth. She wanted more than just a Gudgel relative calling the governor a scumbag. Kate wanted something that would make Gudgel think twice about any more moves against the park. She wanted to end his career.

Online research using Rod Gudgel and Montana as search terms had yielded too many stories to read at one sitting. She found stories on Greatland that Mila Edwards had mentioned, and she hoped someone would fill in details.

At the Billings airport, she rented a small Nissan SUV and headed down the gradually sloping road toward downtown. Patchy clouds hung over the city, and judging by a nip in the air, bare trees, and remnants of snow in the shadows, Billings was struggling to embrace spring. Kate checked into the Blue Spruce Hotel, something of a Billings landmark. She had a comfortable early dinner in the dining room, then checked the address of the destination for her first Gudgel "family talk."

The Betty and Jay Safewrights lived on a numbered street in the western section of town. Betty met her at the door, and Kate knew Betty was a Gudgel. She had the governor's high forehead and narrow face. When she smiled, the likeness faded.

"Welcome, Kate. Please come in."

She introduced her husband Jay, and they settled in the family room. She offered Kate coffee and homemade pie.

"Thank you, but I just finished dinner. I appreciate your inviting me tonight. Safewright?" Kate said. "I have that right?"

"I know," Jay said, "it sounds like the windshield company. I always have to spell it for people. It's an ancient Scottish name."

His chunky build contrasted with his wife's slender one. His tightly cropped gray beard would disqualify him from playing Santa, but he otherwise fit the bill. He relaxed onto the couch next to his wife.

"Betty told me about your call," he said. "I'm interested to hear exactly why you're here and what you're looking for."

"I work for Nostalgia City, as you know. Have you been there?"

"No," said Betty. "We'd like to someday. We've been to Disneyland."

"We're a theme park like our better-known neighbor in California. And recently Governor Gudgel has made derogatory remarks about the park and about the people who were murdered. We don't know what to expect next."

"We read about the shootings," Jay said, "the death of your employees. They were hate crimes."

"Not according to the governor. He seemed only concerned about his campaign headquarters."

Betty glanced at her husband. "We can certainly tell you that my cousin is often vindictive. We grew up together here, and I learned to be careful with Roddy. If you did something. If you criticized him. If he even just *thought* you told his mother on him, he would remember and get back at you. It might be a week later and for no reason, he'd start a nasty rumor or steal something."

Sounds like him. Kate nodded.

"When he was elected to the legislature," Betty said, "we think he used his position to support legislation to benefit his corporate clients. He was a full-time attorney while in the legislature."

"Being an attorney and a legislator is not inherently dishonest," Jay said. "A number of legislators are practicing lawyers. But most don't mix the two the way Rod did."

"And if anyone threatened to expose him," Betty said, "he was ready with unsavory, incriminating details of others' lives that he dug up."

"From his character, it sounds as if Nostalgia City can expect more attacks from him when we stand up for decency. I was hoping to find out something specific he *did* here."

Betty looked at her husband. "We could tell her about Great Falls Greatland."

"That could have been a billion-dollar boondoggle for Rod," he said, "but the whole thing collapsed before it got anywhere."

"Long story," Betty said. "It involves a development company that wanted to build a mini-Las Vegas in Great Falls. Hotels, casinos, amusements. It required several major pieces of legislation to make it all legal and give the company tax breaks and other incentives."

"The company would get all of these breaks," Jay said, "and Roddy would earn substantial *legal fees*."

"Bribes?" Kate asked.

"Essentially, but he didn't sponsor the legislation. He got some fool representing Great Falls to do it so he could seem out of the loop. But he lobbied for it until it came out that Roddy had recently represented the development company. So he immediately backed out, claimed to be neutral, and stopped supporting it—in public."

"Tell her about the funding," Betty said.

Jay smiled impishly, reinforcing his Santa similarity. "Turns out the development company got its funding from the Saudis who were running the whole shebang. They'd flown Rod back to Riyadh, the capital, more than once, to encourage his continued support. When the source of funding was uncovered, it soured everyone and the legislation went down the tubes."

"But Rod Gudgel got paid," Kate said.

"Not nearly what he was expecting. And the shell corporation disappeared."

A marvelous story, but how can I substantiate this? "Did Roddy—Gudgel—tell you about this?" Kate asked.

Betty shook her head. "Not in so many words, but he bragged about what a grand project this was."

"But all the details?" Kate said.

"The family grapevine," Jay said. "And sometimes Sheila, Roddy's wife, would say too much at parties, especially after she'd been drinking."

"The papers covered the story, too," said Jay, "but we liked the family's slant on it."

Citing a family grapevine about a 20-or 30-year-old failed scam would not shake the foundations of a powerful governor, even if it did confirm his penchant for corruption. Would throwing the word *Greatland* in his face be worth anything? At least she picked up a psychological profile of a malicious, revengeful child who became governor of Arizona.

At the door, she thanked her hosts.

"You're going to see Angie and Dan tomorrow?" Betty asked.

"Oh, did they tell you?"

"Oh yes. Our ad got the whole family talking. And Mila told everyone about you."

CHAPTER 28

April 13

Rat-tat-tat. Rat-tat-tat.

Unmistakably the sound of a machine gun. A big one.

Lyle could hear it over the sound of Kansas doing "Dust in the Wind" on his car radio as he steered down the dirt road.

Too far away to see what was happening, Lyle slowed his Mustang even below the speed of its hesitant crawl over the potholes. Jake had given him directions to the place where he and his friends took target practice. He neglected to explain the journey included a few miles through open, scrub-covered desert on a trail better suited for a different type of mustang.

He approached a rise dotted with piñon pines. Around a slight curve, he saw a string of vehicles—mostly 4WD pickups—parked just off the road. Lyle pulled over and listened as he got out of the car. Machine gun blasts occasionally interrupted small arms fire. Holstered on his hip, Lyle wore his Charter Arms .380 revolver, and he carried a small box of ammunition. The odor of gunpowder hung in the air. He crept along the edge of the road, unsure if he should take his gun out. As he got closer, he saw a row of people, mostly men, with their backs to him, firing toward a line of makeshift targets on a low hill. Lyle pulled his shooting earmuffs from around his neck and fit them over his ears. At the end of the row, he saw someone sitting on the ground behind a tripod-mounted machine gun.

Many of the shooters fired handguns; a few held AR-15-style rifles. Two wore black tactical helmets with front mounts for night-vision goggles. A knot of men stood behind the noisy firing line trying to talk to each other but mostly gesturing and laughing. Two of them drank beer from bottles.

Lyle strolled along behind the shooters, noticing CBA patches on jackets and a CBA tat on a forearm. He noticed a tall, blond-haired guy firing a pistol at a bulls-eye target suspended from a wooden stand about 30 feet away. He lowered his dimpled chin and took aim using the Weaver, an angled shooting stance. The blond coolly put a succession of shots in a tiny pattern in the bullseye.

Watching the collection of armed CBA shooters, Lyle thought of them as potential—or actual—murderers. Did one of them kill and injure the demonstrators and possibly shoot Lightfoot as well? These people knew how to handle weapons, and most seemed to belong to an identified group. *You wanted to know about hate groups, Deming. You found one.*

Before he reached the end of the firing line, Lyle froze.

Behind the .30 caliber machine gun sat a young girl. She used both hands on the gun, firing short bursts. The weapon chugged and shook as it spit steel-jacketed bullets at 2,800 feet per second. Empty shell casings tumbled out like quarters from an old-style slot machine. An unarmed man in a denim jacket stood behind her and patted her on the back when she finished the barrage. She turned and smiled. She wore earplugs and a pink t-shirt with a pistol on it.

Lyle stared.

She looked to be no older than eight or nine. Was the girl this man's daughter? A captive? What kind of person teaches a child of that age how to fire a deadly—and probably illegal—machine gun? Lyle couldn't move. The entire scene was dangerous. A sharp pat on his back surprised him enough to make him slap his hand down to his holster.

"Whoa," said a smiling Jake. "Didn't mean to startle you. That's unusual, isn't it?" He gestured toward the girl. "She's only eight."

"Cease fire," the marksman with the Weaver stance shouted from the other end of the firing line, and a dozen men and one woman stopped shooting, lowering their weapons.

Lyle still couldn't fathom the eight-year-old machine gunner. He turned away and watched as the man who called the cease fire walked to the two beer drinkers.

"What th' hell are you doing?" the man said. "You know there's no alcohol here." He stood ramrod straight, holstered his semi-auto, and rested his fists on his hips. "Put your weapons back in your trucks. Or better yet, get the fuck out of here."

His sharp, but controlled voice penetrated Lyle's ear protection. "Who's that?" he asked Jake, as he watched the two drinkers shuffle back to the parked trucks. "Is he the range master?"

"Sort of. That's Wylie. He supervises things out here."

Lyle wanted to pump Jake about the machine gunner, but not within earshot of the girl. With the firing stopped, Lyle and Jake wandered over to folding tables that held gun cases, ammo boxes, bottles of water.

"What the hell," Lyle said. "What's an eight-year-old doing firing a damn machine gun?" Lyle had other questions too, such as where did anyone get a GI belt-fed machine gun, where did the ammo come from, and what the hell did they plan to do with it? But he settled for just his one question now.

"Yeah, it can be kind of a shock. Her name's Sonya, and that's her father. I've only seen them out here once before."

"Is this a gun club, a private range, or what?" Lyle asked.

"It's a group of people who like to shoot, you could say. We do other things, too."

"I see Cadre Brave patches. Is that—"

Wylie gave the signal, and shooting resumed. Jake raised his voice and told Lyle he could use his target. He led him to a position on the firing line opposite a reinforced cardboard refrigerator box with several targets pasted to it.

Lyle fired six times, doing better than he expected. As he reloaded, he looked over to the machine gun emplacement. Father and daughter were dismantling the gun.

Lyle fired another cylinder's worth of rounds, again getting his shots approximately where he wanted them to go.

He stepped back and let Jake take over with his Glock. Glancing down the line to his left, Lyle saw Andrew, the muscular HVAC tech from the other night, firing at a target in a tree with a large caliber semi-auto. After destroying the target, he started in on pine cones on the ground—not a safe idea. The abundance of rocks could lead to dangerous ricochets. Next to Andrew, a guy blazed away at a paper target with a long-barreled Colt .44 magnum, a weapon slightly smaller than a howitzer. The paper target carried a caricature of a national political figure.

After he'd fired off two more cylinders, Lyle ran out of ammo. He lingered, watching the other shooters—all white. He used his phone to take a few quick pictures of *suspects*. Was one capable of slaughtering innocent people?

Dressed in casual clothes, several in camos, the shooters ranged in age from twenties to fifties and many handled their weapons like pros, pumping rounds into bullseyes. The one woman in the group, a thirtyish redhead, fired, picked up her brass, reloaded, and fired again like she'd done it for years.

A guy in his forties attracted Lyle's attention as he fired. Shorter than average and thin, he had light brown hair and a bland, flat face making him look remarkably ordinary. Except this man's sizeable ears stuck out almost perpendicular to his head. He wielded an assault rifle, aiming and screwing up his face in a frown, as if he were angry at the target. The guy squeezed off rounds almost as quickly as full auto. He was one of two on the firing line shooting at targets, similar to those used by police, showing the outline of a man rather than a bullseye.

Big ears and several other shooters exchanged weapons. Guys with pistols got a chance to fire assault rifles and vice versa. Jake gave Lyle a chance to shoot the Old West style six-shooter he'd just purchased. It reminded Lyle of a plastic gun he'd had as a child.

As the crack of gunfire faded, people gathered in small groups. Jake introduced Lyle to three other guys who chided him on his choice of a revolver over a semi-auto.

"I'm comfortable with it," Lyle said, "and it's a little easier to clean, even though I have to scrub each cylinder. Then there's the jamming issue with semi-autos."

"That's bullshit," said one guy.

They talked ammo loads, gun manufacturers, and dreaded gun control. Lyle couldn't imagine Arizona gun laws any looser. Anyone over 21 could carry a concealed, loaded weapon. No permit required.

"Well, we'll all be ready when the time comes, won't we?" said a short man in a denim vest as the conversation lagged. They all nodded in agreement. "The deep state is getting more and more powerful," he said, "but slowly."

"Yeah, we all know the quote," said a thirtyish guy in a t-shirt that revealed a CBA tat on his lower arm. "And before you realize it, the state has taken away your rights."

CHAPTER 29

First Prairie Bank's headquarters occupied a six-story grey stone building in downtown Billings. From the decorative keystones and other embellishments, Kate guessed the building had been there for some time. Up close, the numerals 1-9-2-2 over the main entrance also helped date the structure. She smiled at herself as she pulled open the heavy brass-framed glass door at four minutes past nine o'clock on a dark, cloudy morning.

Dan Meacham, VP for commercial loans, had told her the branch office on the ground floor would be open and she could take the elevator to his department on the fourth floor.

A tall, paneled wooden door with scrollwork and a frosted glass window opened into his outer office. Meacham, a fiftyish man of average height, stepped out from his private office and introduced himself. His round face and open expression gave him a guileless look. He wore a sport coat, slacks and an open-neck shirt. *Banker's casual?*

"Rod Gudgel and I are almost the same age, but I'm his uncle," Meacham told Kate as they walked into his office. "My sister, his mother, was much older than me."

Kate took off her overcoat and draped it on a chair. "Thanks for meeting me on Saturday," she said.

"I had a little backlogged paperwork to take care of, so no problem."

Kate started to explain her quest, but Meacham stopped her, filling in details himself. "I know your mission," he said. "We've been talking, the family has.

"I've thought about this a lot." He toyed with a fat gold and black pen on his desk. "Sadly, my sister passed a couple of years ago. I never really knew if she—if she understood her son was unequivocally not a good person. She was proud he was Arizona governor but didn't talk about it much."

His arms resting on his desk, Meacham looked at the fat pen. After a moment, he tapped it on his desktop and looked up.

"I know what Rod did here in Montana and have followed his so-called career in Arizona. Not all of us who signed the ad disagree with his politics, but we all agree someone without a moral compass doesn't belong in power. That's why I'm willing to help you." He looked past Kate to the office wall and took a deep breath. "He's family, but we're appalled."

"I share your view, or I wouldn't be here."

"I understand, but regardless, I have to ask you to not use my name as a source in any way."

Everyone signed the ad. What have they got to lose? "Okay, Mr. Meacham." *Is this going to be good?*

"Call me Dan. You'll be able to confirm much of what I tell you from newspaper files. Although it's old news, if your goal is to defend yourself from him, to stop petulant reactions to imagined slights, then you might mention the Sunnyside State Building."

First Great Falls *Greatland,* now Sunnyside State Building. Kate wondered how many touchstones from Gudgel's past it would take to create an avalanche of grief for the governor.

Meacham set his jaw and glanced at the door to his office. Did he want to close it even though the entire floor was deserted?

"May I take notes?" she asked.

He nodded, and she pulled out a small pad and pencil.

"You know Rod rigged bids," Meacham said. "He didn't do it right away, but by the time he became chair of the appropriations committee in the legislature, construction companies knew what they needed to do to get a state contract. Many of the jobs were small and Rod didn't make much in 'commissions'. Highway contracts were more lucrative.

"The new state office building in Billings promised to be a sizable job." He lifted the pen he'd been holding and gestured with it at Kate. "The state received bids from companies across Montana and one of Gudgel's local favorites turned in the lowest bid. What a surprise. Obvious clues in the process should have raised red flags. Maybe he became careless, having evaded detection so many times before."

Meacham explained the winning bidder, McFee Constructors, hired a sub for the framing. During construction, floor supports gave way injuring two people, one seriously. A fall crushed the legs of carpenter Bruno Venner. At first, the accident was investigated as attempted murder due to previous fights among the workers.

"Venner was in the hospital for surgery on his legs and internal injuries," Meacham said. "As insurance claims were being sorted out, Venner told the McFee company and the sub-contractor that he knew McFee bribed Gudgel to get the contract *and* that the sub used cheap, inferior materials and took other dangerous shortcuts. Shortcuts that Gudgel and the McFee folks knew about."

"How did you—" Kate said.

Meacham held up a hand. "I know. I'll get to that. The crux of the matter was that Venner had complained to supervisors that the work was unsafe. They told him to keep his mouth shut and do his job. So, from his hospital bed, Venner became a blackmailer."

Kate looked up from her notepad. *Bribery, malfeasance, negligence. What else?*

"You're wondering how I got this information. It's a small town. I knew some of the players."

Meacham looked across the room. "I can't remember the exact order of things. Let me call my wife for a minute." Rather than use his desk phone, he pulled out a cell phone and in less than a minute was talking to his wife.

"Angie, I'm talking to Kate Sorensen, the woman from Nostalgia City. You're on speaker. Do you remember how old man Venner blackmailed everyone? Wasn't that attorney involved?"

"Hello Ms. Sorensen. Is Dan giving you the lowdown on Roddy?"

"Hi, Ms. Meacham," Kate said. "Thank you for your help."

"So, it was that ambulance chasing attorney from Spokane, remember?" Mrs. Meacham said.

"That's right," her husband said. "He came into it when the murder investigation was canceled and building inspectors went back to work. One of them had been bribed, too."

"Yes," Mrs. Meacham said, her voice echoing off her husband's desk. "He had to be bribed twice. First during construction, then later after the accident."

"Who paid Venner's blackmail?" Kate asked.

"Just about everybody," Mrs. Meacham said. "The builder, inspector, the sub of course, but Roddy had to pile in the money, too. Old man Venner threatened to expose everything. Even the bank was involved to some extent."

Dan Meacham nodded. "Rod tried to run a blackmail within a blackmail, forcing McFee to pony up more than its share of the extortion money. But Rod no doubt took a bath anyway because he'd finagled the bidding process in the first place and had to cover his behind. The attorney turned out to be the bagman."

"Poor old Venner," Angie Meacham said, her voice softening. "He spent the rest of his life in a wheelchair. Never really recovered from all his injuries. He died a few months later."

Kate jotted in her book adding *negligent death* to Gudgel's criminalities.

Meacham thanked his wife and clicked off the phone.

"So what happened to all the principals?" Kate said.

"The subcontractor went out of business shortly thereafter, and I guess they moved. The other guy who was injured got a small piece of the pie because he didn't know enough to be a big threat. And the key building inspector retired. Of course Venner died. His son still works in construction here. Has a small company that does mostly subcontracting work. McFee is still one of the largest builders in the state."

"Sunnyside State Building," Kate said, mulling the details in her head. She put away her notebook. *How can I use this information?* "So Gudgel was partially responsible for the injuries and maybe Venner's death."

"His corruption started the chain of events," Meacham said. "I consider him culpable."

CHAPTER 30

Suspicion, distrust, and curiosity tugged Lyle in different directions. He stood at the desert gun range and plucked his wrist rubber band. He had soaked up everything he saw, heard, and smelled during the rapid fire and later. Visions of the child behind the machine gun made him want to smack the father or just hop in his Mustang and put the entire group in the rearview; still he wanted to know more.

Many of the shooters headed to their trucks; a few remained. Lyle pulled out his phone, hoping to take quick, unnoticed photos of the few guys left.

Crack!

One gunshot and a cry of pain grabbed the stragglers' attention. Lyle spun around and saw a man drop his semi-auto and fall to the ground clutching his leg. Lyle dashed to the middle-aged man and knelt over him. *The idiot shot himself.*

Blood quickly soaked the man's right pant leg. Lyle

saw the bullet hole and groped for a spot to apply pressure. He wondered if he'd severed his femoral artery.

Jake and two others stood over Lyle.

"Gimme a knife," Lyle said.

"Here." Jake flipped open a large folding knife.

Lyle grabbed the knife and cut away part of the man's pant leg. Using the loose fabric, he applied pressure to the wound.

"He might have cut an artery," Lyle said. "Call an ambulance."

"Out here?" Jake said. "The closest fire station is a long ways away. I don't know if they'd find us in time."

"Help me," moaned the man on the ground.

"I can drive," said another man. "I have a Suburban, and I know the way to the hospital."

"Get your truck," Lyle barked.

As the guy ran off, Lyle pulled off the wounded man's belt and slipped it around his thigh. He pulled it tight, but couldn't fasten it. The buckle was useless cinched up this far. Lyle gripped the belt firmly and almost stopped the blood flow.

He leaned close to his patient. "I'm Lyle. What's your name?"

"That's Bobby," said the other man standing over Lyle. Bobby's eyes pleaded with Lyle for a miracle.

"We can use this blanket," said Jake, who appeared in Lyle's line of sight holding a large striped blanket someone had been sitting on.

The Suburban crunched toward them in reverse over the rocky soil. "Okay you two, spread out the blanket next to Bobby. One of you take his shoulders and the other his legs and lift him onto it."

The men followed his orders. Fortunately, Bobby stood probably five feet six and was not a heavy load. He groaned and screamed as they lowered him onto the blanket while Lyle held the belt. The Suburban driver jumped out and opened the rear door.

"I need something for a better tourniquet," Lyle shouted. He shifted his grip to keep the belt tight, his forearms covered in blood. "You got any rope?"

Jake grabbed a coiled cord from the back of the Suburban and threw it to Lyle.

"That's great." He cut the cord and wrapped it around Bobby's thigh, replacing the belt. But blood flowed again. He needed a way to keep it tight. "Hey, give me that stick." Lyle pointed to a stubby broken branch. Jake handed him the branch. He looped the cord around it and twisted. The tourniquet held. "Get him in the truck."

With the back seats down, the two men slid Bobby through the rear door of the vehicle as Lyle scooted in beside him, holding Bobby's leg and the tourniquet. Lyle found a backpack and shoved it under Bobby's leg. Jake jumped in the passenger seat and waved off the fourth man.

Lyle held on. The Suburban crawled, swayed, and bumped over the dirt road as Bobby groaned. Once on pavement, the driver turned on his emergency flashers and drove as if he were at the wheel of an ambulance. Lyle kept an eye on the wound. Bobby had lost blood, but not a critical amount, he hoped.

When the Suburban screeched around a corner, tires

lost their purchase on the road. The rear swung one way, then the other like a saloon door.

Bobby screamed in pain, then shouted. "Don't kill me 'fore we get there."

"You shot yourself asshole. I'm trying to save you," the manic driver said, regaining control of the careering vehicle.

Soon the highway heroics paid off, and they arrived at the ER in half the time it took Lyle to drive to the shooting range.

White coats transferred Bobby out of the Suburban with practiced care, onto a gurney, and through the ER doors. Walking alongside, Lyle let go when a nurse took over the tourniquet. Just inside the emergency room, Jake explained to the nurse that Bobby had shot himself. He provided Bobby's full name but didn't know his Polk address or exact age. He explained how they had transported him from a shooting range in the desert.

Lyle felt self-conscious bringing in a gunshot casualty while still wearing his revolver on his hip, his arms and chest painted with the victim's blood. There had been no time for him to stash his gun back in his car, and he knew a gunshot wound would trigger a visit from a sheriff's deputy. Jake and the driver—who turned out to be *Ed*—left their weapons in the Suburban.

After Lyle washed off as much blood as he could, a nurse told him and the other two to stick around and for Lyle to keep his gun out of the hospital. Lyle told her they weren't going anywhere. The ER crew worked on Bobby. Lyle, Jake, and the hotshot driver stood outside— Ed wanted to smoke.

Lyle found a spot downwind near the building, and the other two leaned on a railing that ran around the ambulance ramp.

"I should have picked up his gun," Ed said, exhaling smoke. "It was lying right next to him."

"We can get it when you take us back to pick up our cars," Jake said. "If someone else didn't get it."

"Wylie's going to be mad," the smoker said, taking another drag.

"He left early," Jake said. "Bobby was careless. We all saw what happened."

"Who is Wiley anyway?" Lyle said.

Jake glanced at Ed. "We're members of Cadre Brave." He pointed to the CBA patch on Ed's jacket. "You probably saw other guys wearing this. Wiley is in charge in the county."

Lyle said, "What's it all about?"

"We're patriotic citizens," Ed said. "We stand up for America. We need to stop citizens' rights from being sacrificed by government control. It's not good."

"CB is all about returning to the real American standards, the way we grew up," Jake said. "We respect and honor our history, the Constitution, and what the founders of the country intended, and I'm not ashamed to talk about it."

Ed took the cigarette out of his mouth. "We also don't want them teaching kids about queer sex in schools."

Jake's glance at Ed might have been reproving. Was he telling the outsider too much? "We're organized to stand up for the little guy," he said.

"Little guy?" Lyle said.

"The average white male," Jake said. "He's lost today in our mixed-up society."

"*American* family values," Ed said.

Lyle translated, *straight white male values*. "I'm all for traditional values." He could see where this was going and decided to take the ride.

Lyle nodded as Ed ticked off problems that showed him the need for an alert group like the Cadre Brave: Hispanic immigration, gun control and, of course, the deep state.

Ed took a breath to continue, then stopped when a San Navarro County Sheriff's cruiser pulled up to the ramp. He and Jake turned from Lyle as Rey Martinez got out of the car and walked toward them.

CHAPTER 31

As the bank lay only a mile from Kate's hotel, she'd walked to the meeting with Meacham. As she stepped outside, she felt a chilly wind whoosh down the street. Clouds blocked the sun. She buttoned up her coat. The brisk walk back warmed her up, but she still paused in the hotel lobby in front of a coffee bar for a hot cup.

One man stood in front of her, but he stepped aside and motioned for her to place an order. When she had a steaming cup in hand, she turned and the man who had moved aside stood ten feet away staring at her. A frown tugged at the corners of his mouth. Coupled with his lowered brows, his expression made Kate think he wanted to inflict bodily harm. But as she walked past, his face changed to an impassive gaze.

"Ms. Sorensen," he said, "I need to talk to you."

Kate's usual height advantage disappeared. This man was as tall as Kate and bulky. Thankfully, this was no dark alley. The lobby bustled.

"Let's go outside," the man said.

"I have a feeling you're not inviting me to lunch," Kate said, "so you can talk here." She strolled over to a high table and chairs near the coffee bar. She set her cup on the table but did not sit.

She looked at the man across the table and noticed a slight Gudgel family resemblance. He was younger and heavier than the governor, but his hairline and perhaps his demeanor struck a familiar chord.

"Why are you here?" he said. "It's to cause trouble, isn't it? You're just like Dan and the others, trying to destroy. Is it politics? Were you involved in the advertising?"

"How did you know who I was?" Kate asked.

"I figured it out."

"You know who I am. Who are you, and what do you want?"

"Mickey, Mickey Gudgel. I want to know what you're doing, why you're here." He put a beefy arm on the table.

"First of all, it sounds like you have a difference of opinion in your family. That's for you to work out. I'm not a part of it."

"Yes, you are the problem."

"I don't respond well to being accosted like this, and I have no need to share my business with you."

"You're just trying to dig up old lies and stories." He put his other arm on the table and cast a feral look at Kate. "You'd better be careful. Accidents happen."

Kate wondered how she would break it off with him, but he solved the problem by storming out of the hotel.

She found the safety of her room, locked the door, and took a deep breath. Obviously *that* Gudgel did not sign the advertising.

Laying down her coat, she glanced out the window at billowing awnings on buildings below. At the desk, she set up her laptop and got to work. First, she took Meacham's advice and dug into Billings newspaper archives. Rather than just using Gudgel's name, she now had search terms such as Sunnyside State Building, Venner, McFee and others.

After reading through the stories about the Sunnyside State Building, Kate found Meacham's account to be essentially correct. "Old Man" Venner, Bruno Venner, Sr., died four months after his 'accident'.

News sites also yielded stories on Greatland. First publicly endorsed by Gudgel, then abandoned, according to one article, Greatland did not generate interest among the public or legislators, especially as it was funded by a foreign country. An editorial called it a 'half-baked idea.'

In the *Billings Monthly Broadside,* she came across a story headlined, *Ariz. governor's family knows the real Rod Gudgel.* Certainly not a Gudgel puff piece. She called the editor who authored the article, but wound up talking to voicemail. She explained—briefly—who she was and asked if she could see him.

Using "Venner Construction" as a search term, she found an address in Laurel, a small town southwest of Billings. On a hunch, she called and discovered that "Junior" Venner was the owner. The recording said the office was open five days a week, but Kate took a chance that he'd be there. Owners of small companies didn't always keep regular hours.

After a twenty-five minute drive, she parked in front of a metal industrial building with the name Venner over the door. The sun had come out, so she left her coat in the car. Finding the office deserted, she wandered around the side of the one-story building and saw rows of stacked lumber stored under metal shelters. A yellow forklift idled in one corner. Three men stood around it talking.

In her dark mauve suit she thought she might look like an attorney or maybe a banker, certainly not someone often seen in the storage yard. Only one of the men watched her approach.

"Excuse me," she said. "I'm looking for Mr. Venner."

A long-legged man in jeans and a western shirt turned. "That's me. What can I do for you?" He looked at her as if he saw a six-three blonde in a business suit every day on construction sites.

Kate told him her name and asked if they could talk. He glanced at the others with a smile and pointed toward the office. She guessed Venner to be in his early 40s, making him twenty-something at the time of his father's fall. As they walked, Kate told him who she worked for and that she was checking into Gudgel's background.

Before they reached the office door, Venner stopped. "Why would I know anything about the governor of Arizona?"

"Your father—" she started to say.

"Okay, I know where you're going. You want to know if he was involved in my father's death."

Kate tried a sympathetic smile. "I believe there's a connection, and I wondered what you remembered about that time."

"Why, what difference does it make? That was over 20 years ago."

She explained Gudgel's campaign against Nostalgia City and his comments after the shootings.

"Three innocent people were killed, three injured, in hate crimes, and Governor Gudgel said it was 'woke' to lament their deaths. Was he equally unconcerned when your father got hurt?"

"I get it," Venner said. "You want me to tell you Gudgel is a crook and responsible for my dad's death. Yes, he *is* a crook. He tried to make a bundle on a rigged, hazardous construction job that resulted in my dad's accident and death. But I'm not going to give you a statement blaming Rod Gudgel. I'm sorry other people died. I am. He's a lowlife. But No. I'm done talking about this. I live and work here. No."

"I'll do the dirty work to get the governor exposed and, we hope, out of office. I just need—"

"Sorry, Ms. Sorensen. I have kids. I've lived here all my life. I have a business. Sorry."

Kate told him she understood and would keep him out of it.

He turned and walked away.

CHAPTER 32

When Lyle saw Rey get out of his car at the hospital ER ramp, he thought his brief flirtation with Cadre Brave was over. He could imagine Rey calling him by name and asking him—facetiously—if he shot anyone.

Rey made eye contact with Lyle. With the two Cadre Brave members' backs to him, Lyle met Rey's gaze, frowned, and shook his head.

"Are you the three who brought in the gunshot victim?" Rey said as he reached the top of the ramp.

"Yeah," Ed said. "He shot himself in the leg. It was an accident."

"You, with the gun," Rey said. "May I see it?"

Without a word, Lyle pulled out his revolver and handed it to Rey.

"We were at a shooting range," Ed said, taking a half step toward Rey, "so his gun was fired, but he didn't have nothing to do with the shooting. He probably saved Bobby's life, okay?"

Rey looked from Ed to Lyle and back. Lyle still thought his friend might make a smart remark. Instead, he asked everyone to give him their names. A second sheriff's car arrived, and a deputy joined Rey.

"The deputy is going to take your statements," Rey said. "I need to go inside and talk to the doctor."

Carrying Lyle's handgun, Rey walked into the emergency room, and the deputy asked Jake to walk with him over behind one of the black and whites.

Out of earshot, Lyle and Ed watched the deputy question Jake, taking notes as he did.

"Damn Mexican cop with the fancy uniform," Ed said in a low voice. "I think I seen him before. Don't like 'im. He better not try anything."

After a couple of minutes, Rey appeared. "Looks like your friend will survive," he said. "He won't be running any races for a while, but you got him here in time."

Rey looked up when Jake walked back to the group, followed by the deputy. "I'll talk to, uh, Lyle," he told the deputy. "You finish up with him." He pointed to Ed.

Rey walked toward the ER doorway and motioned for Lyle to follow him. He opened the door for Lyle, then turned to Jake. "Stay put for a few minutes, please."

Inside, Rey had scoped out an empty exam room where he and Lyle could talk. "Okay. What's going on?" he said as soon as he closed the door.

Lyle leaned against an exam table. "It's just as they said, that guy shot himself. Was he decocking his gun or what, I don't know. The shooting party had broken up. Most everyone had already left, and no one was firing. Then this guy shoots himself in the leg. He bled like a son of a bitch, so I put on a tourniquet and held on. These other guys helped get him here."

"By *these other guys,* you mean Cadre Brave members. I saw that guy's patch."

"Yup."

"Where were you shooting?"

"Some out-of-the-way place toward Cottonwood. Middle of nowhere on a dirt road."

Rey pulled Lyle's gun from his belt and set it on a counter. "Guess they're not great shots."

"Obviously, Bobby doesn't know how to handle a pistol, but there are dead shots in the group. I saw a guy almost put three shots in the same hole on a target with a nine mil. And another guy was as good with an AR."

"*Dead* shots, eh amigo?"

"Well, they have a lot of weapons, like you told me. And they swapped, so just about everyone had a go with an AR." Lyle decided not to tell Rey about the machine gun just yet. They might figure out the new guy blabbed. He didn't want to turn in the owner of the family machine gun nest just yet.

Rey walked over to a paper towel dispenser and pulled a sheet out. He handed it to Lyle, pointing to a blood smear below his ear. "And what were you doing there?"

"Just checking it out."

"Going to join?"

Lyle knew the official shooting investigations had not yielded promising suspects. He'd inspected the security of Sam's apartment and talked with friends at the Phoenix and Tempe police departments to ask about security at Arizona State, not only for Sam, but Olivia Lightfoot and the others. His concerns assuaged, what else could he do? Nosing into the local hate group might help the investigation, head off more violence, or who knows what else. Was he crazy?

"Join? You think they'll they ask me?"

"Look, Lyle—"

"I know. I just want to see who these guys are. I won't get in the way. I'll be in the background."

"You think they were involved in the murders?"

"And you don't?"

"The FBI is tracking hate group involvement. Officially, I'm telling you to stay out of it."

"Unofficially?"

"I'm telling you to stay out of it." Rey stared at Lyle for a minute. "But if you don't follow the sheriff's department's orders and get involved—"

"Then we never had this conversation."

"And you'll tell me everything you do, everything you hear."

CHAPTER 33

On the return drive to Billings, Kate remembered, not for the first time, what Lyle told her about detective work: full of disappointments, wasted legwork, and frustration. You talk to many people and *maybe* pick up something useful.

Back in her hotel room, she reviewed her notes and research. The homophobic hubbub at the NC fast-food restaurant had made her forget to ask Joann if she'd discovered anything about the PI she'd met. She started to call her, then remembered it was the weekend. She texted. A bit less intrusive.

She called Drenda's cell to chat and find out if Gudgel had tried to outlaw theme parks while she was gone. The call went straight to voicemail.

Moments later, she received a text from Joann, succinct as usual. Her secretary said she didn't have her notes at hand, but from memory she could tell her that Hurt's firm offered surveillance, background checks, handled divorce cases, and assisted attorneys. His office was in

Glendale and he was not a member of the BBB. AI searches revealed only that Hurt had testified in court on corporate liability and custody cases. He must be good at keeping his name out of the press or internet, Joann noted.

What a report from memory. Kate wished she could carry so many details in her head at once. Right now, *her* head was packed. She needed to let her subconscious sort it out.

She looked out the window. The afternoon weather didn't look too ominous. Sunshine peaked out here and there. She'd go for a run to unwind.

Far from a marathoner, but a regular runner—something she shared with Lyle—Kate craved exercise at times like these. Online, she found a nearby bike and jogging trail in a park where the Yellowstone River rushed by the eastern edge of town. Wearing a sweatshirt and running shorts, she brought along sweatpants in case the weather shifted.

According to the map, the trail snaked through a few stands of trees, but mostly she'd be jogging in open fields. On the drive to the trail she glanced in the rearview mirror to be sure that Mickey G., who accosted her at the hotel, wasn't angling for another talk. She found one of several parking lots along the trail and pulled in next to two other cars. As always, she went through stretching exercises. She leaned forward with one leg extended behind her, then the other. After a few knee bends, she was eager for the trail.

Her university basketball coach had regularly leaned on the team during practice. They would run from one end of the court to the other—and back—again and again. During games, if she wasn't dribbling down the court with the ball, she was dashing forward to receive a pass from the point guard, or lunging ahead on defense. Years later she kept in shape by running, working out, and by walking most places at the park rather than taking public transit.

Now she looked up and down the trail and headed north. After about five minutes, she passed her first jogger—going the other way. He gave a slight wave as he passed and continued to pound the paved trail, breathing heavily. Kate thought not about the Gudgel family or the governor, but focused on buds on deciduous trees, the gurgling of the river, and her body's response to the exertion.

Around a gradual curve, she ran through a small stand of trees. She noticed a man jogging close behind her. Had he been there before she ran into the shade? She tried to look back—without appearing to gawk. The man was athletic and lean. He wore sweatpants and T-shirt. He looked nothing like Mickey G. She relaxed and maintained her pace.

Amid the trees lay another parking lot with a cluster of vehicles, one of them a commercial pickup with a painted sign on the door. As she got closer, she saw the name McFee.

She slowed for a moment and the guy who had been behind her suddenly lunged forward from around a curve. "Hey Sorensen, stop," he shouted. "Where you goin'? You better stop."

CHAPTER 34

With Kate in Montana, Lyle driving his cab, and Governor Gudgel ominously silent, Drenda thought it was time. But first, she needed to build a persona. It didn't have to be CIA quality, just enough to get by.

She'd kept her married name—Adair—after her divorce, so her last name would be fine. It wasn't *Maxwell,* her maiden name. *Drenda*, however, wouldn't do. Too uncommon. She'd use her middle name, Ann. The melodious alliteration might draw attention, when she wanted to be unobtrusive, but it matched the name on her driver's license, not that she'd ever need to show it.

Next, she needed a Phoenix address. If she registered as a Gudgel-for-Governor volunteer and said she lived in Polk, people would immediately think of NC. And they'd wonder why she would drive two hours—in *light* traffic—just to hand out bumper stickers or answer the phone.

Her first choice for help, Jane, a friend who worked as assistant collections administrator for the Maricopa County Library District, agreed to permit Drenda to use her Phoenix address. Drenda explained, in general terms, that she was conducting a little political investigating. As her friend shared Drenda's opinion of the state's dreadful governor, she also volunteered her spare bedroom if Drenda needed it.

Jane's generosity permitted Drenda to offer to do volunteer work two days a week at Gudgel headquarters without having to drive hundreds of miles over two days.

With her spurious background ready, Drenda appeared at the Gudgel campaign's central headquarters. Neglected landscaping surrounded the broad, low-slung office building. The letters forming the name of an electronics firm had been removed but were visible in the building's otherwise faded paint. Above it, a white and red Gudgel banner flapped in the light breeze.

Inside, Drenda was taken by the spacious yet sparsely furnished office. Past an unoccupied reception counter, a dozen desks in small clusters, many divided by low partition walls, spread out in an area that could have held fifty. They looked like islands dotting a small sea. Along one wall bright, indirect lighting showed a row of glassed-in offices, a few occupied, plus a conference room with a long table and chairs. Campaign posters adorned doors and walls. A busy hum of voices floated in from a wide corridor off to the right.

Drenda approached one island of desks, some stacked with literature, signs, and political buttons. Campaign buttons, she knew, reached a peak in popularity and production in the late 1960s. The historical NC connection amused her. A woman at one desk looked up.

"Are you here for the canvassing orientation?" the

woman asked with a glare. "It started a little while ago, but you can go in." She pointed to a hallway.

"I could," Drenda said, "but I wanted to volunteer for something more than knocking on doors Saturdays."

The woman's frown disappeared.

"The upcoming election is *so* important," Drenda said. "I'm familiar with word processing, spreadsheets, statistical analysis."

"You could work *during* the week?" Her emphasis sounded encouraging.

"Yes, my job is flexible, and I could work a day, possibly two per week."

"I'm special assistant to the governor. I don't coordinate volunteers, but I know we can use additional help, especially during the week. Not for statistical analysis, but other things."

She looked back over her shoulder at a neighboring island of desks. "Landon," she shouted, "can you come 'ere for a minute?"

A gangly young man, early 20s, ambled over with a pencil in one hand and a sheaf of papers in the other.

"This is Landon," the seated woman told Drenda.

"I'm Ann," Drenda said. "I'd like to volunteer for any office work you might have."

The woman and Landon exchanged glances. "Yeah, we can use help." He gestured for her to follow him.

Drenda sat across a desk from Landon. He put his papers to the side. "So what kind of work can you do for us? Just weekends?"

"Oh, no," Drenda said. She repeated she was available during the week.

"That's great. We need office help especially during th' week. Most everyone is a volunteer and they disappear after Sunday night."

"Well, I'm glad to help. I'm really dedicated to this election." She'd practiced ways she could appear to be a Gudgel supporter without saying she was. Her backup plan, lying as convincingly as possible, however, caused her no grief.

"We'll be staffing up as we get closer to the election, but now is the important prep work." He explained their online voter registration files needed to be checked and updated, precinct maps had to be prepared, volunteers contacted and scheduled, and all related activities that arose as the campaign progressed would require attention.

Drenda again repeated her office skills.

"I supervise the volunteers and can use help." He pulled out a paper form. "I'd like to get a little information from you."

Drenda glanced up at a column of wires that hung from above through spaces between ceiling panels and then spread out along the floor among the desks. Each desk cluster had a similar column of wires.

"Oh yeah," said Landon. "Those are network and phone line connections. They were strung up after the computer company moved out. Looks kind of weird in here, huh?" He waved his hand across the open floor space. "The building owner leased the place to the campaign for peanuts."

Landon slid the form across his desk. "Would you fill this out? It's our volunteer info sheet and waiver. We need to know how to contact you."

Drenda pulled a pen from her purse and scanned the form before she began. Two questions she'd not anticipated caused her pulse to inch up. Her thoughts worked overtime as she filled out or omitted parts of the form. She knew her bogus address and used her own cell phone number. She left the line for her office phone blank.

She also left blank the line for her email address. All her current addresses ended with *@NostalgiaCity.com*. Since she'd planned to use Jane as her work supervisor, she couldn't use her as an emergency contact. She invented a name, relationship, and phone number. No one would call.

She passed the form back across the desk. "I left the email address blank because I'm changing providers. I can update that in a few days when I get it straightened out."

Landon didn't notice the blank space for her work phone. She planned to give Jane's office number—after clearing with her friend. She would add that info later, saying she'd forgotten to fill it in. If she were lucky, her job might entail maintaining volunteer files, and she could update hers as necessary.

"Does the governor ever come in here?" she asked.

"Oh yeah. Meetings. Campaign strategy." Landon pointed to a spacious, glassed-in office. "That big office there is his."

Drenda looked at the corner office. *Governor Gudgel, right there. Fascinating.*

CHAPTER 35

A man yelling and running after a woman attracts attention. But if both wore sweats and running shoes, an onlooker would see two joggers.

Kate's mind worked as fast as her legs. Was this another disgruntled Gudgel wanting to shut her up? A McFee Constructors' owner seeking the same end, permanently? Kate passed the empty McFee truck and kicked up her pace. The man ran seventy-five yards or more behind her. Not an experienced runner? Out-pacing him would not solve the problem, however; she knew the path did not loop back to her car. She'd intended to run about four miles, then turn around.

A woman in street clothes and a child walked toward her at a leisurely pace, pausing occasionally to examine the vegetation. For a split second, she considered stopping to talk to the woman in hopes her pursuer would not try anything with others around. As she reached the woman and child, she realized she might involve them in something dangerous. She looked around and saw the man had gained ground.

"That man is trying to get your attention," the woman said.

"I can see that." Kate took off at a sprinter's pace.

"Kate, we just want to talk," the man shouted.

We?

Kate kept up her pace for the next half mile, her legs thumping the path. Ahead she saw another parking lot and through a clump of fir trees, a building at the edge of the park. A parking lot and a building meant a road close by. She stopped at the edge of the trees and looked for an escape route. Her hesitation cost space between her and the guy racing toward her. She could hear his guttural exclamations.

She thought about stopping to "talk" then surprising him if he made a move. She kept in shape and knew how to take care of herself. Was more than one person after her?

About thirty yards ahead along the edge of the trees, she saw cars and trucks parked. Again, she paused. Two trucks in the lot wore McFee signs. A man in work clothes emerged from one of the trucks and looked at Kate. He wore a work belt and carried a wrench in his right hand.

Kate ran toward him.

"I think I need help," she said. "This guy's following me."

The man in work clothes stepped forward. Kate stopped next to him and turned around—in time to see her pursuer dash past as if on a routine jog.

"You sure he was after you?" the worker said.

"Yeah."

The building she'd seen through the fir trees was half finished and she quickly realized the reason for the McFee trucks: a construction job.

"D' you want to call the police?" he asked.

"No thanks. I'll be okay."

Kate recognized the nearby street as the one she drove getting to her starting point. She jogged back on the edge of the street and, in less time than it took her to jog the circuitous trail, she reached her car. She started up and moved away. As she drove, she weighed the value of talking to the police. The only way she could get them to consider it anything but a potential mugging would be to explain why she was in Billings. Would the police start talking to Gudgel family members? Would that improve her circumstances? Getting out of Dodge would be an improvement.

After a quick shower at her hotel, she sat back at her desk. What a day. She powered up her computer, and the story from the *Billings Monthly Broadside* appeared. The editor, Hank Fisk, had not called her back. She tried again.

"Hank Fisk," said a gruff voice.

"Mr. Fisk, I called you earlier. This is Kate Sorensen."

"Yes. Got your call. Been busy."

"I work for Nostalgia City—the theme park. Your piece on Rod Gudgel got my attention." She explained NC's conflict with the governor. "I'm here in Billings to look into his past."

"And find out what breed of snake he is? Not a bad idea."

"That's what I thought." She asked him if he'd been in the news business for a long time in Billings, and he told her he remembered when Gudgel was a law student. She explained she had a plane to catch the next day and wanted to know if she could meet with him early in the morning. She counted on his curiosity. It worked.

CHAPTER 36

April 14

Do people still smoke cigars? That was the first thing that came to Kate's mind when she met Hank Fisk at his home in an older section of Billings. A bit over-weight, the sixtyish Fisk welcomed Kate and led her to a gold and avocado green kitchen. He wasn't smoking, but the house was.

"Ya want coffee? I gotta have coffee."

"Okay."

Fisk pulled a cup from a dish rack. He poured coffee into her cup from a large drip carafe and filled a mug the size of a beer stein for himself.

"This way." He led her down a hallway. "Ever since the paper went to monthly," he said, "I've done every-thing from here."

The office appeared as Kate expected, a room full of file cabinets and stacks of books, a desktop littered with papers, and an ashtray holding cigar butts. She took a bentwood chair and Fisk settled into a swivel chair behind his desk.

"I used to be a reporter," Kate said, "and I figured if anyone in Billings would know the Gudgel family, it would be a veteran newspaper person."

"Guilty as charged," he said. "I've been in journalism for nearly forty years.

"Your opinion piece in the latest issue got my attention."

"I thrashed about for ideas, and I saw slippery Rod was running for re-election in Arizona and most of his family was telling people not to vote for him."

"The article made it pretty clear what you think of him."

"Oh? I tried to be restrained." He smiled and scratched at the ring of brown hair that circled his otherwise shiny head. His affable demeanor seemed at odds with his rumpled, bushy-eyebrowed, cigar-smoking, grouchy newspaper editor looks.

"I came here to learn if there's more to Governor Gudgel than what it says on his campaign website."

"That's a gem, isn't it? Sounds like that son of a bitch cleaned up all the corruption in Montana, then moved on to give Arizona the benefit of his political perspicacity."

"Something like that. And nothing about the bid rigging you mentioned in your article."

"That's his forte. As you read in his bio, he was—at first—a reformer in the legislature. He exposed bid rigging in government contracts.

"As a young lawyer and legislator, Gudgel learned the forms of bid rigging." As he spoke, Fisk reached into a desk drawer and produced a cigar. He held it up. "Okay?"

She nodded her head, but her expression said, "really?"

"Okay. Not now. I get it. They're smelly, but I love 'em. Only a few a day. My wife puts up with them. She's a wonder.

"There's several forms of bid-rigging," he continued, "such as *bid suppression* and *phantom bidding*. One of the most common is *cover bidding*, Gudgel's specialty. One contractor is determined in advance to be the winner. So other bidders prepare proposals that are higher, sometimes much higher, than the estimated costs for a job, or they have conditions they know will be rejected. This makes the winning bidder look attractive, even though the price might not be. It looks like a fair process."

"And Gudgel uncovered it."

"Often it's not too difficult." Fisk gestured with his cellophane-wrapped cigar. "These contractors are not Rhodes scholars. They used the same terms and wording in supposedly separate bids.

"And uncovering this gave Gudgel a reputation as a white-hat crusader and made it easier for him to rake in a piece of the action once he learned the ropes. He covered for the cover bidders and showed them how to write better phony bids," Fisk said. "He was no Supreme Court justice, but his corruption was pretty outrageous."

"Like the Sunnyside State Building?"

"Yep. Did you get that information from Dan Meacham?"

"I'm here like a reporter, keeping my sources confidential."

"Okay. Likely it was Dan. He probably didn't tell you, but his bank at the time had a part in that debacle, so he knew about the state administrators, inspectors, and others in Gudgel's pocket. Dan was clean. Don't get me wrong. He figured out the schemes—after the fact—and he left that bank.

"How did Gudgel escape criminal charges? Ass-kissing?"

"That's a part of it. As he gained experience, he made friends and bought friends. People expect a certain amount of malfeasance from elected officials, and in Montana, your actions have to rise to a certain level to attract scrutiny.

"This is not to say no one tried. The local DA started investigations until slippery Rod and his friends bankrolled an opponent in the DA's election. Reporters I knew looking into Gudgel's shenanigans found witnesses refused to go on the record. At least, that was the reason the publisher gave when he ended the probe.

"Eventually, Gudgel would have been nailed. Now, 20 years later, nobody around here cares."

Fisk pulled the wrapper off his cigar. "Does this give you a more clear picture of his stellar background?"

Kate looked at her watch and set her coffee cup on Fisk's desk. "A person I talked to called Gudgel, 'a philanderer' was the word she used. You know anything about that?"

"Is he still married? I wonder why? He was definitely interested in extracurricular sex, the younger the women, the better."

"Sorry, I need to get to the airport. I really appreciate your help. I'm still left with one question. Everything I've learned about the Arizona governor, everyone I've talked to, *everything* paints a dark picture of this man. Everyone has *some* good qualities, don't they?"

"You're asking the wrong person. I'm no shrink or member of the clergy. I don't understand everyone's motivations, but in my years of reporting I've run across Gudgel types. They may be kind to their dogs and their children may love them, but they have a large part of their psyches that's walled off. *It's* in charge and focused on getting power and a share of everything. Whatever it takes. Consequences be damned."

Fisk lit his cigar.

On the way to the front door, Kate paused. "Mr. Fisk, I wouldn't like for it to get back to the governor that I came here to look into his past. It might happen anyway, but if you write a story about me, that will put it on the record. If you hold off, I promise to let you in on whatever actions, legal or otherwise, we decide to do."

"I'm happy if I've helped you derail slippery Rod. You keep in touch, and I'll keep mum."

CHAPTER 37

Lyle did not know what to expect from Kate. She'd be back from Montana any moment. During the weekend, they'd only had time to exchange voicemail, and the night before, they'd talked briefly. He hadn't told her the details of his shooting adventure. Sounded too scary. And he neglected to mention the barbecue invitation.

"Lyle," Kate sighed as she walked through the door to her apartment, dropped her bag, and threw her arms around him.

"Feels good," she said as their embrace lasted.

He held her tight, kissing her neck, her lips. When they parted, he picked up her suitcase, and they spoke simultaneously:

"What did you find out about Gudgel in Montana?"

"You didn't actually join the hate group, did you?"

"Okay," Lyle said. "Let me put your case in the other room and we can compare war stories."

"That sounds ominous. Maybe you should go first. Where's Trixie?"

The cat appeared from the bedroom as Lyle walked by. When he returned, Kate sat on the couch, the cat rubbing against her ankles.

"Drink, coffee, leftovers?"

"Nothing just yet." She patted the cushion next to her. "Gudgel is as low as we imagined. His relatives' newspaper ad was understated. But you go first."

They traded accounts of their last few days, Kate gasping at Lyle's machine gun story, the mad dash with the wounded shooter, and his close call when his friend Rey pretended not to recognize him in the company of the hate group shooters.

"So I was associating with racists and homophobes," Lyle said, "but you were getting chased by parties unknown. And you didn't go to the cops."

Trixie jumped up on the couch next to Kate. "Am I ignoring you?" she said, scratching the top of the cat's head.

"No point in going to the cops," she said. "The guy who accosted me in the hotel didn't break the law. He looked like a thug. I think, however, he was just a slow-witted person trying to defend his family or some such nonsense. Nothing serious. The guy who chased me? A different story. Another Gudgel? There are lots of them in Billings, and not all of them share our opinion of the governor. I couldn't have identified him."

"But that means Governor Gudgel probably knows you visited Montana asking about him."

Kate shrugged. "I guess it was bound to leak out with a big family involved. Maybe this will keep him more restrained."

"Or not."

After an hour of nonstop recapitulation, including Gudgel's involvement in the Sunnyside State Building accident that cost Bruno Venner his life, they decided to plan their next steps in the morning.

■ ■ ■

April 15

Lyle awoke first and after admiring Kate asleep, her long hair in beautiful disarray over her pillow, he made coffee and brought it into the bedroom along with his trusty lined yellow pad, ready to strategize.

"Look at you," Kate said when she opened her eyes. "You brought me coffee," she purred. "I see you also have your yellow pad all set."

Writing, putting things down with pencil and paper, helped Lyle think, to plan, to solve problems. Kept him focused.

"You may remember," he said, "last night we never got around to deciding what we're going to do next with the information we gathered."

Kate fluffed up her pillows and sat up. "Right." Her voice shifted from dreamy to tactical. "And Drenda's coming over this morning."

"She is?"

"Relax. Not for a while."

Trixie jumped on the bed seeking attention. Kate made space for her and rubbed under the cat's chin as she continued. "Drenda sent me a text yesterday. She wants to talk about Gudgel and she doesn't want to meet at the office. 'Walls have ears,' she said."

"Hmm."

"And she said she has a hate group expert for you. What does that mean?"

"We'll see. And speaking of that," Lyle said, trying to sound conversational, "I've been invited to a barbecue at the home of the guy who's in charge of the local Cadre Brave group."

Kate sat up straighter in bed, her lips tight as she stared at him. Trixie looked put out and rearranged herself on the comforter.

"I'm going to be super careful" Lyle said. "I've talked with Rey. He says the FBI is investigating the Cadre Brave—I don't know how—and looking into other groups."

"And Rey thinks it's okay for you to be socializing with armed racists?"

"Not really. He doesn't want me to get in the way of investigations, but I promised him I'd keep in close touch. I didn't hear anyone mention the killings at the shooting range. That's why I'm going to their barbecue."

"*Lyle.*"

"It'll be okay. It's a casual get together. I just want to mingle and listen."

"Are dates invited? May I come?"

"I'm pretty sure this is a guy thing. I think the group's a tad misogynistic, too."

"Wonderful."

"Now about Gudgel." Lyle held his pencil over the lined tablet, not sure what to write.

"As I said last night," just *digging up decades-old dirt*, as one of Gudgel's relatives put it, is not enough to stop him."

Lyle said, "Let's put him out of business for good."

"Based on his MO of bribery and fraud in Montana, we can assume he's doing the same here only on a larger scale. And as governor, he has many opportunities for graft." She motioned for him to start writing.

"First, in Montana he seemed fond of public works projects. That's almost a given. Second, the governor appoints people to influential state boards and commissions."

"Like the airport board?" Lyle asked.

"Just like that," Kate said, pointing to his pad. "Then you can add political endorsements for candidates or causes. Of course, he proposes legislation, appoints state judges, and promotes the state economy by encouraging companies to build a plant or relocate here."

Lyle wrote quickly to keep up with Kate's list. "You've really thought about this."

"I had time in my hotel and on airplanes. As chief executive, the governor, through the chain of command, controls all state agencies and issues executive orders and grants clemency and directs the Arizona National Guard."

"Oh, the guard," Lyle said, shaking his pencil at Kate. "Forget about the National Guard. Gudgel controls the Arizona *State* Guard. Remember those guys in camouflage uniforms we see at his speeches?"

"Yes?"

"They're the Arizona State Guard. His bodyguards and private army reporting directly to him."

Kate stared at Lyle.

He explained the guard details he learned from Howard. "I also talked to a guy who works for Howard in the Control Center. He was an officer in the State Guard when it was formed two years ago.

"He said he quit when the guard became Gudgel's private, armed militia. He said certain units drive Humvees, carry assault weapons, and are training for combat. According to a Gudgel statement I found, the guard can be used for aiding law enforcement and for immigration control." Lyle stopped and looked at Kate. He could see her jaw muscles tighten.

Kate leaned back against her pillows and looked straight ahead. "This is really unbelievable. What's he going to do with his army?" She thought for a moment, then pounded a fist on the bed. "Election security?"

"I thought of that. And a couple of other things."

"This doesn't sound legal."

"It is. Something like eighteen other states have what are called state defense forces or state military reserve. But none that I know of operate like Arizona's. Most people don't even know their state has a guard, except the National Guard."

She glanced at Lyle's list. "Now we have to move full speed. We know the type of graft he's trafficked in before. We need to find people who can help us expose his form of kleptocracy in Arizona. I'd like to find ex-staffers, legislators, disgruntled employees I can talk to."

"How about campaign staff? They often know a candidate's weaknesses, and they turn over, too, as political fortunes rise and fall."

"We have to get leverage on him, quick."

CHAPTER 38

Lyle opened Kate's apartment door. Drenda wore one of her '70s outfits, a red coat and matching skirt with a wide pink stripe down the front of the coat and along the hem. It reminded him of a flight attendant uniform from the long-defunct Pacific Southwest Airlines.

"Drenda, welcome to our clandestine meeting to discuss the problem of the governor."

She flashed him a mischievous grin. "Kate told you about my conspiratorial-sounding text message, didn't she?"

"Yes, I did," Kate said from the kitchen. "Hey, Drenda, there's more coffee."

Drenda accepted a cup, and they settled in the living room, Lyle and Kate having showered and dressed.

"I wanted to talk about the mole in the park," Drenda began.

"Mole?" Lyle said.

"I forgot to mention it," Kate said with a slapping her forehead gesture. "So much going on. I'm not sure how, but Gudgel heard we were considering a Gay Pride event." She explained Gudgel's comments, her suspicions, and the risks of questioning park officials about it.

"Okay, so what do we do about it?"

"Drenda suggested we strike back by infiltrating the governor's office."

"Yes," Drenda said. "I'm now a Gudgel office volunteer."

"You volunteered?" Kate asked.

"You volunteered?" Lyle echoed. Drenda looked as if she were trying to hold back a grin by keeping her mouth closed, but Lyle saw smiling eyes. "You're proud of yourself. What are you going to do?"

"Answer phones, keep records, make calls to volunteers, and be an office drudge. The campaign headquarters is in a large disused one-story office building off Thomas Road near the Heard Museum."

"That's in Phoenix," Kate said.

Drenda explained she picked the Phoenix office, rather than Polk, because she wanted to be closer to the decision-makers. With help from a friend, she established a local Phoenix address and could work two days a week.

"My little department here can function without me occasionally."

"Did you use your real name?" Lyle wanted to know. *Is she going to muck things up? Nice to be enthusiastic, but realistically?*

"Yes, but I'm going by my middle name, Ann." She turned to Kate. "Adair is common enough and I'm never quoted or mentioned in the news like you are, and I'm not on the park website.

The continued glimmer in Drenda's eyes told Lyle she was eager to help nail Gudgel, and it sounded as if she'd planned for contingencies. *She's intelligent and maybe she could pull this off. But does she know the potential downsides?*

"Do you have any qualms about working for Gudgel's campaign?" Kate asked.

"No. I'll do what's expected, but you know how lackadaisical I can be."

"Are you thinking of sabotaging the office?" Kate said.

"My primary aim is to gather information."

Lyle raised his hands. "Drenda, this is risky enough. Best thing to do is be silent, keep your head down and—"

"Spy?" Drenda offered.

"Let's say *observe*. That's what I do. Just hang out and listen."

"I may have opportunities to do that. The governor has a big corner office with windows, so he can see the campaign drones at work. They said he comes in for regular meetings."

"On ways to sabotage Nostalgia City," Lyle said. "Did you see any surveillance cameras in the office?"

"I didn't look for them. But I don't plan to rifle desks or listen at closed doors."

"Maybe you should," Lyle said.

Kate laughed. "He's just kidding."

Lyle smiled. "Caution should temper your actions."

"There's one other exigency I need to cover," Drenda said. "My online presence. I need to block, disable, or remove my information and posts from several websites and substitute a history for *Ann* Adair."

She's bright and *creative. This could work.* "I know several techies, engineers who program rides. One in particular would love to do this and he can probably handle it on his lunch hour and still have time for a meal. And Rob is absolutely trustworthy."

As he thought about his tech friend's resources, Lyle had an idea. "Drenda, may I see your glasses for a moment?"

With a puzzled look, she handed them to him. Lyle turned them over in his hands, noticing thick, plain black frames. He handed them back.

"Maybe it's nothing. I can talk to Rob. But I know he can set up a new online presence for you. Just send me your account information and pictures he can post without jeopardizing your identity."

"Thanks, Lyle. That will help, just in case. And I can reciprocate. I found a hate group expert you can talk to."

"Is he or she a psychologist? Because I don't understand these hate mongers at all."

"Actually, she's an NAU history professor and has done extensive research on these groups—and published a book. She's a former university colleague of mine."

Before the top secret meeting ended, Lyle cautioned Drenda about telling *anyone* else about her new identity, "especially if we have a mole in the park."

"Another caution," Kate said. "We discovered that

those guys in uniform we see at Gudgel rallies are offi-cial Arizona State Guardsmen. They report to Gudgel."

"Sounds sinister, especially considering historical parallels, Huey Long's bodyguard units, Blackwater con-tractors, and others. So I will be watchful. I'm ardently invested in the cause. I even thought about putting a campaign bumper sticker on my car." She gave a mock shudder. "But I decided against it. And judging by the cars in the parking lot, most other people did, too."

CHAPTER 39

April 16

Kate researched former employees of the governor, and it brought her to the zoo.

Using news site archives, she created a list of Governor Gudgel's former assistants, department heads, and anyone else prominent enough in state government to warrant a news story when they resigned—or better yet—were fired. She had met one person on the list.

Lisa Oberon had been Gudgel's deputy press secretary during his first two years as governor. According to a news story, Oberon had been one of several casualties of a "shake up" in the governor's staff. Kate didn't know her well. They'd met at Public Relations Society of America meetings in Phoenix. When Kate phoned, Oberon, who now managed communications for a zoo, guessed the call related to the governor-versus-theme-park row. She'd be happy to talk.

"Lisa?" said a middle-aged woman in the zoo office. "You'll find her in the capybara enclosure."

"The what?" Kate said.

"Just go out these doors and turn left," the woman said. She handed Kate a map of the Philips-Arizona Rescue Zoo.

Kate wandered along a landscaped path past ostriches, alpacas, and goats until she saw a sign for the capybara enclosure. She found Oberon sitting on a low stone wall, petting a small animal Kate had never seen before. Oberon pulled treats out of her khaki jacket for the brown furry animal.

Oberon, perhaps a little older than Kate, looked entirely different from Kate's memory of her in a suit. She greeted Kate like a friend, not a business associate.

"Hi Kate." She stood, extended a hand and invited her to sit. "Good to see you." She wore a little makeup, her short hair parted on the left and swept across her forehead.

Kate sat next to her. "What a peaceful setting."

"It is. And you won't see any cages. We try to provide natural environments for our rescued residents."

"As you know, my environment at Nostalgia City has not been quite peaceful."

Oberon nodded. "And the horrendous shootings. Has anyone been arrested? I haven't heard."

"It's a tragedy and no arrests yet."

"And the governor's comments haven't helped."

"Helped? He ignored the deaths of innocent people, mocked minority groups, and attacked Nostalgia City because we're inclusive. He…"

Oberson smiled. "I get the picture. He's a disgusting individual."

"Sorry for going off like that, but we're at wits' end. He's more than disgusting, and we're trying to fight back by finding proof of his graft and corruption that I'm sure is going on."

"How can I help?"

"Sounds like you share our opinion of the governor."

"He fired me and a handful of others just to make it look as if he was streamlining government. We figured Gudgel wanted more yes-men, although I can't imagine he needed *more* sycophants."

"Not surprising." Kate said.

"I was planning to leave. Maybe that's what everyone says when they get fired, but it was true in my case. I'd already interviewed for other jobs."

"Difficult to work for?"

"He abandoned decency in public office and propositioned me twice." She frowned, but momentarily, and continued. "But it was a good job. I learned a lot. High pressure at times, exciting. As time passed though, I saw the governor was extreme in the worse sense of the word. But you know that."

They sat in the warm sunlight that passed through branches of a green palo verde tree. "Yes. He's—" Kate stopped when one of the squat, blunt-nosed capybaras set its head on the wall next to her.

"Look at this creature," Oberon said, placing her hand on its head. "He's a herbivore from South America and one of the most gentle creatures on earth. Doing PR for animal rescue like this is a joy. Dirty politics nowhere in sight."

"Looks peaceful. I'll trade you."

Oberon continued to pet the capybara, her serene look shifting to a focused stare. "You have your hands full."

Kate explained she'd collected information on the governor that showed he engaged in bid rigging and other graft before he came to Arizona. "He specialized in public works projects. Construction contracts can be lucrative not only for the contractors, but for the politicians who take a cut."

Oberon stopped petting the capybara, though the animal remained near. "I know when I worked in the governor's office he had developers, large corporations, and others begging for his consideration."

"In exchange for a hefty bribe?"

"That was the sense of it. Someone—including me—should have looked deeper. Sometimes we were told not to publicize actions he took, like issuing a pardon or pushing through huge financial incentives for companies to relocate. Many projects we *did* promote, of course, like solar energy and the big data centers. Others were low key, off the record. I could list a few questionable ones."

"That would be a help. I'd also like to look into large construction contracts, current and going back a few years."

"ADOT would be one place to look. They award hefty road construction and repair contracts. I had to learn about that when I worked in the capitol."

"Arizona Department of Transportation," Kate said. "Right, where do I start?"

"Let's go into my office."

CHAPTER 40

Fuzzy stuffed critters and posters of animal babies decorated Oberon's office. As they entered, she pulled a visitor chair up behind her desk so Kate could see her PC screen, and she got busy.

"I worked with the ADOT public information office, among others, so I know some of this," Oberon said, "but it's been a while. We'll start with the ADOT home page. From here, you can choose one of eight regions in the state."

She clicked the back button and then through a series of pages from *construction projects* to *contract types* to *bidding opportunities*.

"You have to go through many layers. They don't make it easy. Sometimes setting up an account is necessary—as you can see."

Oberon wiggled her mouse to highlight the heading on the next page. "Here are the bid tabulations. If you click to the sidebar, here, you can find details for each of these jobs listed, including the winning and losing bids.

You can also see what the state estimated the cost to be and the winning bid's over or under percentage."

They read details on a variety of costly construction jobs. Another click and they saw a message:

Further information on bid tabulations for thirty
days after the state transportation award date
is available by making a public records request
through the Office of Safety and Risk Management.

"You're frowning," Oberon said.

"I'm wondering how common, how routine these requests are. If I request a bunch of files from months and years ago, would that raise a red flag? Would he send the Arizona State Guard after me?"

"The guard. You know about that? You might be careful, but I don't know how many record requests are received. I do, however, know somebody at ADOT who could answer that question, and he might help you short-cut the bureaucracy to get the files you want. Tim has been counting the days—"

She paused and glanced through her open office door, then lowered her voice. "He's waiting for the voters to oust Gudgel and set the government straight again. I'll give him a call. Would you close my door?"

Kate listened to her friend's side of the conversation and after a few minutes, Oberon ended with, "Okay, I'll send her over."

"Lisa, I don't know exactly what to ask for yet."

"That's okay. Tim said he wanted to meet you first and find out the *type* of information you're looking for.

I'm sure he can help. And I'll try to find whatever I can on those 'off-the-record' projects I mentioned."

■ ■ ■

Before she left, Kate thanked Oberon, congratulated her on a rewarding job she obviously enjoyed, and acknowledged more than a little envy. "I'll trade you a governor for a capybara any time."

Back at her car, she programmed her GPS for the address of the ADOT office in downtown. Glancing at her backup camera view as she reversed, she noticed a small, muddy-looking SUV. Dull, flat finishes seemed to be a trend in new cars. Didn't that car pull into the lot an hour ago when she did? As Kate backed toward him, the man behind the wheel looked away.

She pulled onto the street. So did the SUV.

Was this guy following her? Gudgel put a tail on her already? For the last 85 miles from Nostalgia City? Not possible. Even if they discovered where she lived. Toward what end? A confrontation like the one in the Billings hotel? *At least this isn't a State Guard vehicle behind me.*

She drove east several miles toward the freeway. The car stayed behind her, sometimes dropping back, so she had a hard time seeing it in her rearview. But it was there.

She pulled on the interstate, checked the mirror. No car.

Lisa's friend Tim worked in an ADOT building in the central city, miles away. Kate stayed on I-17 south. Traffic was heavy—as is usually the case in the fifth largest city in the country. She monitored the rearview mirror when she could, but didn't notice the gray SUV.

Offices of many state agencies clustered within a small area east of the interstate in downtown. Following the GPS voice directions, Kate turned off the freeway, made a quick left, then a right turn. Pursuer still gone.

On a hunch, before she reached the ADOT building, she pulled into a parking lot and cruised, ostensibly looking for a space. No SUV in the rearview. She crept down a row and pulled into a spot. After a minute, she saw the dull gray SUV with a male driver pulling into a space one row behind her.

Damn. In the event her pursuer could see her, she made a show of punching buttons next to her GPS screen, then talked to herself aloud—Lyle style—as if she were on the phone. Would he think she got lost? Calling for help?

She knew she could not meet her ADOT contact now. If her follower worked for Gudgel—and who else?—she didn't want to expose her source. Lisa's friend Tim wanted to meet Kate in person, perhaps check her out, even before she knew exactly what she wanted. His caution reinforced Kate's.

She started the car and drove randomly downtown, craning her neck, looking at buildings, finally finding a shopping mall. She parked and noticed the SUV pulling into a space many cars down in her row. Of course, there had to be more than one SUV of that make and color in Phoenix. Rationalization. This was *the car.*

To reach a mall entrance, she had to walk past the gray ghost. As she passed the rear of the car, she repeated the license number several times to herself as she typed the plate into her phone and continued into the mall.

Inside, she looked at clothes in a dress shop. No men in sight. She bought a coffee to go and walked outside.

This SOB was not going to chase her any more. It was a bright afternoon and people wandered about. She'd march up to his car and have it out with him. Maybe take his picture. If he got physical, she'd throw hot coffee in his face, knee him in the groin and, if necessary, punch him in the nose.

The SUV was gone. But he could have moved to throw her off. She paced a few aisles, her coffee at the ready, but saw no one. Before heading out, she texted Lyle:

> On the way home from Phx. Got good source for investigating G. Also picked up a tail, like they say on TV, but hope I lost him. Home soon.

Driving back, Kate kept one eye on the road and one on the mirror. She saw her pursuer in her mind, but not actually on the pavement behind her.

She hoped her visit to the mall had confused her tail so he wouldn't know her purpose in driving downtown. But the guy in the funny-colored SUV knew she visited the rescue zoo. He couldn't know why she went there, but Kate worried she might have exposed her friend Lisa to Gudgel reprisals.

CHAPTER 41

"Of course I can do it," Rob Napier said. One of NC's engineers who created the programs *and* hardware for the park's AI-controlled attractions spoke with a note of excitement. "This sounds like espionage equipment."

"Let's say an *observation* device," Lyle said, "but this has to remain between you and me. People's safety may ride on it."

Napier would keep his secret, Lyle knew, but that didn't stop him from getting enthusiastic over detective work.

Napier's office and mini laboratory sat in the inner reaches of NC's Park Attraction Development building where engineers, programmers, and others brainstormed and created new rides. Next to the engineer's minimalist desk—two monitors, keyboard, and a gizmo resembling a bar code scanner—sat a table filled with assorted metal and plastic parts, several with wires attached.

"What's this?" Lyle asked. "Did you take apart a computer?"

"Just a minor project I'm fiddling with."

Lyle had met the talented engineer, programmer, and out-of-the-box thinker while working on one of Max's investigations. Napier's logic and ingenuity were unmatched. He was an asset as long as Lyle could persuade him to temper his exuberance. Lyle reached in his coat pocket and pulled out a pair of black-framed glasses.

"These look a lot like yours," Lyle said, gesturing to the engineer's plastic glasses. "I've seen these smart glasses demonstrated online and I think they're ideal for our purposes. They just need a few modifications."

"A lot has changed," Napier said, "since the early smart glasses came out. Those were spooky looking and obviously more than just glasses." He picked up Lyle's glasses. "These could fool anyone except for the tiny warning lights at the corners."

"I'm assuming you can remove or turn those off."

"Sure. And we'll need a little more creative work to disguise the camera lenses."

"Now the cameras transmit to the cloud and we can download and watch, right?"

"With a little tweaking, yes. I'll test it out."

"And it records?"

"Uh huh."

A ding from his phone told Lyle he had a text, but he ignored it. "I think it's difficult to use the on-off switch," he said. "Can you make it a little easier?"

"Maybe." Napier took off his glasses and tried on the other pair. "I see. It is a tight fit."

"The person who will be wearing them is much smaller than you are, but the switch might still be an issue."

"I know how these work," the engineer said. "Anything else?"

Lyle could tell Napier was hooked. "Yes, but one part of this may be beyond the lab's capabilities here."

"Hmm?"

"I need to have prescription lenses in them. I have the prescription here. It's just single vision."

"I know an optometrist in town. We can get these tomorrow."

"Rob, you're a genius."

"If there's any other, you know, spy stuff you need, just come by."

Lyle mentioned the online request he needed for Drenda.

"Simple."

As he left the office, Lyle pulled out his phone and saw a text from Kate. Outside the building, he called her.

"Are you all right? Who's following you, Gudgel?"

"You can relax, I think. I saw my friend Lisa at the zoo and noticed that someone had pulled into the lot when I did, and he was still there when I came out."

She explained her seemingly successful efforts to lose the gray SUV and its male driver, and she told Lyle her ETA.

"You haven't seen him on the highway?"

"No. I've been looking."

"See you at my place."

CHAPTER 42

When Kate drove into Lyle's condo parking lot, he stood outside plucking the rubber band on his wrist.

"That son of a bitch," he said in the midst of a welcome hug. "Damn."

They sat at Lyle's kitchen counter as Kate described her visit at the zoo and her afternoon adventure.

"Can you imagine someone following me all that way from here? What if I was going to the grocery store? Would he follow me there, too?"

Lyle could feel his anger rising, but shoved it down so he could evaluate the situation. "Did you see him following you all the way back here?"

"No. I pulled into a shopping mall and went inside. He stayed in his car, I think. When I came out, he was gone. I didn't see him again. I got his license plate. Maybe you can find out who he is."

"Can do." He typed the plate into his phone. "I have

another idea. Let me call Gayle at the garage. I bet she'll help us."

A few minutes later, Lyle and Kate pulled into the NC garage in Kate's hybrid SUV. As soon as they stopped, Lyle saw Gayle LeBlanc, the heavy-set garage manager. Dressed in a shop coat that would cover a queen-sized bed, she stepped down from her desk situated on a platform so she could see down the rows of autos being worked on in the hangar-size building.

"Hey Lyle honey," LeBlanc said in her Louisiana accent, "y'all think ya got a bug attached to this buggy? Where'd you pick it up, Kate?"

"Wish I knew," she said.

"Well, let's take a look," LeBlanc said. "Carlos over there will help us out. Just pull into that service bay with the lift."

She turned from Kate and raised her voice. "Hey Carlos, this is the infected car. Can you direct her into the space?"

A guy in remarkably clean work clothes waved. Kate got in the car and drove in his direction.

Lyle knew LeBlanc's teased hair and heavy make-up disguised her automotive wizardry that made the NC restoration garage efficient enough to keep a fleet of fifty- to sixty-year-old cars running like new. She wasn't a bad judge of character, either.

"So, Lyle honey," LeBlanc said as Kate drove past them. "Are you guys onto somethin' again? I mean, there's lots of talk around here after the shootings."

"Gayle, we're trying, but we're working on several things at once. We're poking around, asking questions, and looks like we got someone's attention. I think they're tracking us. Let's take a look."

He and Gayle walked to the service stall where Kate's car was now six feet off the ground.

"I've seen a few of these nasty gadgets before," LeBlanc said. "Sometimes they use 'em t' track wayward spouses. Know what I mean?"

She walked under the car with Lyle. Kate joined them with her head bowed. Carlos looked on from outside.

"It's dark in here," LeBlanc said. "Carlos, how about a work light?"

Carlos grabbed a tripod-mounted flood light, adjusted the height, and rolled it to LeBlanc.

The shop manager directed the light to the rear of the vehicle and she and Lyle paced, looking for something that didn't belong.

"*This* wasn't factory equipment," LeBlanc said, pointing to a small metal box, lacking the coat of grime the rest of the underside wore. She reached to grab it.

"Wait Gayle," Lyle said. "I've been thinking about what to do if we found a tracker. Rather than pull it off and stomp on it, let's attach it to one of our cabs. May we do that?"

Gayle smiled. "Pretty sharp. Yeah, that way whoever's following Kate will think she's just driving around the park all day."

"Let's put it on a cab that won't be going back into service for a day," he said. "D'you know if this model will send a signal if it's detached?"

"No idea, Lyle honey. Only a real expensive one would have that. This looks like they bought it online for less than a hundred bucks. Self-contained, attached with a powerful magnet."

Lyle looked closely at the device.

"'Fore we pull it off," LeBlanc said, "let's look 'n' see if it has any cousins hanging around."

Kate moved the work light, and the three of them searched under the front of the car.

"Looks clean," Lyle said after a few minutes of scrutiny.

"Carlos can pull the tracker off and stick it under that cab over there," LeBlanc said. "That okay?"

"Let's take a chance. Thanks Carlos."

"Whoever bugged my car didn't need to follow me from here, did he?" Kate said.

"That's what I thought. They wanted to know whenever you got near—what? Something in Phoenix? The governor's office? Or were they just generally looking to see what you're up to?"

"I think the latter," Kate said. "In that case, maybe your Mustang ought to go on the lift."

"But I'm not the spokesperson for the park, just a cab driver."

"Y'all take care of yourselves," LeBlanc said as Lyle and Kate drove off.

■   ■   ■

"I have to get ready for my Cadre Brave meeting," Lyle said as they walked into his condo,

"Getting dressed?" Kate said. "Did you iron your sheet?"

"No, it's not a formal dinner." Lyle chuckled, but

every time he thought about the Cadre Brave, his equilibrium wobbled like a seismograph needle during a 7.0 quake.

She pulled him close. "I know you're going there to check them out, see if you can get a hunch about who might have been the shooter." Arms around him, she squeezed and met his eyes up close. "Don't take chances. Come home."

"Just a barbecue for a bunch of guys. Okay, maybe neo-Nazis, but they invited me, so I'll be cool. Really. He returned her firm squeeze and pressed his lips on hers. Of course I'll come home."

Before he jumped in his car, he took another dose of what the Stones called Mother's Little Helper.

CHAPTER 43

Lyle listened to Jim Croce singing "Time in a Bottle" as he accelerated. He wanted to get to the barbecue early to make it easier to meet people as they arrived. Apparently, a handful of other guys had a similar idea.

Lyle parked in front of a broad adobe Southwest territorial style home. A gravel drive led around the side of the house and continued through heavy oak gates opened wide. Brick-bordered cactus gardens connected by narrow gravel paths circled the backyard that covered a half acre or more. In the middle, conversation groups of teak tables and chairs, shaded by umbrellas, surrounded a curving, lighted swimming pool.

At the far side of the pool, a clutch of five men in casual clothes stood talking near a fire pit. As Lyle approached, his shoes crunching on the gravel, they all looked up and the conversation ebbed. The words, "I mean it, man," died in the air.

"C'mere Lyle." The guy Lyle remembered as Ed, the wild Suburban driver, motioned to him.

Lyle recognized Wylie, the supervisor—and dead shot—from the shooting range. The man extended his hand.

"Lyle, I'm Wylie," he said with his dimpled-chin smile. "We owe you a thanks for your quick thinking to help save Bobby's life. Saved him from his own carelessness."

"Jake and Ed helped. Took all of us to get him treated."

"Glad you could make it here tonight," Wiley said. "You can meet the guys and find out about us. And about our mission for the country."

"That's why I'm here." Lyle studied Wylie's face, wondering if his name was an appropriate adjective.

"We tol' him some about CB," Ed added.

Wylie pointed to a galvanized tub loaded with ice and beer in bottles. "Help yourself, Lyle."

Floodlights along the edge of the house and around a ramada next to a large, smoking barbecue supplemented the setting sun. Lyle looked at the three other men in the group and introduced himself. For a moment he forgot where he was. The clink of glasses, the smell of meat searing on the grill, the light shimmering on the pool surface made him imagine a barbecue with guys who might be in the same bowling league, softball team, or Kiwanis Club. But they were hate group members, possibly killers. He tried to remember the faces.

Lyle wandered to the ice tub and helped himself. He planned to circulate and collect information—casually. His back to the fire pit, he set his beer bottle on a table. He pulled out his phone and, pretending to do something innocuous, he took several pictures of the group. Enlarged, the photos might provide decent mug shots.

"Keeping up on Instagram?" a voice behind him said.

Lyle lowered his phone and turned it off in one motion. "Hey, Jake. You just come from work?" Lyle pointed to his shirt and tie.

"Yeah, working late on specs for a new commercial development. Citizens are worried about more traffic."

Lyle turned halfway round, looking at the grounds. "This is a beautiful place."

"Wylie does all right. So you took the invitation to come."

"I'm interested in the Cadre Brave and would like to know more. What are you guys concerned about?"

"I guess *concerned* is a good way to describe the group."

"So help me understand. What's wrong with the country? What does Cadre Brave want to change?" Lyle picked up his beer and held it in front of him.

"It's like what Ed and I said the other day. We want to maintain American values. They're slipping away. The values that our forefathers fought and died for. You think George Washington fought so drag queens could read books to students?"

Yes, exactly. He helped guarantee freedom of self expression. "Did they have drag queens then? The guys did all wear wigs."

"Seriously, it's what our heritage represents," Jake said. "But today, values and priorities are shifting. Back in Washington and here.

"Look, I'm not a racist, but can't you see how our cities, our culture, are being diluted by the mass of immigrants, illegals? I was lucky to get my job with the county. I have a degree in urban planning, but they said they needed diversity, and I'm white, so that put me at the end of the list."

"So how did you get hired?"

"I was a senior planner in the LA area and got good reviews. And my boss here knew my wife looked after our kids and my income was all we had. Lots of these Mexicans have two jobs, the wives work, too. They're not really nuclear families."

"Don't a lot of Hispanic immigrants need more than one job to just make ends meet? They're just like any poor folks if they don't have an education."

Jake stared blankly over Lyle's shoulder for a moment. Was he considering it?

"Don't you see?" Jake said. "I was lucky. I found someone who *understands* the challenges of white males these days. That's how I got the job. The deep state is controlled by officials who—"

"Wait a sec Jake. *You* work for the government. When we first met, you said you work to balance the interests of homeowners and developers."

"Yes, growth is going to happen, but it shouldn't be at the expense of working people. That's part of my job."

"So you help average citizens. Are *you* part of the deep state?"

"No, that's different."

"How?"

"Creating livable spaces."

"To help *everyone?*"

Jake looked off into the distance.

"You telling him about the great replacement?"

Cody, the NC bus driver, said as he interrupted, beer in hand.

"He's trying to understand Cadre Brave," Jake said.

Who is trying to persuade who?

"It's white American males who are getting dumped on," Cody said. "As the immigration wave continues, more and more of us will be replaced by cholos."

"Lyle," Jake said, "there's just *too many* people flooding the border. So we hold rallies to stop immigration."

"What it comes down to," Cody said raising his beer, "is that straight white guys are victimized, by government, minorities, the women's movement." His passion increased. "Instead of Gay Pride or Black Power, we have straight white men's pride, white power."

Cody wandered off and Lyle wanted to mingle, but he paused for a moment. "Jake, how about we have lunch together sometime in Polk? You can tell me more. My schedule is flexible." *He wants to help people. Why does he need a hate group?*

"Okay. I'll call you."

Lyle put his empty beer bottle in a trash can and wandered toward four guys talking by the pool. He paused about 20 feet away, pulled out his phone, and held it up. He took quick photos of the four guys and of another group nearby. Then he randomly punched the screen several times, muttering to himself as he put it away.

"Problem with your phone?" asked Ed, as Lyle approached the group.

"My sister-in-law keeps sending me alerts about

baby videos, but I never know if it's maybe an important message instead."

Lyle joined Ed and three others he didn't know, although he recognized one from the shooting range, a guy who blasted away at a senator's picture with a .44 magnum.

"Hey you guys," Ed said, "this is Lyle. He's the one who helped us save Bobby. He's interested in joining."

A short, balding man with an America First t-shirt looked at Lyle as if assessing his suitability. The man had one eyebrow higher than the other, giving him a look of perpetual alarm. "We're a tight group," he said.

Lyle waited for more, but that was it. "You're close knit," he said. "I can appreciate that."

"You should, if we want you to join."

"He saved Bobby," Ed repeated.

"Is that in his favor?" asked another CB member, drawing chuckles.

After a couple minutes of random talk, Lyle sensed he could slip in his question. "So what did you think of the shooting the other day?" He said it in a casual tone.

"They didn't catch anyone, did they?" America First said.

"I don't think so," said .44 magnum.

Lyle watched and waited for more responses, but a guy with a beard wearing a red ball cap joined the group and said, "Are all you guys going to the Gudgel rally?" It's next weekend in Prescott." The man gestured with his drink. "You gotta support him."

One grunted concurrence. "We gotta support

Gudgel f'sure. He's fighting the gay, faggot, anti-American, woke bullshit at Nostalgia City."

"Hey," said America First. He pointed a finger at Lyle's chest. "You *work* there, don't you?"

"Uh huh."

"Whacha do out there, anyway? Are you working against the governor?"

CHAPTER 44

"I drive a cab." Lyle said.

The inquisitor glowered, and the others watched.

"What?" Lyle said, "you think some executive calls the transport department and says, 'lemme talk to a cab driver so I can decide what to say about the governor.'"

Two guys laughed.

"It's just a fuckin' *job*, man."

Everyone looked up when Wylie announced food was being served. Lyle found a table with Ed and big ears from the target practice, introduced as Morgan, and three others. Morgan wore a t-shirt that said, "If you know how many guns you have, you don't have enough guns." One of the other men at the table looked like the father of the eight-year-old machine gunner. He considered asking him, but wasn't sure he could keep his mouth shut if the answer was "yes."

White-coated servers brought out platters of brisket, cornbread, beans and other dishes and set them on the tables. Lyle and the guys at his table helped themselves.

"I'm new here," Lyle said to the guy on his left after everyone had a plate of food. "Why did you join Cadre Brave?"

"Why did we join, eh Ed?" asked the man.

"The other day," Ed said, gesturing with a slab of cornbread, "we told you we're patriots. We want to protect the country. It's our duty."

"We're protecting ourselves, too," said Morgan, "from them."

"Yeah," said a rangy fellow with a neatly trimmed beard. Dockers and a long-sleeved sport shirt made him the dressiest CBer except Jake. "The country is not just being run by those guys you think get the votes, but by the deep state. People in high places. Not good Americans. The FBI is involved. And other agencies."

With everyone digging into dinner, the table fell silent. "So what did you think of the shooting?" Lyle asked as off-handedly as he could.

"Think of it?" said the tall, bearded man, the first to speak after several seconds. "Some gays got whacked." He shoved a hunk of brisket in his mouth.

"It sends a message," Ed said, "to leave children alone."

"There were *two* shootings," someone said. Lyle looked to see who had spoken, but food occupied everyone's attention, except Morgan. He looked at his plate when Lyle made eye contact.

Lyle wanted to keep the subject alive, but one of the guys asked, "How's Bobby doin'?"

"He's okay," said Ed. "Has to stay off that leg for a while."

"Idiot," someone said.

When most of the guys at Lyle's table were finishing their food, Lyle noticed Morgan had left.

Lyle wondered aloud if Wylie was going to address the group.

"He usually has something to say," said one guy.

Looking over the man's shoulder, Lyle saw Wylie standing by himself under a patio cover near the house. He had his back turned and was talking on the phone.

Lyle got up mumbling about getting another beer. He wandered in the general direction of the beer tub but took the long way around the pool toward Wylie. Pausing for a moment in a shadow, he pulled out his phone, glancing at it as an excuse to stop and listen. He strained to hear.

"I'm telling you now," Wylie said into his phone, "I don't know who did it. But you can give us credit if you want. Tell Bannach we're dedicated."

Wylie turned slightly, so Lyle continued to the beer tub. As he bent over to help himself, Wylie stood right behind him.

"Like our group?" Wylie asked.

"Ah—"

"Hey, Wylie," said a voice close by.

Lyle turned to see Andrew, the muscular guy he met at the bar. "Lyle here's an ex-cop. Used to be a detective."

Wylie looked at Lyle. "That true?"

Lyle turned to Andrew. "Where'd you hear that?"

"Well," Andrew said, "Is it true?"

"Of course. I worked for the Phoenix PD."

Wylie patted Lyle's shoulder. "That's great. We like

ex-cops and guys in the military. You were pretty good at
the range, I remember."

"Fair."

"If you want to join us," Wylie said, "let me explain
what I'd like."

CHAPTER 45

April 17

Kate took no chances. Even if the GPS tracker was attached under an NC taxi back at the park, she still kept looking at the rearview mirror as she drove south on I-17 through Phoenix. She'd also altered her appearance with drab, almost-to-the-point-of-ugly makeup, clear fashion glasses, a long dress to make her legs look shorter, and horizontal stripes she believed made her look wider, shorter.

At the state transportation department building, Kate found an office, one in a row of spaces with windows to the outer office, and a solid door. The glass next to the door bore the name Tim McKenna.

"I understand why you wanted to meet me first before we conducted any *business,*" she said when she sat opposite his desk. "Sorry for the delay."

"Yes, you were concerned about being followed," said McKenna, whose hair was the color of an Irish setter.

"I dealt with it," she said, "but didn't want to take the

chance of being followed into your office. This doesn't mean I expect you to do anything prohibited or unlawful to help me, but as the spokesperson for Nostalgia City, I thought I might be persona non grata in state offices."

"Not in *my* office you're not," he said smiling, his light freckles making him appear younger than he probably was. "Pardon my asking, but you don't look like Lisa described you. You're tall, but...."

"Just my idea of protecting both of us," she said. She peeled up a corner of the dark wig she wore to display a wisp of light blonde.

"In addition to being odious," she said, "the governor is powerful and dangerous. I've seen his private army at his rallies. I wanted to be careful."

"I work for the people of Arizona, not Governor Gudgel. I'm doing my work in their best interests, not his."

Obviously not a politician, McKenna is here to do a job. Refreshing.

"I'm sure Lisa told you what my goal is."

"To get back at the governor because you advocate for minority groups and he doesn't."

"Concisely put." Although the tip of an exceptionally cold iceberg. "He's used his position to disrupt park operations, too. As Lisa may also have told you, I don't yet know exactly what I'm looking for. But I suspect somewhere in his Arizona political career—up to the present day—the governor has elevated his lifestyle through graft."

"And so you thought the highway department would be a good place to look. You're right. The difficulty in detecting bidding schemes varies with the skill of the scammers."

"That I've learned."

"Now I don't work directly with contracts and bids. I'm on the engineering side." He gestured to a striking framed aerial photo of a collection of freeway ramps snaking over each other, traversed by blurred automobiles.

"But," he continued, "that doesn't mean I don't have access to the kind of information you're probably looking for. But you'd have to give me a starting point, a particular highway, job number, dates, things of that sort."

"But you must hear things, or know about certain jobs that could be suspect."

He leaned back in his chair and gave her an assessing look.

Made up to look frumpy and forgettable, Kate discarded a coy smile as a persuader. "There could be a connection between the murders at Nostalgia City and the Gudgel administration. People we work with were shot."

McKenna frowned.

"We don't know, of course, but he degrades people and does not condemn violence."

"Okay. Give me a few minutes." McKenna typed into his computer, stared at his screen, typed some more. When he finished, pages streamed out of his printer.

"Here's a list of large, expensive jobs, a few complicated with delays and overruns. I don't know if any of them are rigged. Maybe none. But if you suspect anything funny on one of these—or others—I can get you the files, bid documents, whatever else is available."

He handed Kate three pages. She scanned them, biting her lip thinking how much time it would take her to examine each job, using the procedures Oberon taught her.

"That first page is the more likely candidates," he said." McKenna swiveled in his chair and glanced out the window. "You have your work cut out for you."

"I'm very grateful for your help."

He swiveled around to Kate. "Now, you did not get this from me. I don't know who you are. You're in disguise. Maybe you're from the auditing department."

"I understand your position fully, which is why I took precautions. I appreciate your help Mr.—I don't even know your name."

"Let's not meet here again. Lisa can tell you how to contact me at home if you need something."

CHAPTER 46

Kate's incognito get-up wasn't designed only for Tim McKenna. She had a date with Drenda. So intrigued by her friend infiltrating the Gudgel campaign, Kate wanted to see for herself.

Had she exaggerated telling McKenna that Gudgel could have had a hand in the shootings? Maybe, but Lyle had come home from the barbecue with stories about Cadre Brave members hoping Gudgel would crush gay-loving Nostalgia City.

To get to her rendezvous with Drenda, she took a circuitous route downtown, once hopping on a freeway. When she arrived at the campaign office it appeared as Drenda had described it: an empty high-tech company building surrounded by unwatered vegetation and a large and largely empty parking lot. She noted a few shiny luxury cars—and a dull gray SUV. She did a slow, cautious pirouette, then headed for the campaign door.

Even with her wig and other changes, Kate wanted only a quick look around to see where Drenda worked, and evaluate the facilities. Lyle had suggested she look carefully for surveillance cameras, particularly indoors.

Drenda sat at the reception counter in front of a low partition. Kate asked about a campaign yard sign in case anyone was listening.

"You're fine," Drenda said. She gestured beyond the counter to the wide-open office space occasionally punctuated by clusters of desks, many unoccupied. "No one can hear us. That skinny guy over there is paid staff. He supervises volunteers. I work for him, in a manner of speaking. We can go over to my desk if you like. I can tell you about volunteer opportunities with the Gudgel campaign."

"Yuk. Of course I'd like to learn about it."

As she crossed the open carpet, Kate scanned the ceiling, corners, anywhere a camera could be installed. They sat at Drenda's otherwise deserted cluster; her supervisor sat 25 feet away. Kate saw the separate offices, all with interior windows, across an opposite wall.

"Most of those offices belong to campaign staff," Drenda said. "The one past the conference room is Gudgel's office."

Kate saw the governor's broad desk with a telephone and stacks of papers. Turning back to Drenda, she saw two men in Arizona State Guard camo uniforms walk in. They spoke with someone in one of the private offices.

"Are they Gudgel's bodyguards?"

"Not necessarily. I've seen guard members here every day I've worked. Once the governor was here for a short time, and the State Guard was all over the place. Like a military bivouac. Is it supposed to be reassuring? It had the opposite effect on me."

Kate watched the guard members finish their conversation, walk around a corner, and disappear down a corridor. "Who's in the office next to the governor's?"

A thirtyish guy with long blond hair sat behind a glass-topped desk looking at a computer screen while talking on a land-line phone.

"He's the campaign manager, Steve Vaughan. He's been here about two months. Gudgel fired the first campaign manager."

"One reason I wanted to see this place," Kate said, "—oh my God. He can't see me here."

Kate watched as a man she recognized walked out of one of the private offices, talking and joking with a woman in a business suit. Relaxed body language told her the two were comfortable with each other. They walked toward the main entrance and stopped at a desk cluster. Kate turned her back.

"What are they doing?"

"They sat down and are looking at a bunch of papers."

"I was foolish to come here."

"The woman he's talking to is Beth Montagne. She's special assistant to the governor. I don't recognize him. You can wait and see if he leaves. Who is he?"

"I'll tell you later. But if he walks over here, it'll spoil everything. I'm dead. Where can I hide?"

Drenda looked over Kate's shoulder. "There's a ladies' room back there. Seclude yourself, and I'll let you know when it's clear."

Kate chanced a glance at the two who were engrossed

in their work, but were too close for her to relax. She nodded to Drenda, and as unobtrusively as possible walked into the ladies' room.

The restroom held six stalls along one wall and three adjoining from the corner—obviously designed to serve an office full of corporate employees. A row of sinks and long-spouted faucets sat on a broad counter that looked like granite.

Kate's first instinct was to see if she was alone. The room *felt* empty. Her steps echoed as she walked down the row of stalls, doors slightly ajar. Should she hide in a stall? Would the governor's special assistant—or anyone—recognize her?

She chose an end stall and closed the door behind her. She stood hoping to hear Drenda's voice soon. After five minutes had passed, she looked at the toilet seat. It appeared clean. She hiked up her long dress slightly and sat on the edge.

She pulled out her phone and scrolled through email until she heard the restroom door open. When she didn't hear Drenda's voice, she realized from the person's stride it was someone else. *Guess I'll sit tight, so to speak.*

The woman selected a stall two doors down. She finished quickly and flushed. Kate heard her wash and dry her hands, then silence. As the silence persisted, Kate assumed the woman was looking in the mirror, perhaps applying makeup. After a minute, steps headed to the door. But the door didn't open. The woman was listening.

After a few seconds, the restroom visitor said, "huh," and left.

Alone again, Kate texted Drenda. No answer. Then,

Coast is clear.

Kate texted a thumbs-up emoji and made her escape. In the parking lot, she noticed several cars had departed—including the cloudy SUV.

CHAPTER 47

Lyle couldn't tell if the secretary of the Northern Arizona University's history department was a student or employee.

"Good morning," he said, "I'm here to see Professor Jolley."

"Do you have an appointment?"

"Yes."

"Awesome."

"My name's Lyle Deming."

The receptionist glanced at her computer screen. "Perfect."

"My appointment's one o'clock."

"Perfect."

Awesome, perfect? Is she a university *student?*

"Dr. Jolley is awesome. I just had her for Civil War and reconstruction. Her office is down that hall."

"Perfect."

After his Cadre Brave party, Lyle still had more questions than answers. Perhaps Drenda's friend could help.

"Glad to meet you," Dr. Jolley said after Lyle knocked and let himself into her office. "I was pleased to hear from Drenda. It had been a while."

A bit younger than Lyle expected, Prof. Jolley, probably in her 40s, pointed Lyle to one of the two guest chairs in her office, the other stacked with papers. "Drenda told me you were a Phoenix police detective and now do security work for Nostalgia City."

"Trying to keep the park intact would be a better way of putting it. You know what's been happening down there. Two of our employees were killed and one injured. It's a hate crime, but is a hate group involved?"

"I don't think I can answer that question, but I can give you background on hate groups."

"Yes, where do we start?"

"Anywhere you like."

"Okay, I know hate groups are, by definition, racist or against minority groups, but…"

"I think most level-headed people know about prejudices," she said. "We all have them to some extent, but what does it take to build a movement and organization around hatred?"

"That's my question."

She scooted her chair forward and put both arms on her desk. "Why don't I start at the beginning and you can ask questions as we go."

"Great."

"The SPLC, Southern Poverty Law Center, is the leading hate group research and advocacy organization in the country. It estimates there are more than 1,400 hate groups and anti-government organizations in the US."

"Holy shit," Lyle muttered under his breath, then put his hand over his mouth.

Jolley smiled. "A common reaction. It is a frightening number."

"You said hate *and* anti-government groups."

"Correct, although it's a challenge to keep them in neat categories. The SPLC has many more categories than that. But to keep it simple, which it really isn't—"

She smiled at herself.

"The SPLC and the FBI do have definitions for hate groups. In short, it represents animosity, hostility, and malice against members of a group, generally people with immutable characteristics. You can't change your race, your ethnic group."

"And the anti-LGBTQ groups," Lyle said, "erroneously claim homosexuality is a mental disorder that can be cured."

Jolley nodded. "Now anti-government groups are just that. They believe in various conspiracy theories that assert the legitimate government has been co-oped by nefarious actors, including bureaucrats, industrialists, Jewish leaders, and others who make up the deep state." She brushed her blonde-streaked brown hair off her forehead. "Details of the conspiracies vary with the dissimilar groups."

"Kidnapping babies and drinking their blood?"

"That's one of the older ones, but it still has adherents. Incidentally, hate groups may espouse anti-government sentiments, but they masquerade as patriotic organizations intent on protecting the Constitution."

"Hate group members say they're trying to protect

themselves against discrimination," Lyle said. "They think straight white men are getting the shaft. At least, that's what they told me."

"Accurate observation. A common characteristic of hate groups is a culture of victimization and grievance. They're victimized by government corruption, by immigrants who are stealing their jobs, by gay people who molest their children, by Black people whose lives matter more than theirs. And there's grievances against Muslims, Jews, Asians, Hispanics, and of course women, whose feminism is designed to emasculate men."

"Why do people join these groups?"

"For many reasons. Studies have been conducted, many since January 6, to assess the appeal of hate groups. Those who have been rejected for military service join a hate group or a paramilitary group. People seek belonging, a sense of purpose. Their grievances and prejudices are reinforced by others. The most unfortunate to me are those who join with the mistaken idea they are serving their country."

"Why don't they join Boy Scouts or the Red Cross?"

"Joining a hate group to oppose supposed threats by minorities or others might, in a peculiar way, give you the same rewards as being a Red Cross volunteer."

"And the next step is violence?"

"That's one reason you're here, isn't it?"

"Yes, the Cadre Brave. Uh, one of the local groups—"

"And the biggest in Arizona."

"Yes, I've uh, met several of these marvelous guys, but maybe they're not involved in violence. Maybe it's just a—"

"Lone wolf?"

"Yeah, some nut job."

Dr. Jolley shook her head. "The news media often attributes hate crimes to lone wolves. It's a fallacy and one that has played into the hands of hate groups for decades. Attributing a mass killing to one lone gunman obscures the source of hate. Lone wolves are *a product* of hate groups."

"I can see—" Lyle began.

Dr. Jolley help up a hand. "People spread conspiracy theories on TV. Hate groups use social media, rallies, guns shows, and other events to encourage and connect people all over the country. They validate the sense of victimization. Sorry, I didn't mean to cut you off."

"Okay, understood. Groups like the Cadre Brave are spreading hate like it was COVID."

"Yes, and the it-was-only-a-crazy-lone-wolf explanation diminishes the perceived threat of hate groups."

Lyle thanked Dr. Jolley for her time.

"Mr. Deming, I don't know how you're investigating. You've obviously met Cadre Brave members. But all I can say is, these people are unpredictable. Don't try to fool them."

■　　■　　■

Two hours later, after making a quick stop at Nostalgia City, Lyle stood in the common mailbox area of his condo. He opened the box. Nothing but advertising.

Lyle heard a footstep behind him, then a punch to his kidneys slammed him against the wall of mailboxes. He dropped his mail and spun around to face his attacker.

Before he could bring up a fist, the heaviest of the three men facing him landed a punch in his stomach. Lyle tried not to double over, but then thought it might be a good defensive move.

As he bent, one of the men leaped behind him, grabbing his arms and pinning them to his back. Then the two other attackers took turns on his stomach, side, and chest. With what little energy he still possessed, Lyle threw himself back against the man holding his arms and kicked at the other two.

The youngest—and strongest of the three—wore heavy work boots, and he used them to kick Lyle's legs while the man behind him dropped Lyle on the concrete. Boots was about to kick Lyle in the ribs when the one person in the group Lyle recognized—Andrew—stopped him.

"That's enough," he said, raising an arm. "Okay Deming, just being sure you're committed to our cause. This is step one. Everybody does it."

CHAPTER 48

Working in the enemy's camp—Gudgel for Governor headquarters—kept Drenda on her toes. Hiding Kate from a sinister figure gave her a thrill. But when she walked into Lyle's family room after the drive from Phoenix, she recoiled. Kate was applying ice packs and cold rags on ugly bruises across Lyle's bare chest and stomach.

"Oh Lyle, what happened?"

"Initiation rite of the Cadre Brave," Lyle said. "Ooh, that's cold," he groaned as Kate moved the ice pack from one bruise to another.

Lyle pulled his shirt off completely and eased back into his chair. "I got this crazy idea that I would ingratiate myself with the hate group and find out if they were involved in the shootings."

"Lyle went to a hate group's barbecue last night," Kate said, "and *this* was his reward." She smacked him on the chest. "Tell me you're not going to mess with them again."

"*Your* reward hurt as much as theirs. How could I get involved further?"

"It didn't hurt."

"Oh yeah? Drenda, did Kate ever tell you about the time we were captured in a Provincetown, Massachusetts motel by two organized crime thugs? One guy held a gun on me, another stood guard at the door. Kate crept up quietly—the second guy was about shoulder-high to Kate—and she hit him in the face with an elbow. Crack. I could hear his nose breaking from across the room. He fell down flat and dropped his gun. The other guy looked away, and I nailed him. We tied them both up and left them for the police. So where were you today, huh, Kate?"

"Want me to smack you again?"

Drenda looked from Lyle to Kate. "Is that story true?"

"More or less. But Lyle got us in the mess in the first place."

Lyle shook his head. "Kate can be dangerous. But today my beating was a routine formality. No offense is intended. They just want to make sure you're tough enough."

Drenda felt helpless as she watched Kate's ministrations and listened to Lyle's groans.

"Shit. Ow." Lyle moved around in the chair.

Kate shifted the ice packs, then handed one to Drenda. "Can you hold this on his shoulder while I get more ice? Incidentally, please keep all this hate group stuff to yourself."

Drenda pressed a flexible ice pack against Lyle. "Luckily, they didn't hit your face."

"Yeah, or I would look like I did 10 rounds with Rocky Balboa. That's how I feel."

"Is it worth all this?"

"To find the people who killed the innocent victims, yes. But as I told Kate, I'm not sure I found out anything useful."

"Is the governor connected to the Cadre Brave?" Drenda said.

Lyle groaned again. "I don't know directly, but they go to his rallies."

"It's not difficult to believe," she said, moving the cold pack to a different place as Lyle grimaced.

"I didn't need to get beat up to find out how hate groups operate. I talked to your friend Dr. Jolley today. She warned me about the Cadre Brave just before this happened."

"Did Kate tell you about *her* adventure today?" Drenda said.

"She told me she had to hide in the bathroom at Gudgel headquarters, but we didn't get much further than that when she noticed what happened to me."

"I saw Gregory Hurt, the private investigator I told you about," Kate said from the kitchen. "I had to hide in the ladies' room. I didn't want him to see me."

Kate came back and settled on the arm of Lyle's chair, pressing one ice pack on his left shoulder, another on his right side. "When I met him, Drenda, he made me think he was investigating the governor, but it looks like he's working *for* him."

"I heard a few words of conversation," Drenda said. "It sounded like he was reporting on Nostalgia City."

"That fits Gudgel's history," Kate said, "hiring investigators to dig up dirt on his adversaries. I think Hurt was the person who followed me. I saw the Gray SUV in the parking lot when I drove in, but it was gone after Hurt left the campaign office and Drenda freed me from life in a toilet stall."

Drenda turned to Kate and raised a hand. "After he left—I forgot to tell you about this—I heard Beth, that's the governor's special assistant, talking on the phone and she said something about alerting ICE. I assumed that meant immigration."

Kate said. "Did that have to do with us?"

"I'm not sure."

"They could have been talking about an unrelated issue," Lyle said. "Besides, immigration is the feds."

Drenda saw Kate's pained, *what next?* expression. "Common sense doesn't deter Rod Gudgel from making trouble." Kate said. "I'll have to check this out. Somehow."

"Too bad I'm not there working all the time," Drenda said. "I'd have a better chance to eavesdrop."

"I have something that may help you on the days you *are* there in Gudgelville," Lyle said. Moving slowly, he reached over and picked up a small box sitting on the coffee table. "I think the naproxen is kicking in. Feels better anyway. Remember when I asked you to send me your eyeglass prescription?"

Drenda had texted him the prescription but wondered then, and now, what he had in mind.

Lyle opened the box and handed her a pair of glasses that looked remarkably like the ones she was wearing.

"This is the latest generation of smart glasses. A

generic version is commercially available, but I had my engineer friend Rob make changes, and he had prescription lenses installed."

Drenda took off her glasses, put on the new pair, and glanced around the room. She moved her focus from Lyle's face to across the room and out a window. Her vision was sharp and clear. "They're the same as my glasses."

"Except these are a *little* different." Lyle reached out a hand and Drenda took off the glasses and passed them over.

"In the upper corners here are little cameras. They're very sensitive and they will record and broadcast everything you see." He pointed to other spots on the glasses. "Microphones here record all the sound. Everything is sent to the cloud and we can download through our phones in real time. Sounded complicated, but Rob set it all up."

Record everything I see and hear in the office? "I wonder if I'll be self-conscious? No, I don't think so. Those feel like mine. Much of the video will be boring, however. Just me typing or making routine phone calls."

"Obviously, we won't need all of that. In fact," Lyle said, "you have to be careful how you use it because battery time is limited. There's an on-off switch here. It's hard to see."

Lyle took over holding the ice packs, and Kate moved to another chair.

Drenda picked up the new glasses and put them on slowly, holding them by the edge of the frames with both hands. She opened her eyes as wide as she could and stared at Kate.

Kate laughed. "I don't think you'll be able to read minds, Drenda."

"Unfortunate," she said with a mock frown that turned into a smile. "This will be sufficient, regardless."

"See Lyle," Kate said, "I told you Drenda has a sense of humor."

"Dry, like a martini," she said with a wink.

"If you see the private investigator again," Kate said, "try to record him."

Lyle moved an icepack to his right ribs. "Rob also fixed up your social media, Drenda. Did you receive the access information he sent?"

"Yes, I'm officially Ann Adair."

"You should now be secure in your *information gathering*."

"He means spying," Drenda said.

"Did either of you see surveillance cameras at the office?" he asked.

Kate said, "I looked closely and didn't see anything."

"Neither have I," Drenda added. "They don't have cameras, but they're always looking for bugs."

"Bugs?" Kate said.

"Every day, often in the morning, an Arizona State Guard person goes through the offices with a device that looks like a radio. I asked my boss, Landon, what was happening, and he said they sweep for listening devices and hidden cameras. The guard pays particular attention to the governor's office and the conference room."

"In that case," Lyle said, "If you're there when that's going on, power down the glasses. I'll check with Rob about it."

Drenda wanted to get back to the headquarters with her new spy glasses as soon as she could. "When I get back there, I'll linger and listen. I'll hang out in the coffee room." She tapped the edge of her glasses. "And see what I can pick up."

CHAPTER 49

April 18

A Lincoln SUV had taken a long ride along a guard rail, leaving a trail of black paint and gouged metal until it slammed into a heavy traffic barrier. Paramedics loaded the driver into the back of an ambulance. A sheriff's deputy directed traffic, and Lyle watched as uniformed Undersheriff Martinez paced down the edge of the state highway.

Lyle caught up with him past the accident site where Rey had parked his cruiser.

"Your office said you were here, and they told me you'd be tied up the rest of the day, so I am reporting as ordered."

Rey walked around his car and leaned on the passenger side, his back to highway traffic. "You talking about the hate group?"

"Si." Lyle leaned against the cruiser next to Rey. "Why are you out here on an accident call?"

"The victim you just saw getting attended to by the EMTs is a bigwig here in town."

Lyle glanced at the accident scene and the backed-up traffic. He hadn't decided how much to tell Rey. He knew the shooting investigations were moving no faster than the black Lincoln impaled on the guard rail. Shell casings and slugs turned up nothing. He'd hoped his venture into the world of hate would help. So far, not much.

Rey crossed his arms on his chest. "So what do you have to tell me? I'm a little busy today."

"Okay. I went to a barbecue at the home of a guy named Wylie. He's apparently the boss in this area. I counted seventeen guys there, some I knew from the shooting range. I found out about the group in the first place from a shuttle bus driver in the park who invited me for a beer. We met at West's Bar. You know the place?"

"Yeah. We're called there about once a week."

"It could be their hangout. Looks like whites only. I found out the bus driver is a CB member and I met two others. That's how I got invited to the shooting range."

Rey kept his arms folded. "And?"

"At the barbecue, I asked guys why they joined and what the group does. They all think society is against them, so they band together to take on the *deep state* when the time comes."

"Anybody mention the shooting—the shoot*ings*?"

"No one brought it up, but I did. Didn't get much. One guy said it sent a message to LGBTQ folk to leave children alone."

One of Lyle's ribs hurt. Maybe they broke it. He shifted his position against the car. "I kept thinking—well, first I thought, what the hell am I doing there?"

Rey stared at him.

"But then I thought that any of them could be the killer. Or none of them. If one of them did it, he's not talking about it. They're not real open. Maybe because I'm a stranger.

"I overheard this Wylie guy on the phone telling someone, words to the effect, that if their group wasn't responsible for the killing, he'd take credit for it anyway. Fucking awful street cred, huh?"

Lyle started to cross his arms like Rey, but stopped when he touched a sore spot.

"'S matter with you? You hurt?"

"I found out that getting beat up is part of the Cadre Brave initiation. Nothing too serious. They just hit me here, and here, and here, and over here. Kate told me to stay away from them."

"Smart woman. You should listen to her."

"I do. Hope I'm not committed already. You know, the group includes the kind of guys I expected, but some look ordinary, whatever that is, white collars and professionals. Not your common ignorant, neo-Nazi, skinhead types. This Wylie is someone to watch. I don't even know his last name."

"It's Tanner. Wylie Tanner. I'm going to haul him in again today for *questioning*."

"Uh, are you—"

"Don't worry. I won't mention you." Rey uncrossed his arms and rested a hand on his gun butt. "Deputy Beard died this morning at Flagstaff Memorial. Too much tissue damage from the AR."

CHAPTER 50

Kate got to work early. She needed to address her biggest concern of the moment, the possibility of an ICE raid. Drenda's overheard conversation had to be taken seriously, but who could she tell? That was the trouble with secrets. They got in the way.

But no need to tell anyone about Drenda's tip. She called the park's legal expert. "Morning Austen. You're in the office early, too."

"Patent issues. Always fun."

"Sounds fascinating," she said sarcastically, dragging out the last word. "My excuse is, I'm losing sleep imagining what dirty tricks our governor is planning next. And I thought about an ICE raid. Does that sound foolish?"

"Not at all. I've thought of that, too."

"Really?"

"Part of my job is to anticipate legal problems and obviate them."

"I guess PR is a little the same. So, should we be concerned about immigration?"

"I think the chances of a Gudgel-generated immigration raid are extremely slim. The governor should know a little more now about jurisdictions—in this instance, state versus federal—and presumably, someone in his inner circle might remind him that we fight back. The Phoenix City Council certainly wasted no time killing the crazy proposal to limit our airport bus access."

Kate relaxed—a little.

"And as for the legal status of our employees," Danvers said, "my department reviewed our I-9 immigration forms and policies with HR a few weeks ago and we're in good standing."

"One less thing to worry about," Kate said, thanking Danvers and crossing her fingers. If ICE *wasn't* a threat, she knew Gudgel would plan *something*. She remembered what Billings banker Dan Meacham called Gudgel's *petulant reactions to imagined slights*.

Clicking the email icon on her computer, she soon found more positive news. Lisa Oberon came through. Oberon's email carried the subject line, "shopping list." When Kate opened the file, she realized the subject was Oberon's idea of humor, or her way of making the email look innocuous.

Innocuous it was not. Oberon listed eight state government projects, construction contracts, personnel and political issues she said Kate might want to look into. "Thank you, *Lisa*," she whispered. She looked at the list as if it were a mound of Christmas presents waiting to be unwrapped and admired. Of course, they would take research, as they were Oberon's best *guesses* for Gudgel malfeasance.

Oberon's notes included:

- Tax abatement for Shiny Spurs Clothing. This brought the Texas manufacturer to the state. Making clothing can create toxic chemicals. Opposed by residents near the Colorado River site. Lawsuit in the works.

- A $61 million contract a year ago for repairs and highway extensions for Arizona SR 247. The winning bidder, Irwin Construction Co., has ties to the governor. Check the numbers.

- Gary Bresset appointed to Board of Regents. He was a heavy Gudgel campaign donor. Not illegal, but dark money allegations persisted. *Phoenix Standard* investigated, but never published anything. Wonder why?

- Ecoperi, an overseas company, purchased farm acreage in Fremont County a year ago. Gov. G supported the move, but's been low key on it. Now planning a huge expansion. Locals protested the farm was using too much water. See recent Radio Free Gloria podcast about supposed "accidental" deaths.

- Interchange construction for SR 120 south of Phoenix. Bidding process was interrupted three years ago, but job completed by Townsend Inc. way above projected budget. Ask Tim. He may have been involved in the engineering.

By the time Kate finished, Oberon's list sounded like lecture notes for a class in Graft 101. "Accidental" deaths in Fremont County could be serious, but what was the link to the governor? Kate recognized SR 247. She traveled it often. The road crossed two counties and connected to the park. A $61 million budget likely had lots of wiggle room for a payoff.

The ADOT website, daunting as she remembered it, eventually yielded information on the project. Irwin Construction's winning bid exceeded the department's estimate by 42 percent, but she noticed winning bids on many other projects exceeded estimated costs. She copied the data, including the names and prices of the other companies that bid on the job. Of the Irwin company's three principals, two were named Irwin.

Now she needed the job's details, actually anything the ADOT files would tell her. Tim McKenna had told her to ask Lisa how she should contact him—avoiding his office. Kate dialed Lisa's cell phone and immediately heard her voicemail greeting. After leaving a message, she dialed the zoo.

The person who answered the phone at the zoo told Kate that Lisa Oberon was out of the office and wasn't expected back for a few days.

"Oh, is she on vacation?"

"I think so," the woman said hesitantly. "I'm not certain."

Kate left a message.

She moved down Oberon's list. The Arizona farm sounded like a longshot, but if it involved deaths, it was worth checking. The note referenced a podcast.

She looked up Radio Free Gloria, named after a tiny mining town-turned tourist destination, and the podcast did not have a website. She found it via a podcast list, but the Radio Free Gloria link didn't work.

She walked out to her secretary's desk.

"Yes, I know it. I used to listen to that podcast but not recently." Joann told Kate. "It's run by an ex-TV reporter. He talks about politics, local controversies. Sometimes he's funny. I don't know where he gets his material."

Kate explained she couldn't find episodes of the podcast online, then wandered back to her desk. More searching turned up a local phone number that greeted her with a terse message asking her to leave a name and message.

"Hi, this is Kate Sorensen. I work for Nostalgia City. As you may know, we're in the middle of a, you might call it conflict, with Governor Rod Gudgel. A friend of mine suggested I listen to one of your podcasts that mentions a farm in Fremont County. Your podcast link on my phone doesn't work. Could you tell me how I can listen to Radio Free Gloria?"

CHAPTER 51

"Ann, what are you doing here today?"

It took Drenda a few seconds to respond to her middle name. "Work to be done, and I know you're swamped, Landon. I only work part-time at the library district. I asked my boss if I could reduce my hours for a while."

"We can use the help, of course. By the way, the governor asked about you."

"He did?"

"The other day. I just told him you were a hardworking volunteer." Landon smiled.

I don't know if that's good news or not.

She'd made a point of wearing outfits to look professional and attractive, but not overly so. Ms. Average. She knew effective international espionage agents dressed to blend into the background. The flashy James Bond or Emma Peel look was proscribed as counterproductive.

Was she overanalyzing her part?

As Landon walked back to his desk, Drenda realized

she was wearing her spy glasses. The prescription felt like her regular glasses. She would not be self conscious, except perhaps when recording. Her other addition decorated the third finger on her left hand. She had not told anyone whether she was married and decided it would attract less attention if a wife worked scant hours for pay and spent the rest of her time as a political volunteer. She wore a thin silver and stone band she'd bought in Mexico that would have to pass as a wedding ring.

She noticed two Arizona State Guardsmen seated at a distant island of desks and filmed them. With a casual touch of a finger on her glass frames, she began recording. She strolled to the coffee room across the open spaces of the office. A guardsman glanced at her but continued his conversation.

On the way back to her desk, she thought about security while recording. She stopped at Landon's desk to ask about campaign procedures, then said, "are the guardsmen here to sweep for bugs? Is that what you call it?"

"I don't know what they're doing here. Sometimes best not to ask. But the office scans were done earlier."

She'd sensed tension between the campaign staff and the guard before.

As she moved back to her desk, she scanned the office to register a picture of the entire layout, including the private offices. She saw Vaughn, the campaign manager, talking in his otherwise empty office, presumably with his phone on speaker mode. Drenda lamented her glasses could not pick up his voice. She scanned the governor's office next door and looked at the landline phone on his desk. Then she looked up at the tangle of phone and computer cables that spilled out of the ceiling tiles above the clusters of desks. Would one of those wires connect with the governor's phone?

She sat down and visualized scenes from spy movies with secret agents, dressed as service techs, tapping into the bad guys' phones. She turned off her glasses and went back to sorting piles of precinct canvass instructions.

Toward the end of the day, bored and disappointed she had no opportunity to record significant conversations, she watched Beth Montagne, bulky bag in hand, chatting with Vaughan outside his office door. Drenda started her glass-frame cameras, knowing she was probably too far away to pick up the conversation. After a few minutes, she watched Montagne say good night and walk out the building's front door. She'd left her office door ajar.

Drenda lingered at her desk well past five o'clock, trying to look busy. The other campaign clerical workers had gone. The hum of voices faded away. Across the open space, Vaughn still sat at his desk talking on his phone. Now he had wireless earphones in and carried on a lively conversation, at least his side of it.

She got up from her desk, and in a few steps Vaughn was out of sight. Her glasses still recording, just in case, she walked across the office open space toward Montagne's door. On her way, she picked up a folder from Landon's desk. Dropping this off for Montagne would be her excuse if Vaughn came by or if another campaign worker had remained in the office late.

A variety of letters, notepads, and scraps of paper decorated the desk of the governor's special assistant. Drenda wasn't looking for anything in particular, just *something* important. Before she had time to read one document, she heard Vaughn's voice as he talked on the phone. His voice grew louder.

"Yeah, I'm going to head home. I've done as much as I can today," he said. "But—say, Beth left her door open."

Instinct—or fear—told Drenda to hide, rather than offer an excuse for being in the office. She ducked behind the desk. Almost instantly, the light went out, and she heard the door shut with a finite click.

Vaughn's voice grew fainter, and she assumed he'd walked out. Did he lock the main door behind him?

Getting out immediately became more important than searching Montagne's desk. But she evaluated her position. Montage's office locked from the inside so she wasn't trapped. If she were alone and locked in the building itself, well, that was another problem. If her glasses were as good as Lyle said they were, she didn't need to read Montagne's papers. She could simply go through them one at a time, recoding everything she saw. She and Kate could review them later.

Bright light from the main office streamed in through Montagne's windows. Drenda hoped her camera lenses would pick up everything she saw. She paged through a notepad, flipped through reports, and scanned scribbles on yellow sticky notes, careful to leave the desk the way she found it. As she closed and locked Montagne's door behind her, she turned, listening and looking. She was alone.

Grabbing her purse, she headed for the main door and stopped abruptly. Not only did it lock from the outside, making it impossible for her to lock the door behind her, she sensed there might be an alarm system on the door. She stepped back to the reception counter and leaned against it. No one knew she'd been in Montagne's locked office. Could she call someone with the campaign and say she'd been accidentally locked in? That might bring her unwanted attention.

She imagined herself trapped all night.

CHAPTER 52

Kate felt disappointed with her progress. She'd left a second message on Oberon's cell phone. She tried to squeeze any more information she could out of the ADOT site, including details of the other job mentioned in Oberon's list, and she hadn't received a call back from Radio Free Gloria. Maybe that one was a bust.

"Have you heard from Drenda today?" Lyle asked when he walked into Kate's apartment.

"She recorded a bunch of video and photos, but since I didn't get a text from her, I assumed nothing urgent. We can look at them now if you like. Then I have a pleasant surprise. I got a list of potential Gudgel scams from Lisa Oberon."

"I have news, too," Lyle said, standing close. "Not good news. The deputy injured at Gudgel headquarters died today."

"Oh God," Kate said, putting her hands on Lyle's shoulders and moving against him. "To damn much grief and sorrow." She hugged him tight until he groaned.

"Sorry, it still hurts," he said, stepping back. "Rey is obviously taking the deputy's death hard. And, as far as I've heard, no comment from the Gudgel administration."

"Bastard," Kate said. Were they losing control?

Both of them went silent. Lyle untied and pulled off his bowtie and rolled up the sleeves of his white shirt. He mixed himself a drink. Kate sat on the couch, stroking Trixie on her lap. Lyle joined her.

"Let's watch Drenda's video," she said, pulling out her phone.

They first saw scenes inside the office, and Lyle got a look at the headquarters for the first time. Drenda recorded two Arizona State Guardsmen talking among themselves.

They moved quickly through shots of people coming and going in the office and brief conversations about precinct work Drenda had with Landon.

The next scene, through Drenda's eyes, had her rising from her desk and entering a private office. After a moment, the picture turned black and they heard a man's voice mentioning an open door. What followed was a review of papers and notes on someone's desk. Drenda slowly paged through reports.

"We've got to see this on my computer," Kate said, "so we can read everything Drenda is showing us—and save it."

Kate touched an icon on her phone screen, and it looked as if the video was live.

"Can we talk to her?"

"We're supposed to be able to," Lyle said. He touched a button on the bottom of the screen and the image disappeared.

"Dammit. I think I need another lesson from Rob on how to use this." He refreshed the screen, and they saw the glass front door of the campaign office from the inside.

"Drenda?" Kate said.

"Oh, you scared me," Drenda said. "I forgot we could talk on this. Did you see all the documents I shot?"

"Yes, you'll have to tell us about them."

"Right now, I'm trapped. I stayed late to snoop, and I got locked in the office."

She explained her worry about an alarm and inability to lock the door if she walked out. "Oh, somebody's here. I have to move."

Lyle and Kate saw a car pull up in front of the building, then Drenda obviously ran around a corner because the video showed erratic scenes of office walls. The video reminded Kate of the short, jerky shots cyclists and skateboarders posted on online.

"She's in trouble," Kate said, wishing she could transport herself to Phoenix. "And we can't help her."

She and Lyle helplessly watched as the view settled on a wall and part of the office glass door. Then the view moved up and down swiftly, as if Drenda were running. The glass door opened and seemingly, Drenda dashed through it. The image kept bouncing as she ran outside.

"I'm almost at my car," Drenda said.

"Are you okay?" Lyle asked.

Instead of an answer, they saw the dashboard and windshield of Drenda's car.

"I just made it," she said.

Lyle and Kate watched through Drenda's windshield as she zipped through the parking lot and out into a street.

"Beth Montagne, that's the person whose desk I scanned, must have forgotten something and came back into the office. I ran out the door before she saw me."

"I'm glad you're safe," Kate said. When Drenda turned off her glasses, she asked Lyle, "Do you think she's in danger?"

"Maybe, if she keeps sneaking around like this. You heard me tell her again to just hang out, listen, and tape anything she can without exposing herself."

"She's taking this seriously." *But it's damn serious.*

CHAPTER 53

Trying to relax after Drenda's close call, Kate sat opposite Lyle at her dining table. As they ate, she stared at her laptop.

"I don't mean to be distracted," she said, "but I want to read these memos and notes Drenda copied." She stressed over her friend's situation while she admired her moxie.

"Several of these documents are blurry but, *a-ha*. This is our answer."

She was just sprinkling cheese on her spaghetti and it wound up on the table, her keyboard, and a little on her plate. "Darn. Have to clean this up." She picked up her laptop and tried to dump the cheese on her spaghetti.

"Don't laugh," she said, now more excited than worried. "Listen to this. The special assistant to the governor has a note from someone that says, 'Beth, Ramey says ICE is a bad idea. So we move on." Charles Ramey is the governor's general counsel."

"Were you concerned?"

"No, but now I can *officially* relax. About *this* anyway."

"I found out about the gray SUV that was following you," Lyle said. "It was rented by a Gudgel PAC."

"What?"

"I called a friend at the Phoenix PD. He checked and found out the gray SUV was rented by an organization called Freedom for All Arizona."

"What's that?"

"A political action committee funding the Gudgel campaign, mostly for attack ads."

"Does that mean Gudgel's people put the tracker on my car, too?"

"No way to tell."

Would someone *rent* a car to follow her? She couldn't find a reason. "Strange. Before I go out again, maybe I'll ask Gayle to have another look under my car."

Lyle wiped red sauce off his mouth. "This whole mess becomes more complicated by the day."

"And I have more. Maybe dead ends. I don't know. Let's clear the dishes and I'll show you Lisa's list."

Kate made herself a cup of green tea as Lyle put dishes and pots in the dishwasher. She put her tea on the coffee table, sat on the couch, and Trixie jumped up beside her. Absently stroking the cat, she glanced at her phone. She'd received a text message. It came from the phone number where she'd left a message that morning. The text said:

You might be interested in this.

Attached was an audio file. She listened for a moment, then said, "Lyle, come here. You have to hear this. It's a podcast Lisa suggested."

Lyle squeezed onto the couch on Kate's left, Trixie refusing to yield her space. Kate put her phone on speaker mode.

"Good afternoon Central Arizona. Today Radio Free Gloria brings you a story about a farm in a rural county to the west and a Saudi Arabian company that is stealing our water."

A pleasant male voice with an acerbic edge explained that Ecoperi, a Saudi company, owned nearly 1,000 acres in Fremont County where they grew alfalfa to harvest and send back to Saudi Arabia as feed for dairy cows. The rich alfalfa sustained cows in a country that lacked enough water to create the feed itself.

"This little project might have gone unnoticed," the announcer said, "had not local residents picketed the farm and petitioned county supervisors to put the brakes on plans to expand the farm by thousands of acres. Residents worried the Saudi farm would deplete the local aquifer imperiling water for their town and other farms. Surprisingly, except for the biggest metro areas in Arizona, called active management areas by the state water resources people, regulation of water use is almost nonexistent.

"This sounds like a good environment story—given that we live in arid lands—but it didn't cause a ripple in Arizona news. And scarcely little more attention focused on the area when two people who had protested farm expansion died when their car ran off the edge of a road and into a canyon. Authorities ruled it an accident. No sign of foul play, as the cliché goes.

"As of our taping this podcast," the announcer

continued, "the Fremont County Board of Supervisors had taken no action on the farm's growth plans. In order to operate a foreign corporation in Arizona, Ecoperi needed to establish a local business entity, submit an agricultural land use application, agree to a state inspection, demonstrate adequate capital, obtain permits and licenses and satisfy a whole variety of other governmental hurdles.

"The process can easily take a year, or longer. Ecoperi eased through the bureaucracy in a few months. Ditto, it seems, for their expansion goals.

"We reached out to Ecoperi and the governor's office and have received no responses."

Damn, wow, amazing. Kate quivered with excitement mixed with disgust that people died. She didn't know what to do first. This smelled like something to bury Gudgel—but she'd thought that before.

"Amazing," Lyle said. "Imagine the Saudis running a farm in Arizona. Lots of room for kickbacks to grease the wheels of officialdom, but why would Gudgel be involved in the first place?"

"Governor Gudgel has *been* to Saudi Arabia. He was their local attorney back in Montana when they wanted to build a mini Las Vegas. The scheme died, but looks like Gudgel's connections didn't."

"The Saudis went looking for a place in the world to grow their alfalfa—" Lyle began.

"—And come to find out," Kate said, completing the thought, "their friend in the Montana legislature is now the governor of a big state."

"Did he get kickbacks in Montana? Could they blackmail him after so many years?"

"Nah, they knew he was greedy. The kingdom may lack water, but not money."

"But how did he do it? And what about the deaths?"

"I know his methods, but the best way to find out would be a trip to Fremont County."

"Where's that?"

They pulled up a map on Kate's laptop.

"Fremont County is right here," Lyle said, pointing. "Looks like Creosote is the county seat. It's isolated. All the better to go unnoticed. Let's check local newspapers. If this is correct—and it sounds promising—we can go right away. When do you want to leave?"

"I've got too much to do here. I want to check out more items on Lisa's list *and* keep an eye on Drenda, not to mention—"

"I know, running the PR department. So I'll go."

"Why don't you ask Howard to go with you?"

"Howard?"

"I think two former police detectives should be able to uncover felonies and misdemeanors in a small town."

■　　■　　■

Lyle was thinking about calling Howard when his phone chimed.

"Sam, good to hear your voice. Everything okay?"

"Of course. I'm fine. I'd like to come up and see you this weekend."

"Oh, that'd be great, but I'm going out of town for a few days. How about next weekend?"

"I can't. Shoot, I'm working on a project with Mike

and two others for a class. Could you come *here* next weekend? Maybe Sunday?"

"Yeah, sure." Lyle had a funny feeling in his stomach. Sam wanted to talk about something. "Is anything wrong, Sam?"

"No, not at all. It's good. It's…"

"C'mon. You can tell me."

"I wanted to tell you in person."

She's pregnant. She's getting married. She is married.

"Okay. Um, Lyle, I've been accepted to the grad program at Penn."

"The University of Pennsylvania?"

"Yeah, Ivy League."

"I didn't know you'd applied there."

"I didn't want to get too excited about it, because it was a longshot. Completely blew me away. I got *in*."

"That's in Philadelphia?"

"I know Lyle, but listen. I'm getting a partial scholarship and also work through the department, so all we'll have to worry about is the cost of housing."

"That's great, Sam. Fantastic. A graduate program at Penn. You're brilliant, daughter, brilliant." *But it's in Philadelphia.*

"They have a great environmental program," she said. She didn't need to sell it. An Ivy League masters is an accomplishment for a lifetime. She probably didn't want to just stay at ASU anyway. Of course, her other top choice, UC Riverside, is a lot closer. "Sam, you're a grown-up."

"I know you're disappointed. I will miss you, too. But I'll come home on holidays and summer."

CHAPTER 54

April 19

Lyle didn't want to wake up. His first thought was Sam's grad school decision—which he supported and encouraged—but lamented. Kate pushed him out of bed. Howard would be there to pick him up soon. Thankfully, he'd packed the night before. They planned to leave just after sunup, hoping to get to their destination by lunchtime.

Driving to Creosote from Nostalgia City was no mean feat. They took the interstate south for a few miles—noticing heavy traffic at the off-ramp to NC even early in the morning. Rather than taking the interstate all the way to Phoenix and then turning west, they headed southwest on state highways. Lined with conifers through mountains, the highway eventually flattened out and met another two-lane state highway through scrub desert.

With Howard at the wheel of his unmarked NC sedan, Lyle filled him in on the suspicions he and Kate had about Gudgel's malfeasance and confirmed Max's animus toward the governor.

"All you have to do is listen to Gudgel for ten minutes," Howard said, "and you see he's interested in himself first, everyone else a distant second."

"I'm hoping we can find solid evidence of illegal activity out here."

"Hard to believe," Howard said. "Saudi Arabia is growing alfalfa here to send halfway around the world to feed cows."

"The Saudis knew Gudgel from way back and we suspect he helped them dance around the usual approval process in exchange for a piece of the action."

"And we have the deaths of protesters."

"Supposedly an accident, but there was little media coverage."

Howard said nothing for a few minutes, then: "How are we going to play this?"

"I've been thinking about this, too." *And I'm still thinking.* "Lots of options. We could start talking to people who are opposed to the farm or at least opposed to the vast expansion. Kate talked to the leader of the protests and told her we'd be there today...." Lyle's voice trailed off like his train of thought.

"Do we just tell opponents we work for the park and we're in a fight with the governor?" Howard said. "And can you please help us?"

Lyle pulled out a file folder he'd brought with notes and Creosote information. "But I also have contact numbers for the county supervisors. We *could* start with one of them. Tell him Nostalgia City is dedicated to preserving the environment of the state…" He stared at the distant desert hills, looking for inspiration. "We ask directly if they suspect any irregularities with Ecoperi."

"I think I like the first idea better," Howard said. "Talk to farm protesters."

"We also might talk to local law enforcement to find out about the car accident. I have the sheriff's name. It's obviously a small department."

"Do we show him our retired police IDs and try chummy cop-talk so he'll fill us in?"

"Try to sound a little more positive about this, will you, Howard?"

"Okay. In other words, we play it by ear."

"Janie Patel is the person who organized locals in opposition to the farm expansion. We'll see her first. Lyle picked up his cell phone. I'll call to confirm."

When that was set, Howard picked up his cardboard coffee cup and shook it. "All gone. Could use more."

Lyle pointed to the empty space surrounding their position on the dashboard nav map. "I don't think we're going to run into a Starbucks any time soon."

After miles rolled by, Howard asked, "how's it's going with the Cadre Brave? You went to a meeting."

"Uh huh. And next day I got beat up for initiation."

"That why you're moving slowly getting in the car?"

"I thought I had a broken rib. But it's just a deep bruise."

"What's this hate group like?" Howard said.

"Quite a variety. There's one guy named Ed. Talks a lot and has the mental acuity of a Colonel Sanders drumstick."

"Extra-crispy?"

"Uh huh, but there's all kinds, laborers to professionals in many fields."

"You going to join?"

"Hell no. Want me to drive for a while?"

After more miles of empty desert, they started seeing shacks and plowed fields, then the occasional barn and house. The arid landscape turned to planted fields. Lyle watched the giant arched metal frameworks of self-propelled irrigation systems crawling across fields on rubber tires sputtering Arizona water over sprouting green shoots.

"I wonder which one of these farms belongs to the Saudis?" Lyle mused as they passed a sign at the edge of town telling them the population of Creosote totaled 13,562. A sales lot full of farm equipment was followed by a feed store, restaurant, and a variety of stores and small businesses. The state highway formed Main Street lined with old but maintained store fronts and offices. Cars and pickups filled most of the slant-in parking spaces. Pedestrians came and went.

Ocher siding covered the wood-framed Patel house, fronted by a covered porch. As he and Howard stood at the front door, Lyle was glad they'd dressed casually. Two strangers in suits didn't encourage conversation. Lyle added a smile when the door opened.

Mrs. Patel, a wispy woman in her fifties, smiled but kept her lips together as if hiding crooked teeth. She offered them seats in a front room furnished with a mixture of traditional and Ikea. Mrs. Patel sat on a couch facing them. Behind her hung a framed poster featuring a stylized globe sitting in a basket of green leaves and the words *Earth Day 2019.*

"Thanks for seeing us," Lyle began. "I hope Kate Sorensen from Nostalgia City explained why we're here."

"You want to talk about Ecoperi."

"Yes, as you know, Nostalgia City *is* a small city—it was a sizeable investment—and we spent millions to make it as self-sustaining as possible. The company is concerned about the environment." Lyle thought this sounded like so much prattle, but he wanted to ease into their inquiry.

"I'm concerned about the environment, too," she said.

Howard leaned forward slightly. "And we understand you've been leading protests against expanding the Ecoperi farm."

"Water is precious out here. I'm sure you know." She clasped her hands in front of her. "We are concerned that the new farm might compromise the water table."

"Do you have a large group protesting the farm expansion?" Howard asked.

"Not too big. Not everyone is worried about it." She looked from Howard to Lyle and back to Howard. "But why are you gentlemen here? Does a theme park really care about our water?"

Lyle assumed—obviously incorrectly—that everyone in the state knew about the theme-park-versus-the-governor conflict. Her focus was local. On a corner table, he noticed a collection of handmade picket signs, *Ecoperi Sucks.....our water!* and *Turn off the Ecoperi tap now!*

"Mrs. Patel," Lyle said, "the governor is facilitating

Ecoperi in exporting Arizona water to the Middle East. The park believes the governor's support of this is at least deceptive, but more likely illegal."

"The governor has been attacking our employer," Howard said "and we don't quite understand. You must have heard of the horrendous shooting in Polk, near the park. The governor used that as an excuse to criticize gay rights and promote his own political agenda."

"What does that have to do with me and our water?"

"If you believe as we do that Governor Gudgel is bending the law to promote Ecoperi's water theft," Lyle said, "then we're on the same side. If we can prove the governor is profiting from this, it will help you defeat the farm expansion."

Mrs. Patel didn't exhibit the dedication or urgency of her protest signs. Stopping the governor will stop the water theft. What more could he say?

Their host unclasped and clasped hands again. "I don't see the politics. I think this is just a greedy company wanting our water."

"Is there someone else protesting that we could talk to?" Howard offered into the silence.

"You could talk to Aaron Utrecht. He teaches agriculture at the high school. He's involved."

CHAPTER 55

Lyle eased himself into the driver's seat and they left the residential street looking for the high school. "She didn't sound too excited about helping us, did she?"

"She didn't know about the governor's war against us."

"Or she didn't want to talk about it."

"I think you landed on the right tack, though," Howard said. "Help us stop the governor and you stop Ecoperi. All in all, that's the message."

"Let's try it on the ag teacher."

"Maybe two of us were intimidating. Do you want to talk to the teacher by yourself?"

Lyle shrugged. "Okay, I'll try it."

He turned onto a main road and glanced in the rear-view mirror. "Check out what's behind us."

Howard turned in his seat. "That's a State Guard Humvee."

"What's it doing out here, protecting farms?"

Howard snickered. "Maybe pest control?"

"You mean *us*?"

After a mile, the guard vehicle turned down another street. "That looked like it was armored," Lyle said. "And it had the circular opening in the roof for a machine gun."

"The guard picked up US Army surplus," Howard said.

"Do they have tanks?"

"Probably not."

"Cruise missiles?"

Lyle slowed. Moving down what passed for a major street in Creosote they saw "Re-elect Sheriff Findlay" signs. "So the local law enforcement is up for re-election," Howard said.

"Here's the high school up ahead," Lyle said." He pulled into a nearly empty visitors' lot. In the main office, they asked a student behind the counter where they could find Mr. Utrecht.

"He's probably out in field number two. It's that way," said the young man. He glanced up at a big round clock that looked just like the ones Lyle remembered from high school. "But he has a class now."

Howard thanked the student. "We won't disturb him."

Outside, Howard said he'd hang around or take a walk. Lyle found field number two spread out beyond the gym. Small clusters of students probed the soil with hand tools or wrote in notebooks. A tent-like greenhouse, open in front, sat off to one side. A man in jeans and work shirt stood near the entrance. Inside, students worked at tables filled with pots and soil-filled boxes.

"Excuse me," Lyle said to the man. "I'm looking for Mr. Utrecht."

"You found him."

Lyle introduced himself. "Janie Patel said we could talk to you about Ecoperi's expansion and why it's not a good idea."

Utrecht grimaced and wiped his forehead with dirty fingers, leaving a smudge below his shiny dark hair.

"I work for Nostalgia City and I can come back if I'm interrupting your class."

"Nostalgia City, the theme park?"

"Yes, a step back in time." Lyle met his eyes and smiled.

"I've got a few minutes," Utrecht said. He walked into the greenhouse and spoke to several students, then joined Lyle outside.

"Okay, you've got my attention," the teacher said.

"The Ecoperi farm caught our attention, too. Am I correct that you are opposed to the expansion?"

"Yeah, as it stands. I don't understand why you're interested in this, though."

Tell him the truth, Deming, and see what happens. "You see, Governor Gudgel—"

"Oh, this is about your fight with the governor?"

Lyle acknowledged the conflict and gave his one-minute summary of Gudgel's anti-minority, autocratic rule. "There's a good chance the governor is profiting from this. If we can prove that, it will make it easier for you to stop Ecoperi."

The teacher's forehead wrinkled slightly as he seemed to process Lyle's contention.

Lyle tried to effect a casual tone. "I was hoping you might have insight into how the project began. What keeps it going."

"This is a controversial project. No doubt about that. And it's one we have to deal with in Fremont County." He looked down and squashed a dirt clod with his boot. "Obviously, there had to be state approvals to get this off the ground, but I don't know much about that. Is it really going to help us if we get involved in your fight with the governor?"

"I'm not asking you to get involved. Just looking for information."

Utrecht stopped toeing the dirt and looked at Lyle. "This is not an ideal situation, but nothing has been decided yet. Nobody says the farm's getting that much bigger. I'm hoping we'll be able to work something out. Ecoperi has been helping the school. They donated this greenhouse and almost all the plants we're working with this semester. The water is a problem, but they're being good neighbors. Nobody's going to suffer."

"Two young people died recently in a car accident. Were they students here? Did you know them?"

"What's that—" he started to say as his expression darkened. "It was a tragedy for the school. But I don't want to talk about it. I don't think I can be of any more help."

Lyle trudged back across the field. *I really found a sympathetic soul this time.* Before he could moan to himself further, a teenage young man carrying a trowel called to him.

"Are you from the government asking about Ecoperi?"

The young man's words shot out of his mouth. "Do you know what's happening here?" He brushed a shock of blond hair off his forehead.

"I know about Ecoperi." Lyle looked over the student's shoulder and saw Utrecht standing in the greenhouse, engaged with students. "I'm not with the government, but I am investigating the farm and how it came to be."

"You a private investigator?"

"You could say that. I used to be a Phoenix police detective. Now I'm working for a company that's interested in Ecoperi and Governor Gudgel. Do you know about the two students who died in that crash?"

The boy glanced toward the greenhouse and turned back to Lyle. "Yeah, I do. Will and Mary. I hafta to go. You need to talk to Pat Patterson. He runs the farm next to ours, and he's on the county supervisors."

"What's your name? How can I contact you?"

The young man pulled out his phone. "Hold out your phone. I can send you my information." In seconds, the young man pocketed his phone and turned to go.

"My name's Lyle. Thanks."

Back at the car, Lyle saw Howard approaching from a block away.

"Any luck?" Howard asked as they got in the car.

"Yes and no. We need to go see a county supervisor named Patterson. I have his contact information here in my notes." Lyle shuffled through his file folder. "The teacher thinks he can negotiate with Ecoperi. One of his students stopped me as I was leaving. Told me we should contact this Patterson."

"Are we going to get something to eat?"

"Yeah, we can stop. I'll call this guy from a restaurant."

Howard drove out of the parking lot and turned north, back toward Main Street. Two blocks away, Howard pulled up at a stop sign then started into the intersection. Before they'd moved ten feet, an armored Humvee charged through in front of them.

Howard slammed on his brakes, heaving him and Lyle forward against their safety belts.

"He must have been doing fifty," Lyle said, rubbing his neck. "Did he see us?"

"Does it matter? It was a four-way stop."

CHAPTER 56

Kate looked up from her desk when Joann stuck her head in the doorway.

"The assistant manager at the main gate wants to talk to you about freeway traffic."

Kate lowered her brows and pulled her head back from her computer screen. "Excuse me?"

"I know," Joann said. "Crazy, huh? He said they were getting lots of complaints from guests."

When anyone at the park had a question or issue, they called public relations. Kate was one of the most high-profile and accessible senior execs at the park, but why did she get the off-the-wall questions?

"Okay, Joann. Thanks. I'll take the call."

The front gate assistant manager began with a familiar refrain, "Ms. Sorensen, I didn't know who else to call."

He told Kate over the past week they had been receiving more and more complaints about traffic congestion on the interstate at the NC exit. "Traffic is backed up for a half mile at least," he said, "because of highway construction on San Navarro Highway."

And you want me to do what? she thought, but she said, "I'll check into it. I'm sure it's frustrating for our guests."

She hung up and started to smile and shake her head, then a boulder hit her brain. *Gudgel. Duh.*

She grabbed a manila folder labeled "G" in heavy black script. In it she found details she collected on the repair contract for State Route 247—the San Navarro Highway—a major access route to the park. Lisa Oberon had flagged it.

She still hadn't heard from Oberon and dialed her number. "Lisa, thankfully you're okay. I was worried. I tried to call you and couldn't get you on your cell, so I tried your office."

"Sorry. I had a zoo meeting in LA. I kept getting spam calls, so I turned my phone off for a while. Why, were you worried?"

"I started getting nervous after I saw you at the zoo." She explained being followed by the gray SUV and finding the tracker under her car.

"Do you think it was the governor's people?" Oberon asked.

"We checked it out. The car was rented by a Gudgel PAC. And he was waiting for me when I left the zoo, so he knew I'd been there."

"Ah, don't worry. He didn't know you saw me. You could have been visiting the animals. Or maybe arranging for Nostalgia City to make a donation. They don't know we even know each other. Really Kate, I'm fine. Even if we did meet, it doesn't have to have been about Gudgel."

Oberon sounded logical. Kate leaned back in her

chair and tried to relax, although still not one hundred percent certain she hadn't put her friend at risk. "Just to be sure, the park will make a donation to the zoo to cover my tracks. We should anyway. And speaking of tracks, Tim McKenna told me to call you if I needed to talk to him again. We met at ADOT, and he agreed to help me, but he didn't want to connect through his office."

Oberon gave Kate Tim's private number and when to call. Armed with that, she considered buying a burner phone to call him. How far did Gudgel's influence stretch?

Before she had time to ponder further, Lyle called.

"We called it a day. We're settled in a motel here in Creosote."

"Any progress?"

"Very little." He explained their talk with Mrs. Patel and his meeting with the ag teacher. "Didn't get very far, but we have more to do."

"What about the two students who died?"

"The teacher clammed up. I think Ecoperi's been twisting his arm. He said the corporation had donated plants and a greenhouse to the high school."

"Not necessarily arm twisting. Sounds like good public relations. A big corporation moves into town and wants to be a contributing part of the community. You know, NC built an elementary school in Polk as the park opened. We were just being good neighbors."

"Hmm. That's a point. But they named it after Max."

Kate chuckled.

"We have more people to talk to tomorrow, including a county supervisor who may be sympathetic. I'll let you know. Miss you."

Before they hung up, she asked Lyle if he had noticed traffic snarls on highway 247, and he told her of slow-downs he'd seen.

Later, she called McKenna, who agreed to send her anything he could find on highway 247 construction. He told her he'd send it via a secure online site, rather than email it.

On her drive home, she detoured down San Navarro Highway toward the interstate. Traffic heading toward the park stacked up behind the freeway off-ramp for as far as she could see. Before she reached the interstate, the road narrowed from four lanes to one lane in either direction. Traffic crawled toward the interstate overpass. Mounds of rocks, gravel, and sand sat along the edge of the roadway.

Past the interchange, heavy equipment, including a dozer and grader sat in the dirt off the road. Nearby, Kate saw an Irwin Company construction trailer. A company pickup was parked beside it. Someone was home.

She walked up portable metal steps, knocked once, and opened the door. The middle-aged man seated at a beat-up desk near the middle of the trailer may have been expecting someone, but from his expression, not a six-foot-two- and-one-half-inch blonde.

"Good afternoon. I've noticed the traffic backed up on the freeway. It's been that way for at least two weeks." She gestured over her shoulder toward the highway. "Sorry to interrupt. I was just wondering when this construction is going to be done."

The guy at the desk wore a shirt and tie. A hardhat, heavy gloves, and survey equipment sat on a nearby table. By the time Kate had finished her question, he'd looked her up and down, twice.

"It should be done fairly soon. Can I ask why you're…"

"Why I'm asking? Sure."

She smiled, pulled out a business card, and handed it to him. "I'm vice president at Nostalgia City and our guests are getting delayed on the freeway. They have to wait a long time to get to the park. We're getting complaints and we don't know what to tell them."

"I see what you mean."

"It looks as if construction at this interchange has stopped. Nothing's happening." She put a hand on a hip. "Is there a reason?"

"A temporary pause was possible, but it'll get going."

"Problems? I thought this would be complete by now."

"Manpower and other issues."

He looked away. Nervous? "Are you Mr. Irwin?"

"I'm site engineer. The Irwins work in the main office. This is a temporary issue, but we're moving forward."

Kate shifted her feet and stared at him. From the look of things, *nothing* was moving forward.

"Please sit down," he said. "Sorry." He turned in his seat to face her. "We only have so many skilled workers to call upon and, uh, and decisions about redeployment are consistent with the project timeline. We'll be moving forward."

That phrase again. It sounded like obfuscation. "I'd like to tell the president of the park *something*. What should I say?"

"This is a priority, and we hope to have a reasonable estimate soon." Was he scowling or frowning? "There are lots of variables in a complex job such as this, materials, work schedules, interfacing with the state. All of which affect the construction stages. It's detailed in the contract." He spoke slowly. Mansplaining.

"So you're saying the bid contract permits you to move workers from here to another job? But the contract was awarded more than a year ago, and according to that, your deadline is what, approximately? Unknown?"

"It's not quite that simple." He stared out a small, dust-coated window with the expression of someone about to eat something unpleasant. "There are inspections, of course, by the state." He paused and brightened up. He'd thought of more mumbo-jumbo. "In fact, we're still waiting for approval of a minor culvert plan up the road aways."

"On the other side of the overpass, I noticed sand and aggregate dumped next to the road. But underneath looks like finished pavement. I will have a look at that on my way back. So, if you *could* start work right here tomorrow, how long would it take to be finished?"

"I'm sorry. I've told you as much as I can. Now I need to finish up here."

There seemed to be no way to shake the truth out of this guy. She'd done her homework, but she wanted McKenna's information. And she needed to talk to the boss.

She stood. "Okay, thanks for your time, Mr..."

He told her his name and looked relieved she was leaving.

Before she drove home, she stopped at the NC garage to ask Gayle to have someone check under her car again. While she waited, she called Drenda to ask if she had ever heard the name Irwin or Irwin Construction mentioned at Gudgel headquarters. Drenda said she thought she'd heard the name but couldn't remember the context.

That was a help, so was finding out no trackers clung to the underside of her car.

CHAPTER 57

April 20

Farmers get up early, even on Saturday Lyle reasoned, so he'd made an appointment for eight o'clock in the morning. He and Howard had breakfast and hit the road.

The night before, they'd debated about what to do about the guard. The close call with the Humvee was intentional. Options included talking to the sheriff or finding out if a guard base existed close by and calling to complain. Lyle figured they'd be wasting time.

"Do they know who we are?" he said.

"I dunno," Howard said. "You brought a weapon, didn't you? I didn't. Who knew we'd need one?"

"I don't plan to use it, but yeah, I have my SIG semi-auto under the car seat."

Ultimately, they decided to talk to Pat Patterson, the farmer/county supervisor, together.

■ ■ ■

The farm looked prosperous, with livestock grazing and crops coming up in furrowed fields. The Patterson home sat at the end of a long dirt and gravel drive. Wearing jeans, boots, and a wide-brimmed hat, Patterson stood on a broad front porch lined with wicker chairs. Before Lyle and Howard got out of the car, a llama trotted over and stared at Lyle through the side window.

Patterson stepped off the porch and shooed the animal far enough away that Lyle could open his door. He continued to herd the llama away and invited his visitors to join him on the porch.

"Llamas are protective," Patterson said after introductions. "They're good watchdogs for other livestock. They have an amazing cry when they sense danger, and they kick and spit."

"Can we sit inside?" Lyle said.

They walked in and Patterson tossed his hat on a hall tree in the front room. "You guys want coffee?"

Lyle pegged Patterson's drawl as West Texas, but was surprised to learn he was an Arizona native. He served his guests coffee in mugs at a dining table and set the pot between them.

Howard began with the purpose of their visit. Before he'd finished, Patterson said he'd read about the "governor's feud with Nostalgia City." Lyle emphasized they were on a fact-finding mission because they questioned the government's motives for supporting a Middle East farm in the middle of Arizona.

"I'm in the same party as the governor, but this is just plain screwy," Patterson said. "It could drain our aquifer, then Ecoperi moves on, and we'd be sucking sand.

"We wanted them to install meters so they wouldn't be wasteful with our water." Patterson slapped his hand on the table. "The governor nixed that. But some of us also grow alfalfa and we can do the math. Ecoperi wants to lease 10,000 acres. We figure they'll use up enough water every year to supply a town bigger than 50,000 people."

Lyle's eyes widened. *A generous giveaway.* He glanced at Howard, then turned to Patterson. "I don't know if you've heard this, but the governor and the Saudis go back a lot of years. We think they picked Arizona because they'd had dealings with him before, back in Montana." Lyle rubbed his thumb over the tips of his index and middle finger to show what *dealings* meant. "This is just one reason we think the governor is personally benefitting from this project."

"No surprise. They picked a good spot, too. In this climate, Ecoperi can get ten cuttings per year, far more than Midwest farms."

"That's fast," Howard said.

"Yup. Alfalfa grows quick, uses lots of water, and it's rich food for livestock."

"When is the board going to vote on this?" Lyle asked.

"Probably at the next meeting."

"And," Howard said, "you're voting *no*?"

"Won't make no difference. Rest of the board is going to vote for it. 'Sides, Ecoperi is leasing state land, so we don't have much to say about it."

"Why are the other board members in favor of it?" Howard asked.

"The Ecoperi managers are good salesmen. They say

they're going to help the community. It's all just stupid and shortsighted." He reached for the coffee pot and topped off the mugs.

"It's a rubber stamp," Patterson said. "I could talk to the county counsel, but I'd be wasting my time. It's four against one. Maybe you guys can figure something out."

"Local folks protested, picketing Ecoperi. Is that right?"

"Yeah, high school students mostly, and people from town."

"Do you know anything about the two students who were killed in the accident?" Howard asked.

"Everyone in town knows about it. Hell of a thing. They were kids. Sheriff and the State Guard investigated. Said they were driving too fast and skidded off that cliff."

"The Arizona Guard?" Howard asked. "*They* investigated?"

"They help the sheriff out here."

Lyle exchanged glances with Howard.

"Lucas, the young man at the next farm," Patterson said, "he was real close to them. He thinks somebody killed them. Poor kid. Hard to take at that age."

As they left, Howard gave Patterson a business card. "My personal cell is written on the back. If you happen across anything we might be interested in, please call."

They got back in their car with no llamas in sight. Howard said, "We need to talk to the neighbor kid."

"I have his number right here," Lyle said. "Lucas Kidwell. He's the one who talked to me yesterday at the high school."

"It's Saturday, maybe he's home."

They drove out the long farm drive and saw the profile of an Arizona State Guard Humvee against a field of green alfalfa. It sat on the berm of the main road with two men inside. "The kid's farm is that way." Lyle pointed to the right. "So why don't you go left and see what happens."

Howard turned left in front of the Humvee. Lyle twisted around in his seat and watched the heavy, squat State Guard vehicle pull out behind them.

"Son of a bitch. How did they know we were here?"

"Someone could have followed us in a civilian vehicle," Howard said, glancing in the rearview. "Once we left our motel, we made only one turn, then a long, straight drive here to the farm. I saw cars behind us, but no Humvee."

Lyle looked back at the guard vehicle. "They almost ram us, then tail us. What's going on? Why don't we pull over. We can have it out with them right now."

"Forget it. They just turned around."

"Spooky."

"Wait a sec," Howard said. "Now we have a tail. Looks like it could be a local sheriff's car. Has lights on top."

"Coincidence?"

"I dunno. Maybe we can find out. We want to go back toward town anyway, right?"

Lyle grunted "uh huh" and Howard startled him by making a sharp U-turn.

"That's no sheriff's cruiser," Lyle said as they sped past the car in the other direction. "It says, *Ecoperi Security*." He turned in his seat to see if the car followed them.

"Relax," Howard said. "They're continuing."

"Hard to shake a tail in a little town," Lyle said.

"Yup, and the security car just did a U and is tailing us from a distance."

"Let me talk to the kid and see if he can meet us somewhere."

Howard did quick turns on farm roads and drove back to Creosote with a clear rearview. Lyle called Lucas Kidwell.

CHAPTER 58

Activity buzzed at Gudgel campaign headquarters. Drenda could sense a different atmosphere. A mixture of commotion and trepidation flavored the air. Montagne hunched over her laptop, Landon shuffled papers, occasionally stealing glances at the governor who sat in the glassed-in conference room with three people Drenda had not seen before. She made sure to record their faces with her camera glasses.

Angry, muffled words from the governor had escaped the conference room for the past 30 minutes. Drenda looked up when Gudgel screamed words that sounded like, "can't be." The sound eventually died drifting through the cavernous work room. Not everyone heard it. The governor got up from his chair and paced the room twice, glaring at the other participants. He sat down momentarily, then stood again, said something, and pointed to the door. The meeting was over.

Drenda went back to her work preparing recruiting materials to show three organizations how to encourage members to volunteer with or donate to the Gudgel campaign. She'd learned the basics from a manual and added ideas of her own. She hoped the plans would flop but also didn't want to jeopardize her campaign job. Helping to reelect Gudgel taxed her sensibilities and loyalties more than she'd expected.

"Ann," Montagne said over Drenda's shoulder. She turned to see the governor's special assistant's eager expression. By now, Drenda didn't hesitate when she heard her middle name.

"You have experience in statistical analysis," Montagne said, "is that right?"

"Yes, I do. It's not what I'm working on here."

"I realize that, but the governor needs help with survey data, and I told him you knew statistics."

Help the governor directly? She slid her magic glasses up the bridge of her nose with a forefinger and looked at Montagne. "What can I do?"

"Let's go talk with him."

Drenda wondered if her *gulp* was actually audible.

They stood at the governor's doorway, and he looked up immediately. For an instant, Drenda felt sorry for him. He looked up from his desk with creases in his high forehead and anticipation in sad eyes.

Montagne introduced her, and Drenda stood in front of his desk.

"Beth tells me you know statistics. Statistical analysis?"

"Yes, I studied it in grad school."

"Oh, where did you go to college?"

She'd received degrees from two universities, but

didn't want to talk about her PhD. She didn't think it fit her "housewife volunteer" cover.

"University of Wisconsin – Madison," she said truthfully.

"Do you know about polling?"

"I have authored surveys, if that's what you mean." This was the guy trying to ruin everyone's life at NC and beyond. Did she want to help him? Speak to him? Even if he did seem a sad case.

"That's right," he said, offering a thin-lipped smile. "Thanks Beth. Maybe Ann can help me sort out things."

Beth left the office, and Gudgel asked Drenda to take a seat. He asked her what campaign tasks she was working on. When she explained, he said, "that sounds routine. If you can do statistics, you could be more valuable to the campaign."

"How can I help you?" She tried smiling and told herself she was a good actress.

The governor wore a shirt and bright blue tie, his suit coat draped over his chair. "It's these poll numbers. They can't be right."

"Errors?" Drenda offered.

"Okay, let me explain. The statewide polls on TV show I'm six percent ahead in the race. But my pollsters say those numbers are incorrect and that I'm really way behind. These are not the numbers I want to show my big donors. How can I tell who's right?"

Drenda didn't know what to say. Did he want hand holding? "Well, it depends on how your surveys were conducted and many other factors. I—"

"Sure, you have to check validity and reliability. Isn't that correct?"

"Yes, reliability and validity, but…"

"Would you give a look at these reports and tell me what you think?"

"To give you an accurate evaluation, I'd need to see the questionnaires, the methodology, sample sizes, response rates—the raw data."

He held up a bound report and many loose sheets of figures. She expected him to give her an order. Instead, he was plaintive. "Could you look at this and see if there's enough raw material for you?"

He handed her the packet across his desk. "You can work on it here if you like." He pointed to the small conference table and four chairs in his office.

She took the proffered material and didn't know how to address him.

"Thank you, governor. I will look."

"Please call me Rob, Ann."

Maybe she was too wary, but there was a note in his voice she didn't like. Even though Ann was her middle, assumed office name, she didn't like to hear him say it.

Drenda retreated a few steps to the work table and selected a chair that didn't face the governor directly, but at an angle. She looked at the booklet adorned with the logo of the polling company and started reading the executive summary.

How should she handle this, provided she had enough information to make an evaluation? She hoped her comments on this would not result in a meeting with the pollsters. She didn't want to explain her background any more than she already had.

As she reviewed the material, the governor worked at his laptop. Something didn't appeal to him, and he cursed under his breath. Drenda looked up and saw the bellicose expression she remembered from his podium diatribes.

He picked up his desk phone and called to complain about a piece of legislation he despised and wanted killed. Drenda tried to concentrate on the work but didn't want to miss anything useful the governor said. Casually, she touched her glasses to record audio and video.

Gudgel received a cell call from someone, probably his scheduler, that prompted him to cancel one appearance and set up another. Drenda listened while skimming the survey questions. When Gudgel was silent, she looked up and caught him looking at her. He smiled and tilted his head, turning his attention back to his computer screen.

She wished she'd worn a less attractive outfit that day, but on the whole the more she worked, the more comfortable she felt gathering what intelligence she could.

Another cell phone buzzed softly. Gudgel pulled it out of his pocket.

"Yes?" he said. "What's happening Chuck? Who? What are they doing there in town? Nostalgia City? I don't understand. How did you find out?"

Gudgel looked up at Drenda. He held his hand over the phone. "Ann, could you excuse me for a minute?"

"Sure," she said. As she stood up, she turned her back on the governor and slipped off her glasses. She set them on loose papers upside down but pointed at the governor's desk. She set her pen down next to the glasses and walked out, closing the door behind her.

As soon as the door closed, she heard Gudgel firing questions at someone.

CHAPTER 59

Lyle finished his call to Lucas Kidwell. He wanted to talk.

"The kid says to meet him at an antique shop his aunt runs on Saltbush Avenue," Lyle told Howard. "It's near the middle of town." He punched in an address on the car's nav app.

As Howard cruised through downtown, an Ecoperi security car passed them slowly, the uniformed occupants eyeballing them as they passed.

"Ecoperi is a *farm*," Lyle said. "Why do they need security personnel? To guard the alfalfa?"

"I'll make another turn," Howard said, "then we'll park a couple of blocks over from the store wherever we can find a parking lot with a bunch of cars in it. Then we can walk separately to the store."

"Lucas says there's a back door off an alley we can use. Maybe one of us goes in front, the other in back."

They found a nearly full supermarket lot and pulled in. "I watched the mirror. No one followed us here,"

Howard said. "I'll walk this way, and you can go the other way to the store."

Unnecessary perhaps, but Lyle took his semi-auto tucked into a holster at his back with his windbreaker for cover. He walked casually, using reflections in store windows to see who was near him. He backtracked once. No one seemed interested in the stranger. In a dingy alley he found beat-up trash cans, a spot where someone had emptied a full ashtray of butts, and no surveillance cameras. A sign on a metal door identified Creosote Antiques. He went inside.

Kidwell and another young man sat in a dark back room lit by a five-lamp brass chandelier that needed dusting. Lyle joined them at a round wooden table supported by a claw-foot pedestal the size of a barrel. Table leaves, broken chairs, a display case, and shelves laden with bric-à-brac filled much of the room.

"This is Lyle Deming," Kidwell said. "Mr. Deming this is Ben Mathis."

Lyle smiled and shook hands with Mathis, a thin young man with dark hair and a look he probably wore in a dentist's waiting room.

"Mr. Deming is a private investigator. He's here to check out Ecoperi. Mr. Utrecht gave him the runaround yesterday."

"I'm working for Nostalgia City," Lyle said. "The governor has been attacking the theme park, attacking minorities, even making demeaning comments about the protesters who were shot to death. We're here on a fact-finding mission to check out Ecoperi. We think it's one of his personal—and probably illegal—schemes." He looked at Kidwell. "I talked to your neighbor, Mr. Patterson, this morning, and he thinks the governor is giving away your water to the Saudis."

"He *is* giving it away," Mathis said.

"You have someone with you?" Kidwell asked.

"Yes, Howard Chaffee. He's also an ex-cop. He was a commander at the San Francisco Police and is now director of security at Nostalgia City. Howard should be here in a minute. We came in separately. We're a *little* concerned about the State Guard's presence here."

Mathis gritted his teeth. His eyes narrowed.

So this kid is not a fan of the guard, either. Lyle could guess where the story might be going.

A door behind them rattled and Howard walked in from the front of the store. Lyle made introductions. Howard gave Kidwell his business card and he and Lyle showed their retired police IDs. They all sat in pressed-back oak chairs at the heavy antique table. Lyle and Howard sat next to each other, facing the students.

"Are you working with Mr. Hurt, Gregory Hurt?" Mathis asked.

"Hurt?" Lyle said.

"He's also a private detective."

Yeah, a PI working for Gudgel. That SOB governor has his people everywhere. "What has Mr. Hurt been doing?"

"He's protecting Isabel," Kidwell said.

Mathis clenched his fist on the table. "*Lucas.*"

"Isabel's his girlfriend. It's all right, Ben. Mr. Patterson thinks these guys are okay. And you haven't heard from her in a while."

Lyle looked from Kidwell to Mathis. "Why does she

need protection? Does this have to do with the deaths of the two students?"

Kidwell squirmed in his seat and breathed rapidly. "Yes," he said, "Will and Mary." He looked at Mathis. "Go ahead. Tell them. We need to do *something*. It's been too long."

Mathis's lips made a straight, rigid line across his face, and he stared at Kidwell. He got up and walked toward the back door. He turned, leaned against the door, and faced the table.

"The Ecoperi security ran Will and Mary off the road. They killed them. They led the protests against Ecoperi. These crazy security guards had threatened them. Told them to stop." The young man paused and paced slowly across the back of the room.

Mathis explained that he and Isabel, along with Will, Mary, and others, held several demonstrations at the Ecoperi farm protesting the proposed expansion. They picketed at the farm entrance, occasionally blocking trucks from coming and going. Arizona State Guardsmen and security personnel threatened them with arrest, even though they were marching on public property.

"They got in our face and yelled. Called us all kinds of names," Mathis said. "Will and Mary wanted to save Arizona and the world. They started the whole thing. They held meetings at school and got others to join."

"Your teacher, Mr. Utrecht, said he thinks the expansion is tentative," Lyle said.

"Mr. Utrecht used to be with us, but he stopped talking about it. Ecoperi's monster farm is going ahead. Will and Mary proved it."

"It was really cool what they did," Kidwell said. He lowered his voice and looked down. "But that's why they got killed."

A murder case in the middle of a Gudgel project? Does the governor know about it? Is he involved? And what's Hurt doing out here? Lyle sat back and listened. *Howard doesn't know about Hurt,* he thought, *but now's not the time to tell him.*

Mathis wandered back to the table and sat down. "We thought Ecoperi had the irrigation systems all ready for the expanded acreage, even though they told everyone the project was being studied.

"Big metal storage sheds are lined up along their property and surrounded by fencing with barbed wire. Will and Mary fooled the security guards and found a way past the fence one night. They looked through air vents in the buildings and saw big rolling sprinkler systems. Before they left, they sprayed big letters, 'sprinklers' on the side of one building."

"Nobody said anything, you know, officially," Kidwell said. "Security guards were pissed. Ecoperi forced them to paint over the 'sprinklers' sign."

"A few days later," Mathis said, "Mary and Will were dead."

A rattling noise and a thud made everyone jump.

"Oh, sorry to interrupt, Lucas," said a middle-aged woman as she opened the door Howard had used. She looked at Howard and Lyle and offered a hesitant smile. "I just needed to get this." She picked up a cardboard box. "You okay Lucas?"

"Yeah, sure Aunt Phyllis."

"Don't worry," Kidwell said after the woman closed the door behind her. "She's awesome."

Lyle looked at Howard. Who was going to ask the first question? Howard took the lead. "How do you know Ecoperi security personnel are responsible?"

"Isabel," Mathis said. "She said she knows who did it. She has evidence."

"What are her parent's doing?" Lyle asked.

"Her parents are dead. They died years ago," Mathis said. "She lived with her aunt, but she got sick and had to go into a rest home, so Isabel is basically on her own."

"We can help," Howard said in his best law and order voice. "Have you spoken to the sheriff?"

"She tried to, but she was scared," Mathis said. "The sheriff didn't take her seriously. Said she should talk to the State Guard. She sure as shit wasn't going to do that. Then she started noticing people following her. One of them was this guy, Mr. Hurt. He said she was in danger. She quit her job and left town."

"Hurt may have had the right idea, but he's not trustworthy," Lyle said. "We know." He wished he and Howard could have time to talk this over. He could tell him about Hurt and they could strategize. "Where is Isabel now?"

"I don't know," Mathis said.

"Mr. Hurt is protecting her," said Kidwell.

Mathis pushed back from the table. "He said she needed to stay away from town and the guard until she could tell her story."

"To who?" Lyle asked. "How long has she been gone?"

"It's been two weeks."

"Have you talked to her?"

Mathis said that Hurt gave Isabel burner phones she used to call him at a certain time every two to three days. This way, Hurt told her, no one could use Mathis's phone to track her. Isabel finished high school the year before, he said, and worked in a Creosote restaurant.

Lyle smelled a rat. "So you don't know where she's living?"

"No, she's not supposed to tell me. She has to stay safe."

"Has the guard questioned you?"

"No, just the sheriff. I just told him Isabel and me broke up."

"Do you trust this Hurt character?" Howard asked. "Does this arrangement make sense to you?"

Mathis replied with only a pained expression. He hugged his arms to his chest.

"Howard and I need to talk about this, but we can help you," Lyle said. Howard nodded agreement. "Right now, we don't trust the guard, either. Is there a base close by?"

"Yeah," said Kidwell. "About ten miles north of town. They opened it last year."

About the time Gudgel turned them into a militia, and Ecoperi started the farm. "Their Humvees have been following us around town," Lyle said. "That's why I wanted us to meet like this. Let Howard and me talk and make a few phone calls. Can we meet again tonight?"

Mathis and Kidwell looked at each other. Kidwell bobbed his head.

"I dunno," Mathis said. Finally, "All right."

"There's an old drive-in theater on the east side of

town. It's been closed like forever," Kidwell said. "There's no gate, so you can drive right in and there's more than one way to get there. Look at your GPS. If you're followed, you can lose them maybe in the hills near there. Meet you at eight thirty?"

CHAPTER 60

Lyle and Howard went back to the car separately. Lyle got there first and, waiting for his partner, glanced idly inside the car. He saw the case for his dark glasses on his seat. *I didn't leave it there.*

He looked up and saw Howard approaching. Moving in what he hoped looked like a casual stroll, he met Howard. "I think the car's been bugged or searched. I'll explain later."

That was all he hoped Howard needed to keep him from starting a debate on all the questions they had about Isabel, Hurt, and the two young men. When they sat down, Lyle pointed to a cubby hole in the console where he had placed his glass case. Then shook his head. Did Howard understand?

"Did you find anything?" Lyle said. "The gift for your wife?"

"No, not a lot of clothing stores here. I'll get her something on the way home."

Howard backed out and turned left from the parking

lot toward the center of town. Lyle raised his arm, mimicking taking a drink. Howard nodded, and they both looked for a place to stop and talk. Howard must have been thinking of a beer because he slowed in front of the first bar they saw. Lyle shook his head and pointed down the block to a fast-food restaurant.

Sparky's was perfect. In the mid-afternoon the local burger joint was almost empty. "Anybody following us?" Lyle asked as they walked toward Sparky's front entrance.

"I didn't see anyone. If they have a bug in the car, they don't need to be right behind us to pick it up. Good choice here. Lots of windows."

Lyle was happy to hear slightly louder than normal background music in the restaurant, just to cover their conversation. Was that Terry Jacks doing "Seasons in the Sun"?

"Someone moved my sunglass case," Lyle told Howard. "I stashed it in your console. Maybe a bug is near there, or maybe they just tossed the car."

They bought Cokes and slid into an uncomfortable composite and plastic booth.

"First off," Howard said, "who the hell is Gregory Hurt?"

"He's a PI working for the governor."

Lyle explained Kate's meeting with Hurt, and that they later found out the PI worked for Gudgel. He omitted Drenda's role in uncovering him at Gudgel headquarters.

"If he's working for the governor, why is he hiding this supposed murder witness? Is the governor tied into the murder? Does he even know about it? All in all, a royal mess."

Lyle tore the wrapper off his paper straw and stuck it through the lid on his soda. "I don't know the answer to any of those questions. I do know Hurt is not to be trusted. I, too, can't figure out why he's keeping a witness under wraps except to keep her quiet until the land lease is signed. But then what?"

Howard scanned the street outside. "So keeping her safe from the State Guard is a bunch of crap, *if* the guard and Hurt are both working for the governor. Is she being kidnapped? What does she really know?" He held up a hand before Lyle could speak. "I know. We don't have a clue. Let's look at what's before us."

"Ben Mathis knows where his girlfriend is."

"That's obvious." Howard said. "The kids would have found a way. Maybe he's seen her since."

"But they're confused and scared. She's probably in the Phoenix area. That's where Hurt's office is. He'd want to keep her close."

"Hang on a sec," Howard said. "I'm going to get a basket of fries."

Lyle watched him take a circuitous route to the counter, giving him a chance to take advantage of the wide windows and scan the world outside the restaurant.

"You hungry?" Lyle asked when he returned with a heaping basket of French fries.

"Yeah, a little." He shoved a French fry in his mouth. "I also wanted to look at a pickup across the street. It had the Ecoperi logo on the door, but it wasn't security. It's gone now."

"Basic questions," Lyle said. "Why are we being followed? How do they know who we are?"

"We could ask them."

"Yeah, I know, Howard. Good idea. In the meantime, they could have ID'ed us from your license plate or Ms. Patel or Utrecht told them." Lyle looked up from their table to see a car slow down and its occupants turn in their direction.

"The guard and possibly Ecoperi are following us to protect the alfalfa deal. They don't want outsiders rocking the boat."

"Like investigating suspicious deaths."

Howard grumbled in agreement.

"Assuming Isabel—we don't even know her last name—is telling the truth, Ecoperi doesn't want snoopers."

"The guard reports directly to the governor. We know that. But would *they* help cover up a murder?" Howard said.

"Because it's Gudgel's deal? Maybe they don't think it *was* murder and are just following orders to help Ecoperi close the deal."

Howard stopped talking and stared into his Coke. "That makes a little more sense, but this is still a mess. And why are we in the middle of it? To pin something nefarious on the governor?"

"If he's connected to murder, that's a good enough reason, isn't it?"

Howard slid the basket of fries across the table. "Here, help yourself, especially if you think you're not getting enough sodium in your diet."

"I know, Howard, you have another job back at the park. But you're an ex-cop. Let's see if we can make things right here."

"As a matter of fact, this is as challenging as NC security. We need to convince Ben that Isabel could be in jeopardy because Hurt is allied with the governor. What's ultimately going to happen to his girlfriend? He needs to realize what a screwed-up situation this is."

"We need to find out *where* she is and talk to her. Get real law enforcement involved."

"*If* this is all on the level." Howard ate another three fries with a mock scowl.

"We need to hear her story. But two middle-aged guys who look like cops might not get very far with a frightened young woman."

Lyle's cell phone vibrated, telling him he had a text. He read it, then pointed the screen toward Howard.

Gov. G. knows about the Creosote deaths.
Witness says they were not accidental.
He told Ecoperi to lie low.

"That's from Kate," Howard said. "How does she know?"

"I have a pretty good idea. And this confirms the governor's involvement in Ecoperi." He looked at his phone and another text appeared.

Look at Drenda's latest video.
We've got it all recorded.

Do I have to let Howard in on this? I trust him, but I need to see Drenda's video first.

Lyle put his phone away. "Kate will have more details

later. I'll check it out and let you know. If the governor is covering up a murder or even withholding evidence, he can be prosecuted."

"If we prove it was murder."

CHAPTER 61

B ack at their motel, Lyle and Howard spent twenty minutes going through their car.

"Whoever got in here would have been rushed in that parking lot," Lyle said running his hand under the dashboard. "If we can't find a bug, they probably just wanted to search the car or didn't have time to plant something."

When they'd finished with the inside, Lyle used a mirror from his shaving kit to scan under the perimeter of the car. He saw nothing suspicious.

Howard headed to his room for a rest, telling Lyle he would first scour the place for a bug or hidden camera.

In his room, Lyle reached for his cordless earphones. He stuck them in and clicked on Drenda's video.

Here was the governor, upside down, speaking into a phone. Lyle held his phone sideways and looked closely to take in the governor's facial expressions. He could only hear Gudgel's side of the conversation. From the stable camera angle of the video Lyle figured Drenda had set the glasses down facing Gudgel's desk. How did she manage *that?*

"Who told you they were in town?" Gudgel said, his gaze moving around the room, apparently an office.

"Oh, pretty smart. So they're talking to 'em...

"You said they were onboard. So what's the problem?
...

"Stop worrying, I told you. The investigation is over. No physical evidence found. Case closed...

"Yeah, that's what she told the sheriff but the guard says she didn't see it happen. Just heard gossip."

The governor listened silently, scratched the back of his neck, then said, "I *know* what happened. A God-damned tragedy. And we know who did it. But it's over. Closed. Remember, keep a low profile and keep your people in line. Those two guys won't find anything...

"No, that's not a good idea."

The governor shook his head as he listened. He switched the phone from his right to his left hand.

"No." He made his signature gesture, a fist slam on his desk.

"Let the guard handle it. Keep a low profile. Get ready to start planting, and you'll be fine."

Gudgel pursed his lips and stared past wherever Drenda had planted her glasses.

"So yeah, I appreciate it. Yes, that's the amount...

"Because, thanks to you, I have to keep everyone in line...

"No, are you kidding? The Caymans' bank. Do the farm work. Let me handle the rest."

Gudgel dropped the phone on his desk. "Son of a bitch."

He got up and disappeared from the frame. In a

minute, Drenda walked up to her glasses and slipped them on. "I only need them for distance," she told the governor. "I'll get back to this data."

Lyle stopped the video, walked outside—just to be careful—and called Drenda catching her on the way home. She explained she'd been working in Gudgel's office when he received the phone call and asked her to leave.

"I wasn't too nervous. I was in his office because he asked me to do a statistical analysis on his recent opinion poll. TV news says he's ahead but his pollsters say he's behind. Gudgel wants me to review their survey results and report to him."

"Great job. This confirms he's getting payoffs from the Ecoperi farming company. And sounds like he's an accessory to murder."

"Murder?"

"Yes, two school kids. But I don't have all the evidence yet. Would you have time or interest in another assignment to undermine the governor? This one would be simpler, and safer, and not undercover."

"Sure I'd have time. I'm merely an unpaid volunteer at Gudgelville."

"It would involve meeting and talking to a young woman from Creosote and possibly looking after her for a short time. I'll explain the whole thing later."

"Just tell me when and where."

CHAPTER 62

"Have you heard about the traffic delays on the freeway off-ramp?" Max said walking into Kate's office unannounced.

Kate was more surprised by his presence than by his question. She assumed it signified a level of urgency. Max rarely came to visit.

"As a matter of fact, I know about it. Sit down Max, we'll talk."

He turned around and looked at the guest chair before he lowered himself into it. Kate wondered if her office furnishings were up to muster. Her guest chairs were certainly up to supporting her wiry boss who couldn't weigh more than 130 pounds.

"It's taking visitors from Phoenix and south an extra fifteen to thirty minutes to get here on busy days." He slapped a hand on the arm of the chair and gripped it. "They're irritated and cranky when they get here. That's no damn good. Gives them a bad feeling."

"I know."

"Kate, believe it or not, you're not the first person I talked to about this. I called Howard at security and he was out of town. Talked to his number two person—what's his name? Anyway, he claimed not to know about it. I talked to three other people in fact. They all knew about the problem, but no one knew what to do about it."

"Like the weather."

"Ha, I get it. So you don't know either?"

"I *do* know Max, and you probably do too." *In fact that's why you're here.*

"Gudgel."

"Correct. I suspect, well it's more than suspect. I'm sure that the governor has some kind of illegal hold over the highway contractor working on the Route 247 interchange. And you can stop with the dubious look, Max. I'm on this. And I haven't done anything illegal. Well...."

"Maybe I shouldn't ask questions."

"Lyle and I decided—"

"Lyle?"

"Yes, the two of us decided to be a little more proactive. To do preventative measures. You know about my trip to Montana."

Max made eye contact. "You found out what a scoundrel—no, crook—Gudgel has been from the get-go."

"And I found out the type of graft he prefers. Juicy state contracts. I will fix this. I need to talk with one of the owners of the company working on Route 247. They're dragging their feet."

Max got up. "Okay. I'll leave it in your hands. Keep me posted."

"We're working on something else, too, that we hope will get him off our backs for good. And maybe, well, we'll see." *Max needs deniability, no matter how our plan goes."*

■ ■ ■

On her drive home, implications of the Gudgel video about the Creosote deaths stirred up a Phoenix-style dust storm in Kate's head. She cruised by a local strip mall intending to buy a couple of cosmetics and perhaps something for dinner. In the parking lot she saw Irwin Construction vehicles. She'd seen the pickups frequently in the area but never before realized they belonged to the company restructuring the highway. Two Irwin pickups were parked in front of Gilligan's neighborhood bar. Curiosity more than an interest in a glass of wine prompted Kate to go in.

She took a stool and nodded to the Skipper serving customers down the bar. Guests filled several tables. She glanced around the room and spotted someone she recognized.

"What'll it be, Kate," said the Skipper who had walked down the bar. "Glass of white? Where's Lyle today?"

"Ah, out of town. Yes, a glass of Kim Crawford would be nice."

She took her glass and meandered around a seven-foot-tall carved Tiki god surrounded by faux tropical foliage and sat at a small table partially shielded by plastic palm fronds. Through the make-believe leaves she could see two men nearby talking over cocktails. One of them moved his arms while he talked, interlacing his fingers, then rubbing his hands together.

"So we don't have much choice," said the more animated of the two, the man Kate knew. He wore a long-sleeve white shirt with an open collar and loosened tie.

"Look, I understand our position," said the other man who bore a resemblance to his table mate. "But either way we're—" The man paused as a customer walked by their table. "You told me it would only be two weeks."

"I didn't know."

"You know what got us into this don't you?"

"You mean who?"

"I mean greed and laziness."

That sounded like Kate's cue. She stood, picked up her glass, and took a few steps to their table. "Good evening Mr. Irwin," she said to the man she'd met under another name at the construction trailer. "And this must be your younger brother and partner."

The senior Irwin stared up at Kate, speechless.

CHAPTER 63

"Let me introduce myself then," Kate said to the younger Irwin. "I'm Kate Sorensen. I'm vice president of Nostalgia City. The park has a strong interest in getting the traffic bottleneck cleared up. Your brother and I had a conversation about this yesterday except he didn't really have an answer to my question. And he must be shy because he didn't tell me his real name."

The brothers looked at each other, and Kate slid into the booth next to the man she knew.

The younger brother got up. "David, is this how you're handling things? Ms. Sorensen, I can understand your concern. Truly. I'm sure my brother can explain it to you more clearly this time." He looked at Kate and walked away.

"Stan, please," his brother said to his back as he left the bar.

David Irwin looked down at his drink. Kate heard him take a deep breath. "How did you know?"

"Your picture and your brother's picture are on your company website."

He slid over giving her more space. "I'm sorry," he said. "I didn't want to argue any more yesterday."

"I didn't think we were arguing. I just wanted to know when the work would be finished. I had information on this job, and you evaded my questions so I looked up your website. I intended to visit your office."

He took a liberal swallow of his drink. It looked like whiskey. Then he interlaced his fingers around the nearly empty glass and exhaled. Kate noticed he wasn't wearing a wedding ring.

"This way," Kate said softening her voice, "we can discuss this over a drink." A sarcastic, gotcha approach obviously wouldn't work here, as much as she wanted to make him uncomfortable. She slid imperceptibly closer.

"I still can't give you any better idea of the construction timing."

"I can understand the difficulties. Since you're already past the deadline, it causes a strain."

Irwin glanced into his drink, looking disappointed it was almost gone. "Strain, yeah. Stress."

Kate looked up and caught the Skipper's eye then pointed to Irwin's drink.

"You and your brother are at odds. That's not good." She stuck out her lower lip, lowered her head, and looked at him. Long strands of blond hair threatened to cover one eye. She brushed them back.

Irwin sighed and finished his drink just as Skipper arrived with a new one.

"Do you want to tell me about it?" She moved a few

inches closer. "In my job I run into serious difficulties all the time."

"It's too complicated." He took a drink then looked into Kate's eyes. "I really wished we'd finished the job earlier. Then it wouldn't…"

Kate parted her lips and met his eyes. "Then it wouldn't have mattered if someone told you to hold up the work."

He looked at her out of the corners of his eyes, shaking his head, not ready to accede.

"There's two reasons why I know about this. First, Governor Gudgel has been attacking Nostalgia City, telling people our rides aren't safe and pulling other stunts, like jamming the flow of traffic into the park."

He met Kate's eyes, then looked away.

"Second, I know how vindictive he can be. And Nostalgia City is fighting back. We're one of the biggest companies in the state and we're going to stop him. In your case, I thought the only way the governor could get you to clog up the intersection was if he had something on you. I know him. That's how he works—blackmail. All of this is really *his* fault, isn't it?"

She looked at him for a sign of acknowledgement but found none. "Your name came up in the governor's office the other day. Why do you suppose that was?"

He turned and looked at her. She tilted her head and waited, but he remained silent, sullen.

"So I looked at this $61 million construction contract and the bidding process." She tried to sound concerned as she laid out her theory that Irwin, with or without the governor's assistance, *may* have landed the contract through something called cover biding.

"Whatever happened, the governor found out, didn't he? He's dirty. He uses people. Twists arms." She touched his hand momentarily, gazed down and slowly shook her head.

Irwin's shoulders sagged. "This is the first time we ever did anything like this. We really needed this job to pay our employees."

What a noble goal, and you want me to believe this? She worked to maintain an earnest expression. She kept her hand close to his. "So what happened?"

"The governor found out how we got the contract. He said it would be no problem, but we needed to pay a small commission to satisfy legal requirements."

"A bribe."

"A big one. After months passed, I thought we'd heard the last of it. But a few weeks ago, someone called saying he worked in the governor's office. He said they were investigating irregularities in contract bidding."

"After you already bribed the governor?"

"Yeah. I was up against it. But the guy said all we needed to do was delay construction around the inter-change for a few weeks. I didn't know what to do so I shifted our crews and had a front loader move dirt and rocks onto parts of our completed lanes." He looked at Kate, then took a large swallow of his drink. "Then my brother found out."

The despairing look on his face made Kate genuinely want to help him. But she knew he would have to pay consequences. "We can help you."

"I have to do what they say."

"No. You don't. He's blackmailing you and he

accepted a bribe, so he has more to lose than you do, much more. Besides, this is just one of many things we have on the governor. In a short time, you're going to be the least of his concerns. Start restoring the highway. Now. I can assure you the governor will have forgotten all about it.

"And if you do get threats—or even if you don't—your best bet is to talk to the DA, tell him what you did—and the fact the governor has been blackmailing you for it."

"That's what Stan wants to do."

"He's right." She patted his hand. "Talk to him."

CHAPTER 64

Lyle and Howard chose a Mexican restaurant for dinner. Over enchiladas and giant tostadas Lyle explained his and Kate's decision to gather information on the governor.

"Some of the ways we collected evidence about Gudgel may be slightly illegal."

"Meaning *illegal*," Howard said.

"Okay, not admissible in court, but it's an opening to collect further information we *can* disclose to law enforcement and a DA. We started this because we suspected the governor found a way to obtain inside information on NC. So we discovered ways to tap into *his* secrets. We needed to be prepared for his next scheme to torpedo the park."

"Like saying our rides were unsafe. Got it. But how does this Hurt character figure into it?"

"That I don't know. What I do know, is the governor knows about the deaths of the students and that there's a witness—or someone with evidence—i.e. Isabel. And he's trying to cover it up. He's also the state's driving force for the farm expansion despite the deaths. All this in exchange for commissions paid to an offshore account. Does this sound like big-time, mob-style corruption?"

"No shit. We'll need to be careful what we say to Ben because he may repeat it to Isabel, and she might tell Hurt and from there to Gudgel."

Lyle lifted a forkful of refried beans. "We have to tell Ben enough for him to let us contact Isabel. And I know what we can do if she agrees to see us."

"What's that?"

"You know Drenda, right?"

"Sure, mostly from staff meetings. She's the—"

"Don't say nostalgia police. Yes, she's responsible for the park's authenticity, but she's dependable, smart, and knows the score about Gudgel. I called her. She's agreed to meet Isabel and hear her story. If it works out, Isabel can stay temporarily with her until we can put together a case against Gudgel, Ecoperi, and maybe Hurt. And Drenda is young. Isabel is more likely to trust a young woman."

"That's a lot of supposition."

"But it's what we have now. Or we just go back to the park, let the kids fend for themselves and brace for the fallout from whatever Hurt or Ecoperi has in mind for them."

"So, let's go talk to them," Howard said as they finished dinner. They had parked in the rear, but left by the front door, walked a block and doubled back. Not a great move, but it might have thrown an amateur.

■　■　■

Lyle had studied the map to locate the defunct drive-in and plot a roundabout way of getting there. They drove city streets and doubled back once.

"No State Guard behind us," Howard said.

"They're not *that* dumb," Lyle said. "Tailing us with a Humvee is about as stealthy as following us in the Oscar Mayer Wienermobile."

"Yeah, we have to consider civilian vehicles and Ecoperi security."

Lyle saw a movie screen looming ahead in the darkness as they crept toward the theatre on a road with more potholes than pavement. "Coming Soon" said a dilapidated sign on the back of the screen, but the rest of the message was blank. The last line could have said *Ecoperi*.

Howard drove into the drive-in through an opening where a section of fence had fallen in, clearly years before. Their headlights swept the rounded berms that created rows of raised parking spaces. One pickup truck faced the screen next to the boarded-up snack bar. Kidwell and Mathis climbed out as Howard pulled up next to them.

Lyle looked around for a place to sit and found a picnic table that had probably been sitting in front of the snack bar since the theater opened. Fortunately, moonlight bathed the table. Although they might get splinters from the benches, they would be able to see the young men's faces as they talked. Lyle tried to remember the last movie he'd seen at a drive-in.

Howard began their talk looking at Mathis. "This situation your girlfriend is in—and you too—is precarious, potentially dangerous. Can you tell us what you know about Mr. Hurt and what kind of arrangements he's made for Isabel?"

"He's a private investigator licensed by the state," Kidwell said.

"Have you met him?" Lyle asked.

"Ben has."

"Yes, I met him once after Will and Mary died. He said Isabel was in danger."

"How did he know? How did he contact her?"

"He saw her at the restaurant. We thought he was right. Isabel was scared."

"So she went off with him?"

"Uh huh."

"What does he plan to do?"

"I don't know exactly. He told her he's working on a way for her to get away from Ecoperi and the guard for good."

Lyle glared at Mathis. "That sounds like running away. Forever?"

"The way to keep her safe," Howard said, "is to contact legitimate law enforcement. And she should have an attorney, not a shifty PI, looking after her rights."

"Where is she staying?" Lyle asked.

"I don't know."

Lyle shook his head. "If we're going to help you, you have to tell us the truth."

Kidwell nudged his friend's arm.

"Okay. Yeah, I thought about this. She needs to get away from him, but she doesn't know where to go."

He looked at Lyle with a mixture of hope and fear. Lyle waited.

"Okay, she's in one of those suites hotels in Buckeye. I've seen her twice. My parents don't know."

"We figured it would be in the Phoenix area," Lyle said. "The best thing is for Isabel to ditch him as soon as possible. We have evidence he's working for the governor."

Mathis had been toying with a loose piece of the wood tabletop. He moved his hands away and stared at Lyle. "But where would she go?"

"A friend of ours, someone we work with, can put her up temporarily until we get law enforcement to deal with Ecoperi, the guard, and Gudgel. Her name's Drenda and she's a sweet person, understanding. Do you think we could talk to Isabel? Can you call her, and we can discuss everything?"

Mathis looked at Kidwell who nodded encouragement.

"She actually has a phone of her own. She has the one Hurt gave her, but she bought another phone herself so we could talk any time. I ah, talked to her this evening, and she'd like to get away from Mr. Hurt."

"Has he *done* anything to her?" Howard asked with knitted brows.

"No, nothing like that, but he won't tell her anything. He tells her not to go anywhere because she's in danger. Where can she go? She doesn't have her car. And this woman, I think Mr. Hurt's secretary, comes by to check on her. She says she wants to know if Isabel needs anything, but she's really, I don't know, spying on her. Keeping track of her."

"Would you call her now?" Lyle said. "Put it on speaker and we can all talk."

Mathis introduced Lyle and Howard to Isabel who

sounded mature. She reminded Lyle how mature Sam had been at that age. His daughter, who would soon be more than 2,000 miles away.

Isabel Bertran agreed to meet Drenda and discuss the way they would spirit her away from Hurt, as long as her boyfriend came to the meeting. Mathis said he could take off from school for a day or two, having satisfied most of his graduation credits. He'd give his parents a story about visiting a friend.

Having Mathis there would reassure Isabel, and he would help persuade her to go with Drenda. Lyle took down Isabel's phone number and told her Drenda would call her the next day.

Mathis and Kidwell drove out the main entrance and Howard followed. At a county road Howard turned in the opposite direction from the young men. After a mile, a blinding light hit Howard's car, then a Humvee roared out from a dirt road heading directly for Lyle's side of the car.

Howard swerved to avoid the collision and hit the sandy shoulder. Their car fishtailed, then failed to get traction in the sand. The Humvee, with flashing blue lights over its cab, ground to a halt blocking their path.

A camo-clad guardsman hopped down, pulling out his pistol. Lyle's initial reaction was to reach for his semi-auto under the seat, but he slowed himself down. He didn't want to make an erratic motion. He knew of motorists who'd been shot by cops for making the same move.

Howard swore, then put the car in park and opened his door. "Lemme talk to him," he said before stepping from the car. "You might think about getting out your pistol, especially if he shoots me."

Outside the angle of the Humvee's headlights, Lyle reached for his gun as the first guardsman was focused on Howard and the driver was just climbing down from their vehicle. Lyle slipped his gun out of its holster and stuffed it in his belt at the small of his back.

"Out of the car," shouted the Humvee driver. "Slowly."

Lyle opened his door and moved carefully out of the car. Howard leaned on their car's hood with the other guardsman behind him. The guardsman looked to be about twenty years old. He didn't seem to know how to frisk Howard while holding a gun on him.

"Doofus, step back," the driver shouted to the young guardsman. Doofus followed orders and moved back, holding his gun on Howard. The other guardsman, scarcely older than the first, walked around the car and gave Howard a few perfunctory taps on his sides and legs. This duo had police procedures down pat. Lyle was tempted to pull out his SIG Sauer and get the drop on both of them before they knew what happened.

Instead, he tossed his wallet on the hood. "Look you guys, Howard and I are retired cops. There's my ID. But I think you know who we are. That's why you tried to ram us off the road. If you're intent on threatening us for no reason, we'll drive directly to your base and talk to your CO. I'd like find out who conducted your nifty stop-and-frisk training."

"Hold it right there," said the Humvee driver. "I want both of you face down, on the ground." He started to pull out his service weapon.

"I think we scared 'em Howard."

Everyone froze when red and blue lights appeared down the road. Guard reinforcements? Lyle debated what to do with his pistol when a white and blue SUV with *Highway Patrol* on the door pulled to a stop next to them. Two uniformed officers got out.

Let's see what the state police have to do with the guard, Lyle thought.

One of the officers wore sergeant stripes and looked old enough to be the guardsmen's father. "What's going on here?"

"Questioning suspects," said the older guardsman.

"Suspicion of what?"

The two guardsmen spoke at the same time.

"Trespassing."

"Speeding."

"Sounds serious," the sergeant said. "Were they armed?"

"No sir," said the Humvee driver.

"Then why in hell do you have your weapons drawn?" He studied Lyle and Howard in the beam of his SUV's headlights.

The guardsmen holstered their weapons while looking at the sergeant, one of them missing his holster and almost dropping his gun.

"Sergeant," Lyle said. "My friend here and I are retired police. San Francisco and Phoenix. My ID is on the hood. These fine examples of state guardsmanship ran us off the road because we're guilty of not living in Creosote. Or maybe because they need driving lessons. I'll explain."

Twenty minutes later the highway patrol sergeant was

outlining a report that would be copied to the guards-men's superior officer. Howard and Lyle were on their way back to their motel.

"Were you going to shoot one of the guardsmen?" Howard asked.

"Probably. If he shot you."

CHAPTER 65

April 22

Reluctantly, Lyle clicked off the Mustang's ignition silencing K-BOP radio. DJ Big Earl had been playing Linda Ronstadt's "Long, Long Time." Lyle hadn't talked to Rey since he returned from Creosote and was eager to hear anything new on the murder investigations. Happy to be back in a Hawaiian shirt and jeans, he pulled open the bar door.

Inside Gilligan's, Rey sat at a table in the darkest corner of the bar. He wore a light blue work shirt, cradled a beer in front of him, and didn't much look like a cop. The way he liked it when off duty.

The D-backs and Dodgers battled on the TV behind the bar, Arizona down three runs in the fifth at the afternoon game in LA.

"Whatcha have, Lyle, the usual?

"Naw, make it a lager this time," he told the Skipper.

"You out of town recently?" the bartender asked setting a glass and a bottle on the bar.

"Yeah. How'd you know? Small town, huh?"

"Kate was in here with someone the other night. Is that someone who works at the park with you?"

"I dunno." Lyle shrugged.

"They seemed *awful* cozy," he said with a smirk. "She came in alone, then met up with him. Bought him a drink."

Really? "No idea, Skip." He picked up his beer and turned. "Probably business," he said over his shoulder as he made his way to Rey's corner.

"You've been out stirring up more trouble," Rey said as Lyle sat down.

"What, you too?"

"Huh?"

"Nothing. Just something the Skipper said. Yes, I stirred up trouble in Creosote. Trouble for the governor. Two poor kids got killed."

"I read about that. I thought it was an accident. Gudgel is involved in the death of two high school kids?"

"We think he's getting paid to cover up how they died. Just between you and me."

"That's serious. How'd you find out?"

"Still investigating. Ask me in a day or so. At least I'm not associating with the hate group. You're off work today."

"The sheriff insisted."

Rey had probably worked every day for the past two weeks and looked it. "What's happening with the shooting cases?" Lyle said.

Rey's expression turned bleak in a second. "You had to ask."

"Sorry."

"No. You need to know. You're involved. It's just the investigation is shit. We haven't picked up anything like a lead in more than a week. We get calls from the media, from the mayor, from relatives of victims. What can I tell them? *Nada.*"

"The FBI?"

"I don't know if they gave up on the hate crime/hate group theory or not. They couldn't get anything solid, I'm thinking. The CBs are a closed group and Wylie Tanner is a hard-ass. But you got an invitation."

"Only because I saved that guy who shot himself. And then they beat the crap out of me. But you got all my pictures. Weren't they any use?"

"I didn't see many full-face shots. A lot of them showed people's backs as they faced their targets."

"Wait a minute," Lyle said. He looked around to see if anyone was within earshot. "Those were just the shooting range pictures. I also sent the ones I took at the barbecue. I took a lot of groups shots there, with faces. Pretty risky, too."

"I appreciate your sacrifice, but I never received them."

"Shit. Damn. I'm sorry. Maybe it's not me, but I'll check." He pulled out his phone and scanned his outgoing mail. He saw an email to Rey, with but a few files attached.

"I sent you two emails. In the first one, I talked about *two* sets of photos. Didn't you notice? Did you acknowledge? I don't think so."

"There ya go. I was disappointed when I previewed

the shots, so I didn't notice you said you were sending *two* sets of photos. A bad day in a bad week. We had multiple assault cases at West's bar, too. I just skimmed your email. But I didn't *get* your second batch."

Lyle held up his phone. "Okay, take a look." He flipped through group shots, pictures of individuals, diner table groupings. "I even have at least first names for many of these guys. If it's of any use."

"These are good. Send them to me, now. And guard your originals—with your life. Who knows what we might find."

Lyle tapped his phone again and again and sent all the photos, some with captions.

Rey got up.

"Aren't you going to finish your beer?"

The undersheriff was halfway to the door by the time Lyle finished his sentence.

CHAPTER 66

How could Drenda have guessed that her initiative to volunteer with the Gudgel campaign would yield such dividends? And now here she sat to rendezvous with a witness who might be able to connect the governor to murder.

She and Kate had talked at length about the situation in Creosote and then Drenda called Isabel to introduce herself and discuss where they might meet. Drenda suggested they not meet at her hotel in case Hurt or his secretary showed up. Isabel told her about a city park in a residential area walking distance from where she was staying.

"It's a quiet place I like to go to when I need to relax and think," Isabel told her.

Drenda drove by herself to Buckeye, a western suburb of Phoenix on the edge of the open desert. For security, Kate followed and parked on the other side of the neighborhood park where she would listen to Drenda's conversation via her friend's magic glasses. If it worked out, Drenda would drive Isabel back to her condo and Kate would meet her later.

Drenda knew the responsibility she'd assumed, and when she saw the dark-haired young woman in shorts and a light blouse walking toward her park bench, she smiled and stood up.

After she introduced herself, they sat in a comfortable spot where benches were arranged in the shade of acacia trees.

"I just talked to Ben," Isabel said, "and he'll be here in a few minutes."

While they waited, Drenda made small talk, not wanting to probe until Isabel looked comfortable. She knew Isabel to be 19 or 20, but she appeared older, per-haps due to the drama of the past few weeks and the fact she was essentially on her own. She had dark, wide-set eyes, a slender chin, and hair flowing down her back.

Drenda briefly explained NC's troubled history with Governor Gudgel and why he was untrustworthy and not only a threat to the park and its employees, but to the well-being of Arizona. Soon Mathis arrived, parking his pickup in a small adjacent lot. He and Isabel embraced and exchanged quiet words of love.

"Ben, this is Drenda," Isabel said. "She's going to help us get justice for Will and Mary."

Drenda shook hands. "I hope we can help."

Mathis and Isabel sat together on a bench and Drenda took a seat on another bench at a right angle. Drenda looked at both of them in the shade and wondered if Kate could see them in video on her phone.

Holding Mathis's hand, Isabel told her story. She

recounted how Will and Mary and others had protested the Ecoperi expansion and been threatened by Ecoperi security and State Guardsmen.

She explained that Ecoperi obtained their email addresses—possibly through school—and sent threats. They said they knew Will and Mary led the protest and the picketing. They said they had evidence that they spray painted the warehouse wall.

"One email said bad things would happen to them if they didn't stay away from the Ecoperi farm and stop protesting." Isabel looked at Mathis who gave her a sympathetic smile. "Another one said it was 'dangerous and unhealthy' to oppose Ecoperi. I received one of the emails, too, but not as bad as that."

"Did you see the emails that Mary and Will received?" Drenda asked.

"Yes. Some came from personal email accounts, but others came from *Ecoperi.com*. I have copies of all the emails on my phone and on a flash drive."

That's evidence! "You have them here?"

"Yes, all the time." Isabel ran a hand under her collar and pulled out a tiny flash drive dangling from a silver chain.

"Tell her about the security guys," Ben said, "what you heard."

Isabel closed her eyes and took a breath. She bowed her head for a moment then looked up. "I heard them. I heard them at the restaurant where I work. These two guys, two Ecoperi security guards, they come in for lunch at least once a week.

"This time they sat in a corner right in front of a

server's station, you know where we have glasses, water, set-ups, and stuff. I was standing there, right behind them. They couldn't see me, but I heard them fine.

"One sounded really upset. His voice was like, quivering. He said, 'Why did you do it? They were just kids. Weren't hurting anyone.' He sort of cried. 'You forced them off the cliff.'

"The other guy told him to shut the fuck up. He said, 'It happened. We did it. It's over.' Then the first guy says, '*We* did it? You were driving.'

"About two hours later, after the lunch crowd, someone came in the diner and said two Creosote students died in a crash."

Isabel clutched Mathis's hand with both of hers and let out a sob.

"That's when I knew what they did."

"Do you know their names?" Drenda asked.

"I do, their first names. And I wrote down what they said."

Drenda was a history PhD, not an attorney, but she could see a clear possibility for getting one of the guards to flip on the other. "So what did you do?"

"I talked to Sheriff Findlay right away. He said I was hysterical. That it looked like an accident, and if I wasn't there, how could I know what happened."

"Did the State Guard get involved in the investigation?"

"The sheriff said I should talk to them. And he told me to just calm down. How could I calm down when my friends were killed? I didn't trust the guard. They worked with the two guys who killed Mary and Will. And they're not police. Why is the State Guard involved?"

The sound of Isabel's voice and facial expressions told Drenda she was telling the truth. The sheriff sounded like a real miscreant.

"Aside from seeing the security guards in the restaurant had you seen them before, you know, outside of work?"

Drenda knew Lyle and Kate would want to be sure Isabel had no motive to make up a story.

"I don't know what you mean," Isabel said with raised voice. "No I didn't see them outside of work except when they hassled our picket line. They're bad people. I have the emails."

Her indignation sounded genuine. They needed to get her out of there. But one more question. "When did Mr. Hurt show up?"

"No more than two days later he walked into the diner and said he needed to speak to me. After work he told me he was a private detective investigating the so-called accident because he thought it sounded suspicious.

"I told him the story and he, right away says I'm in danger. He said Ecoperi was funding Sheriff Findlay's reelection campaign, and I would never get fair treatment in Creosote."

Drenda shifted on her bench as the sun began to stream past the acacia branches. "Why did you come here with him?"

"I didn't know what to do." She looked at Mathis momentarily. "I was scared. Those security guards looked at me funny the next time they came in. Mr. Hurt said he represented the highest levels of state government and that he would pay for me to stay here until he could find law enforcement we could trust."

The highest level of state government is Gudgel, who's supporting Ecoperi. "So you left your job and came out here?"

"I tried to explain to my boss. I think he understood." She raised a hand palm up. "I'm not sure."

"It would be prudent not to trust Gregory Hurt. Or the governor. Especially the governor. But you're safe now. You can stay with me. I'm single. I live just outside Nostalgia City. I have a spare bedroom. You talked to my friends and coworkers Lyle and Howard. They're former police detectives. We won't wait two weeks to get help for you. We'll do it right away."

She hoped she was correct.

CHAPTER 67

April 23

Rey had been excited to see the pictures from the hate group barbecue, but Lyle hadn't heard from him. The case against Gudgel was building, especially since Drenda had persuaded Isabel to escape Buckeye and Hurt's control, but would it help solve the hate murders?

Lyle filled in a half day driving at the park and later drove into Polk to buy ammunition. He'd used up all his revolver rounds at the Cadre Brave shooting range. No point in having the gun without ammo.

Cedric's Firearms was the largest gun store in Polk and likely to have what he needed. He browsed the ammo aisles noticing the stacks of assault rifle rounds. The shelves overflowed. He knew after the mass shooting, deputies had checked out recent sales and, if they discovered anything, Rey hadn't mentioned it. He bought a box of .380 ammo and headed back to his car.

The store's parking lot wrapped around the front and down the right side of the building. Lyle had parked in front, but as he walked out he glanced to his right and saw Jake, the city planner and CBA member. Lyle hadn't heard from him about lunch and wondered whether to speak to him. Before he'd made up his mind he heard a familiar voice.

"Lyle, get back here," Rey Martinez said in a loud whisper.

As he turned, Lyle noticed that Big Ears was standing next to Jake and both looked in the back of a pickup. Lyle walked a half dozen steps back from the corner toward Rey. The undersheriff wore a suit, and a detective and two uniformed deputies accompanied him.

Rey told one deputy to stand in front of the store's entrance to keep anyone from walking out.

"We want to talk to Clifford, Big Ears," Rey said motioning to Lyle. "Please stay back."

Lyle held up both hands, his box of ammo in one fist, and moved toward his car. Instead of getting in, he walked the length of his Mustang, nosed into a parking space, and crouched in front of the grill giving him a hazy view of Big Ears and Jake through the windshield and then the back window of his car. Rey and his detective walked toward the pickup, momentarily blocking Lyle's view.

"Morgan Clifford," Rey said, "we'd like to talk with you."

Big Ears said something Lyle couldn't hear and started walking toward the truck's cab.

"Don't move. Put your hands where we can see them," Rey shouted as he and the detective rushed forward.

Was Clifford reaching into his truck? Rey and the

detective dashed around a parked car and came at Clifford from different directions. Frustrated looking through two windows, Lyle walked to the rear of his car, standing near the trunk. Clifford waved a handgun, but Rey clutched the smaller man's arm and smashed it against the top of the pickup. The semi-auto fell to the ground.

At the same time, the detective ran into Jake, who blocked him from helping Rey. He slammed Jake against the truck bed. In seconds, three deputies appeared from different directions. Two pinned Jake, the third assisted in subduing Big Ears. Rey had come with overwhelming manpower this time.

Lyle stood among gawkers gathered near the periphery of the confrontation. From his vantage point, Lyle saw Clifford, his large ears framing his angry, but broken expression. Handcuffs bound his wrists.

Rey shoved him to the middle of the parking lot aisle as a black and white rolled up. Two deputies took over control of the suspect and pushed him toward the open rear door of the sheriff's cruiser. Rey spoke to Clifford—probably giving him his rights—before the deputies placed him in their car.

Lyle saw another deputy putting cuffs on Jake.

Minutes later Rey told Lyle, "your photos did it."

CHAPTER 68

April 24

Kate rarely took public transit at the park but today decided on the trolley to take her to meet a colleague from the advertising department for lunch. Although it looked as it had decades before, the NC trolley offered seats that cushioned tourists' backsides better than the original. Otherwise, the car's interior was authentic with its arched ceiling, high windows, and chrome railings. It made Kate smile. Until she saw Gregory Hurt.

He sat toward the rear of the mostly empty car. He smiled—marginally—and pointed to the empty seat in front of him. Kate thought, how convenient.

She didn't even wonder how he appeared there. He might have paranormal insights, but they would not save him. The trolley lurched ahead. Kate sat down quickly and turned in her seat to speak. "Gregory Hurt, showing up like the proverbial penny here in Nostalgia City. You came to see me?"

"Uh huh." On a warm spring day he wore a wool suit

and tie. Kate could smell the tobacco on his breath. He hadn't shaved carefully that morning. Perhaps he'd been concentrating on how he was going to sell her a deal.

"I assume you have things to discuss," she said. "I'm on my way to lunch. Why don't we find a quiet place."

"Yes, I believe I have useful information. Quite a lot of information in fact, that you will be interested in."

Kate pulled out her phone, called her colleague, and apologized she would to have to miss lunch.

"So, Gregory, do you like Polynesian food?"

He winced.

"Good. You'll like the Tiki Kai. We get off the trolley in a few minutes. In the meantime, why don't you tell me about this information you have. Am I correct to think that you want to make some sort of deal and not necessarily *share* information like you spoke of before?"

"I told you when we met that we had many common interests. That's even more true today, and I'm willing to explain in detail. But not here."

Hurt's words, his voice, and his demeanor reminded Kate of an old gangster movie. Edward G. something or other. The trolley clanged to a stop. "Here we are."

The Tiki Kai, NC's homage to the Polynesian restaurant craze of the 1960's and '70s, hadn't yet found a following among park visitors. Kate knew they could find an isolated table. She had one in mind next to a Koi pond with a tinkling waterfall. She really didn't care if Hurt recorded their conversation, but she'd make it difficult just the same.

When they were seated beside the pond and far from the nearest patron, Kate urged Hurt to order a tropical drink. He said he wanted coffee.

"They're really *very* good," Kate gushed. "Rum, coconut, lots of cool ingredients."

He ordered black coffee, but Kate ordered a Tiki Paradise Delight for him, too.

Obviously irritated, he started to light a cigarette.

"Sorry Gregory, this is a non-smoking restaurant."

He stuffed his cigarette back in the package. "Okay, you having fun? You have no idea of the magnitude of information—evidence—that I have. Facts that will make your problems with the governor disappear. I have been systematically collecting material on him."

Kate cocked her head. "For a client, you said."

"Yes. Well, in a manner of speaking, that's what it worked out to be."

"I've been collecting information on Gudgel, too. What a coincidence. One of the things I found out is he likes to hire PIs like you to collect dirt on people. Blackmail material, to keep people in line. I believe you called him a petty tyrant and crook when we last spoke. An apt description."

"He is that."

"Which is why he hired you to follow me. I never got a good look at you in that gray SUV. But later, I followed you."

Kate paused as the drinks arrived, the Tiki Paradise Delight, in a tall, brown ceramic glass, and the coffee.

"You don't wish anything to drink?" the server asked Kate.

"A little later, thanks."

Kate pushed aside her menu and focused on Hurt. "As I said, I followed you. To Gudgel's campaign headquarters. You know what Lyle calls it? Gudgelville. You know who Lyle is, don't you? You know everything about me."

Hurt's face settled into its default scowl.

"You visit the governor's staff," Kate continued, "and give them reports on me and the park. How much did he pay you for that? And now you want to sell *me* information on *him*?"

"Okay. This requires explanation." He took a sip of his coffee and gave the Tiki Paradise Delight the stink eye. "Of course I was working for the governor. That's how I gained his confidence."

Clever bastard you are.

Kate thought he could read her mind because his expression changed immediately. He leaned forward, lowered his head, and pointed at Kate with his index finger. "It was subterfuge. I got close to him to gather intelligence. Yes, information that will be highly useful to you."

"Okay, how much is it going to cost?"

"Please." He started to reach for his cigarettes, remembered, and settled for the coffee. "Let me tell you a little of what I have, then you can judge its value."

A big-mouthed carp stuck its head out of the pond and stared at Hurt.

"For example, starting as a legislator the governor has curried favor with various civil servants who deal with building contractors. He's now at a point where he can command a fee for a state contract."

"Don't tell me. He also teaches contractors how to master the art of cover bidding."

"Yes, well I have documentation, copies of checks, bidding documents. And I know recently your guests have been plagued with traffic trying to get to the park. That's Gudgel's work, too."

Not anymore.

"He's blackmailing the road contractor to sabotage auto traffic access to Nostalgia City. I have that documented, too. I didn't bring paperwork with me, but I have everything on computer files."

"Well, that's handy. Then we could conclude a deal today."

"Just wait until you see the entire case I have against the governor. You'll be satisfied."

Hurt ordered a hamburger. Kate didn't even know they had such a thing at Tiki Kai. Children's menu. She ordered Lomi Lomi salmon.

When they finished eating Kate suggested they continue their "negotiation" at her office so she could see his files.

"You can have a cigarette outside," she said, "then we can catch a cab to the Maxwell Building."

"You'll want Maxwell to sit in," he said. "I'm sure you'll need his authorization to conduct our transaction."

"I'll see if he's in."

"Your boss is scheduled to be in the office all day."

"Good detective work, Gregory, or do you have a connection to another dimension? I need to stop at the lady's room on the way out. I can meet you outside, so you can go ahead and get a smoke. By the way," she said as they got up, "why did you have the Gudgel campaign rent that SUV for you?

"I didn't want to put the miles on *my* car. And they were accommodating."

Also, you couldn't be identified that way.

From a restroom stall Kate called Joann. Ducking into the bathroom had become a habit when she saw Hurt.

"Please set up the department's conference room for us," she told her secretary. "We're going to be meeting with Gregory Hurt."

"Hurt, the nasty PI?"

"The same. Please set up a laptop in the room and see if you can find my little digital voice recorder. Try my top right desk drawer. I'd like to you be in the meeting with us as a witness. Please activate the recorder out of sight. If you can take notes without making Hurt too suspicious, do that. If he gets uncomfortable, just rely on the recorder.

"Also, I don't expect trouble, but call Howard Chaffee and ask him to send one of his best men—not the creepy assistant security chief—to come over to our office and hang out in the waiting area, just in case."

CHAPTER 69

Lyle had let the Skipper's snide comment bother him, but Rey's arrest of Morgan Clifford for the LGBTQ shootings removed every extraneous thought from his mind.

He slapped Rey on the back. "You solved both shootings and made an arrest."

"Not exactly." Rey said. "It's never easy, is it?"

A whiteboard in a corner of Rey's office held mug shots taped up in two rows across the top with names printed in marking pen under each. A list of potential motives was dashed across the board in red. A timeline, beginning with the date of the Lightfoot shooting, and including notes to mark each day since, took up four large flip chart pages pinned to the wall.

His office looked like an incident room. Maybe these were duplicates. Regardless, this was *Rey's* case. And he'd finally arrested the shooter.

"All this," Rey waved a hand over his evidence corner,

"plus your photos, and I'm doubting the guy we have locked up killed the protesters and Deputy Beard.

"But he shot Lightfoot?"

"For sure. He confessed. Okay, sit down."

Lyle plopped in his usual chair. "How did you find Big Ears?"

"Morgan Clifford, as you noted, has prominent ears that help you pick him out of a crowd. We used your pictures, created individual mugs, and started searching."

"Did the FBI find him? Facial rec?"

"Eventually. Clifford didn't have a criminal record, but he was discharged from the army for a personality disorder. That's how he showed up in the FBI files. But I found him first."

Lyle gave him the thumbs up sign.

"Actually," Rey said, "thanks to your photos, your Control Center surveillance techs discovered him—via facial rec—on the recordings from the day of the Lightfoot shooting. His face turned up several times—among the crowds—and twice in the vicinity of Lightfoot and his daughter and friends.

"Sam."

"Yes. He was close by on one ride and ate in the same restaurant. We found his full name and the FBI confirmed. We were tailing him and going to take him at home at the High Desert Apartments, but after work he joined up with the other guy and we thought more guns might be involved."

"They were at the gun store."

"Right, so I decided to take him there. Turns out he had rifles in the back of the truck."

"He confessed."

"Right away. We gave him his rights and he said exactly how and where he killed Lightfoot. He dropped the body in the NC parking lot as a warning to anyone supporting gay rights.

"You should have seen his apartment. I'm not supposed to show you this, but just look at these photos."

Rey opened a folder and turned it around on his desk toward Lyle. Clifford had a six-foot Nazi swastika flag on his wall and a picture of the Führer.

Lyle shook his head, not surprised, but revolted and angry. He glanced at a photo of guns arranged on the apartment floor. Clifford had an arsenal. He shoved the file back to Rey glancing at Clifford's full name, age, and address. "I told Kate you caught him. I knew he was a gun nut, but who knew he was a neo-Nazi?"

"Maybe everyone, except us?"

"What about ballistics?"

"That's the screwy part." Rey hit his keyboard and glanced at his computer screen."

"Clifford's Glock is a match for the gun that killed Lightfoot—*and*—his AR-15 is the gun used to shoot the protesters and Deputy Beard.

"Clifford didn't mention it himself. When I asked him if he used his AR to kill the protesters he paused for a moment, then smiled and said, 'Yes sir, I whacked all the faggots.' He was proud of it."

"Yeah?" Lyle said. "I hear a *but* coming."

Rey leaned back in his chair. "Frankly I would have been happy to tell the DA he copped to the protest shooting, but something was off. I asked him more questions and what he said didn't sync with the facts. He's a small guy and doesn't match the witness descriptions. And he was vague about the timing and couldn't tell us where he stood when he fired."

"So your honesty got in the way of the case."

"Uh huh. We went to the auto parts store where he works and his co-workers said he was in the store the whole day of the shooting. They remember it because they heard all the sirens. Clifford was there at the time."

"So the gun did it, but Big Ears didn't."

Rey nodded. "They trade guns, the Cadre Brave do. Clifford was about to do that when we arrested him. He finally told us the AR-15 that killed everyone was in his home at the time and that he had not loaned it out."

"Someone borrowed it without his knowledge?"

"He says he keeps close tabs on his guns."

"But at the shooting range I saw him exchange guns with someone else—I don't remember who. Several of the shooters did that."

"Maybe he just gave his gun to somebody else," Rey said, "not knowing what he was going to do with it. Now, of course, he clams up."

"But he's going to do life. What does he have to lose? Maybe he could barter with the DA for a shorter sentence."

"I want that shooter."

Lyle got up. "Prints on the gun?"

Rey shook his head.

"Forgot to tell you the other day when you ran off so quickly. One of the Cadre Brave guys has an old GI belt-fed machine gun and he's teaching his eight-year-old daughter how to shoot it. Saw them at the range."

Rey glared. "And you wait this long to tell me? Okay. What's his name?"

"Rich something. He's identified in the photos I sent you."

"I'll check on it."

"Oh," Lyle said at the door, "what happened to Jake?"

"He has no record. He's charged with resisting. Might be dropped if he cooperates. I don't know. He said to give you a message."

"Me?"

"Yeah. He thinks you fingered Clifford. He said you were a traitor against America and dishonest scum. He also had a more crude suggestion for you, but it's a physical impossibility."

CHAPTER 70

"Where's Maxwell?" Hurt said as soon as he walked into the conference room.

"I need to see everything you have so I can confirm it for Max," Kate said. "And we also need to talk money before I call him."

Hurt grumbled and nodded.

Kate introduced him to Joann. "I've asked my secretary to sit in with us. You don't mind if she takes a few notes, do you? Fine."

The PR department's conference table gave them room to spread out. Kate, with her laptop in front of her, sat with Hurt on her left, Joann on her right. Hurt handed Kate a flash drive as if he were presenting priceless jewelry or a rare antique for her appraisal.

"Much of this is chronological," Hurt said as Kate opened the drive and scanned the directory. The files, not included in folders, were jpeg pictures. She clicked on one and saw a photo of herself walking into the Phoenix mall when she was trying to elude him.

"Good thing my apartment is in a high rise," Kate said, "and not on the ground floor. Kinda creepy, don't you think? Looks like stalking."

"It was proof for Governor Gudgel that I followed his orders." Hurt waved his hand erratically over the keyboard. "Go back and click on the first folder."

"Just a moment," Kate said. "You think we're interested in spy shots of me?"

"No, no. Just a mistake."

"What about the tracker? Was that the governor's idea, too?"

"Not really. But you found it. It's irrelevant. Let's move on."

Kate scrolled down the directory of folders clicking on various ones that contained copies of state construction contracts. The bidding files contained handwritten annotations with names and figures, possibly money. Hurt had amassed dozens and dozens of state documents including confidential personnel files.

"Those were necessary," Hurt said, "for deep background on individuals involved in the contract awards."

Meaning blackmail material for the governor.

Kate scanned files and read fine print and annotations on others. Having studied state bidding procedures, she thought Hurt's materials contained bona fide examples of Gudgel's malfeasance. Information that could be confirmed.

Next she clicked on a folder labeled *Ecoperi*. Inside were twenty or more files.

"I'm familiar with this project," Kate said. "It's a water grab."

"Yes. The governor's been pushing it all along because he will pocket regular monthly payments as long as the expanded farm is producing. I have evidence."

Kate opened a file that appeared to be a state environmental form. "Gudgel's fingerprints from the beginning," Kate said.

"I know *Lyle* has been checking out the farm," Hurt said. "The expansion *will be* approved by the county within a week. Do you know about the deaths of two Creosote students?"

"Yes."

"Well, as you'll see, I have documented evidence that Rod Gudgel knew about the crash, knew it was intentional, and has helped to cover it up. That alone should be worth millions. It will ruin his career and shut him up."

"Is that millions with an S?"

"He will never cause you grief again, never interfere." He pointed to the computer screen. "I have a recording here of the governor telling me to locate a witness to the killings and find out what it would take to shut her up."

Kate set aside the computer mouse and rolled her chair back. She walked around the table to a spot opposite Hurt. Joann looked up at her. "Something's been bothering me for a while," Kate said. "I should have put it together long before this. You do divorce work." With her hands on the table she leaned toward him. "I think, in addition to working for Gudgel, you're working for his wife, Sheila. Gudgel's relatives told me they were surprised Sheila and he were still married. Have you collected details on the governor's peccadillos, too?"

Hurt looked defiant.

"So, in addition to getting paid by the governor *and* his wife, you expect *us* to fork over millions for the same research for which you've already been paid twice?"

"*You* are the most interested in what I have, my investigation. You can *prove* the deaths in Creosote were murder. I have a witness."

"No. You don't."

Hurt snorted. "I talked to her this morning. She's ready to testify."

"I'll bet she told you she felt fine and that it was a beautiful day in Buckeye."

"What? You think you know where she is?"

"Yes, and Isabel is not in Buckeye."

Kate walked back around the table, sat down, and ejected Hurt's flash drive. She put it in her pocket. "I assume you have multiple copies. You can still sell it to Mrs. Gudgel."

Kate stood. "Our meeting is over. I don't want to see you again. If I do, I'll send your files to the San Navarro County Sheriff, maybe the FBI, too. There's a nice man outside in a uniform who will show you the easiest way to your car."

CHAPTER 71

April 25

Lyle looked at the jumble of papers spread out on Kate's dining table.

"I printed these out," Kate said. "Documents, transcripts, and other stuff. I spent last night and today going through Hurt's flash drive, his reports, recordings, state forms, everything. And they check out. That is, I think this will stand up as evidence. Mix that with the various malfeasances I discovered and what Isabel can report about the Creosote murders, and we have solid cases."

"Looks impressive," Lyle said, pouring a cup of coffee at the kitchen counter. He was not only relieved that they'd have Gudgel off their backs, but grateful the bigoted, scheming SOB would be behind bars.

"And in the morning, we turn all this over to the US Attorney's office in Phoenix," Kate said.

"That's a good choice."

"Thanks to our NC chief counsel. Austen knows one of the key people. Obviously I didn't give Austen many details, but I said we have evidence of wrongdoing in the governor's office and don't know who we can trust with the information."

"Did you tell him we thought about the Maricopa County DA?"

"Yes, but he said the US Attorney was the best. If they find local crimes better suited to the DA, Austen said, he could forward them. Austen said we shouldn't trust the Arizona attorney general."

"Agreed. Too tight with Gudgel." Governor Rod Gudgel is going to regret he ever tangled with Nostalgia City, Lyle thought, ever talked about *those gays*, ever sent the guard after me and Howard, ever preached hate.

"And, of course," Kate said, "I filled Max in on everything."

"Have you talked to Drenda? How is Isabel faring?"

"Doing well. Drenda says she's eager to see the Ecoperi security guys arrested ASAP. Austen arranged for her to talk to an attorney, pro bono. And speaking of Drenda, she says she's going back to work in Gudgelville tomorrow."

"What?"

"She says she's stalled him too long on a report he wanted about the opinion polls. And she thinks if she just disappeared when we turn over the Gudgel evidence they might think she had something to do with it."

"Makes sense, but I'll be happy when she's out of the vipers' nest." He wandered over and sifted through Kate's printouts. "What's this? A picture of you?"

"Hurt took surveillance photos that day he followed me. I told him I was glad this apartment is not on the ground floor."

Lyle stared at the table.

"What do you think?" Kate said. "I'm safe up here."

"High Desert Apartments."

"What?"

"Is it a coincidence? Not really. I need to see Rey." He gave her a quick kiss. "I'll be back."

■　■　■

Lyle had no intention of getting involved. He'd tell Rey his theory and let him do the rest. But habit made him tuck his reloaded .380 revolver and holster under the seat of his car.

On his way to the sheriff's office, he cruised by a building he'd seen before and stopped for about two minutes. His memory refreshed, he called Rey only to learn he was "out in the field." Rey's secretary told him he could find him "at that new shopping center on the west side doing something with parking."

After touring nearly the whole shopping center, he found Rey, in uniform, standing next to a sheriff's SUV labeled *traffic* and talking with two uniformed officers.

Lyle parked his Mustang where Rey would see him and waited. Rey glanced his way once and frowned. After about ten minutes, his business evidentially concluded, Rey wandered over. He looked down at Lyle still in the driver's seat listening to Big Earl spin the 1965 hit, "Eve of Destruction."

"Is this about Big Ears?"

Lyle shook his head and got out of his car. "I think I know who the mass shooter is."

Rey's usual skeptical expression went blank. "Really?

We grilled a bunch of Cadre Brave bastards and got nada. With the news of Clifford's arrest out, they closed ranks, and the media is calling him a lone wolf."

"That may not matter. I think I we missed the obvious suspect in the shooting."

"Tell me."

"In any murder, who is the first person you suspect? The husband or wife. I talked to Ragsdill about his partner Jordan Nichols and got the feeling he was a resentful guy getting yet another kick in the face by society."

"Detectives talked to him," Rey said. "I didn't. Sounded like what you said. Assuming that makes sense, how did he get the gun?"

"Ragsdill's and Nichols's place is in *the same building* as Big Ears. High Desert Apartments."

"But how—"

Lyle raised a hand. "It takes a little supposition, but hear me out. Ragsdill hated that Nichols made such a campaign out of gay rights. Maybe they had other differences, too. But their apartment is on the second floor and it overlooks Big Ears's. Ragsdill could look out his front window and watch Clifford carry his rifles out to his truck and back when he when he went target shooting or to a gun show, or whatever."

Lyle had Rey's attention.

"I think Ragsdill hated his partner and concocted a twisted scheme to kill him after he found out Jordan would be at the upcoming protest. Ragsdill was in the service and trained with rifles. He knows guns. So—"

"But if he broke into Morgan's apartment, Morgan

would be able to tell. And he might know the gun was recently fired, too."

"All true. Except that if you search Ragsdill's apartment, you might find gun oil and other things to clean a rifle. And as far as getting into Clifford's apartment, Ragsdill works at Superior Hardware. If he's worked in the lock and key department these cheap apartment doors would be easy for him."

Rey crossed his arms on his chest. He raised one corner of his mouth and squinted in a "sounds crazy" expression.

"Ragsdill has a huge head of bushy dark hair," Lyle continued. "At a distance it could be mistaken for a knit cap. Or maybe he wore one."

"I dunno amigo. Sounds possible, the motive I mean. How he did it would take a set of very lucky circumstances."

"You could ask him. I drove by the place before coming here and it looked like he was home."

"How about the ammo?"

"Morgan could have so much ammunition for his arsenal that he wouldn't miss it. Or Ragsdill bought some—or stole it from his store. Or he has his own AR and his own ammo."

Rey started nodding his head, slowly at first then more rapidly. "I'll go see him and let you know."

"Hold it. You're not going alone?"

"I'll radio for a deputy to meet me there."

■ ■ ■

Lyle didn't like the idea of his friend showing up at Ragsdill's door in uniform. Rey would be more than pissed if Lyle followed him, but Lyle knew how to get to the apartment. He'd park in the street next to the building and do what, he didn't know. Snap his rubber band? Pray?

Rey pulled into the parking lot apparently not seeing Lyle because he got out of his cruiser and headed straight for the stairs at the end of the building. He strode along the outside walkway, found Ragsdill's door, and knocked. No sign of his backup.

At the same moment, Ragsdill walked around from the back of the building carrying a small plastic trash can. He looked up and saw Rey at his door. He shouted something up to Rey that Lyle couldn't hear. Rey said something back. Ragsdill waved and started up the stairs. When he reached his door, he unlocked it and pushed it open for Rey to enter.

Thirty seconds later the sound of a gunshot splintered the air between Lyle and the apartment. With his car door already open, Lyle pulled out his revolver and sprinted toward Rey. When he got to the top of the stairs, a sheriff's car arrived. Two deputies jumped out. They saw Lyle carrying a gun trotting toward Ragsdill's door.

"Sheriff's department, freeze," shouted one of the deputies as he leveled a pistol at Lyle. Standing in front of Ragsdill's door, Lyle had no choice but to put his gun down. Before he could identify himself and explain, one of the deputies headed for the stairs. The deputy holding a gun stood next to a cracked concrete tire stop. He took his eyes off Lyle for a split second to check his footing.

Lyle reached behind, twisted the door knob, and fell against the door at the same time. He tumbled onto the carpeting in the apartment. As he fell, he saw what looked like a slow motion scene from an action movie—but it took only seconds.

Rey stood with his hands up, his pistol on the floor and Ragsdill pointing a gun at him. When Lyle crashed in, the bushy-haired suspect turned toward him, and Rey lunged forward. He slammed an arm on Ragsdill's gun hand as he collided with his body. Ragsdill fired one shot harmlessly into a table and, by the time the deputy rushed into the room, Lyle held Ragsdill while Rey cuffed him. Rey was unhurt.

As Lyle drove home, his thoughts revolved like a kaleidoscope. He reached for his rubber band, but it had apparently been a casualty of his tussle with Ragsdill.

CHAPTER 72

April 26

"I bet every major news outlet has a story on the arrest," Lyle said behind the wheel of his Mustang as he and Kate started the long drive to Phoenix and their visit with a US attorney. "And mostly because the shooting was gruesome. If it bleeds, it leads." He still had a hard time imagining the thought process that must have gone on in Ragsdill's mind. "He killed three people and injured two others because he hated his spouse. I've never seen one like this."

"Consequently," Kate said, "it's not connected to Gudgel, except the hatred." She scrolled through news stories on her phone. "This one has Ragsdill as an evil genius planning a mass murder in order to kill his partner and then to cover up everything afterwards."

"Not everything."

"The story quotes Sheriff Wisniewski but doesn't mention you or Rey."

"That's okay. He needs to get reelected, and Rey is fine with him doing the politics."

"Here's a story in a different paper. It says Hudson Ragsdill may have a form of PTSD. He served in Afghanistan and was the victim of discrimination and ridicule because he was gay."

"That's what he said when I talked with him," Lyle said. He held the steering wheel tight remembering Ragsdill's angry voice recounting his 'don't ask—don't tell' experience. "He said he and his partner suffered various forms of discrimination, not to mention ugly words."

"The story says his combination of experiences can produce shame, depression, anxiety, and anger. Here's a quote from this psychiatrist. 'Research also points to the finding that the experience of hate-motivated behavior can result in blaming of and lower empathy toward fellow victims.'"

"Ragsdill was a victim, too," Lyle said. "A different kind of victim. And he'll pay."

"Hate makes society the victim."

They were silent for miles, then Kate said, "Do you think the prosecutor could make a case that Hurt kidnapped Isabel—or illegally restrained her?"

"Maybe. And we tell the prosecutor that Hurt's going to sell his information to Sheila Gudgel so she can file for divorce and blackmail her governor husband into a giant settlement." He chuckled. "How do you suppose Drenda's doing today?"

"I don't know." Kate tapped her phone. "I can take a look."

She opened the video feed and held her phone up so

Lyle could see. They both saw the top of Drenda's desk and her laptop screen.

"Have you talked to the governor, yet?" Kate asked her.

The screen showed Drenda raising her head so they could see someone sitting at a desk near hers.

"Obviously she can't talk now," Kate told Lyle, and the screen moved slightly up and down indicating Drenda was agreeing. "I get it," Kate said, "if you talk, that person will think you talk to yourself, like Lyle."

Lyle could hear Drenda chuckle over Kate's phone. "I was just thinking about something I saw on TV last night," Drenda said, obviously trying to explain her laughing to the coworker.

"She's moving now," Kate said looking at the screen. She must have walked to where she can talk."

"That's correct," Drenda said. "I'm in an empty space right now. Is Lyle listening, too?"

"Roger that, Drenda. But I can't always see your images because I'm driving."

"Right, you're turning in the evidence in Phoenix. Here's more evidence, but not necessarily for the police. This morning I saw another familiar face in here. He wasn't in uniform, but I recognized the NC security assistant chief. His name is Ross."

"That bastard," Kate said. "I never trusted him after he didn't tell the restaurant manager to serve those two girls."

"He talked with one of Gudgel's staff," Drenda said. "They obviously knew each other. I have video."

"Good work," Lyle told their petite colleague.

"Somebody's coming," Drenda said, and she turned to broadcast a woman in a business suit a few feet from her.

"Ann," the woman said, using Drenda's alias, "You haven't talked to the governor today have you? He's not coming in, but he's having a strategy session at his condo-office and wants you to join them. He wants your thoughts on the polling."

"Okay. I can do that. What's the address? I've never been there." The woman told her the address and Kate jotted it down.

A few minutes later Drenda was in her car. "I told you about this place, didn't I? He has a condo near the capitol that he uses when he has a heavy schedule, especially during a legislative session."

"Why don't you turn off your glasses," Lyle said, "to preserve the battery. You can turn it on again at the governor's place."

Drenda's images went blank.

"Howard is going to be pissed to find the spy in his midst," Lyle said. *I pity that guy when Howard gets done with him. I'd like to watch.*

"Ross's got to be the person who leaked our Gay Pride Day idea," Kate said. "I wonder if he overheard my conversation with Howard."

Lyle glanced in her direction momentarily, then his attention was back on the road. "Let's wait until we get back, or tomorrow and talk to Howard in person. He can decide how to deal with Ross."

"And we need to include Max."

After about forty-five minutes, the governor's voice startled Lyle. "Drenda's broadcasting again," Kate said.

Kate muted their voices, but turned up the volume so they could hear Drenda. Electronics in Lyle's aging Mustang couldn't connect with her phone.

"That was interesting," Gudgel said, "and productive. Now, that they're gone, you can tell me about my polling numbers."

Lyle strained to see Kate's phone as Drenda moved her head, panning a large living room with multiple chairs, couches, and low tables covered with papers. The only person in view was the governor. Drenda obviously sat at one end of the room. Gudgel took a chair opposite her. "Would you like a drink before we get started?"

"No thank you governor."

"It's Rod, remember."

Drenda's view focused on a typed report in front of her as she read. "Initially I took note of the polling firm's sampling method. Recent research has indicated data quality problems with opt-in sampling. That means the results don't come from random selection but from recruiting ads in social media. Essentially people select *themselves*. Do you see what I mean?"

Kate held up her phone so Lyle could see the governor's face. "Uh huh, Gudgel said. "You know this is the first time I've seen you out of the office, Ann. You really look quite lovely today. Beauty *and* intelligence."

"Oh shit," Kate said.

CHAPTER 73

"I think we should get over there," Kate said. "It's not far. I put the address in the GPS." *Hang on Drenda.*

While Kate held up her phone listening to Drenda's survey discussion, Lyle pulled off the freeway at the next exit. "Where now?" he said, "Looks like left."

Kate looked from Drenda's video to the GPS map and back to the video. "Yes, left here, then a right and four miles down."

Kate could think only of the governor's womanizing past and history of propositioning employees. *Damn. We put Drenda at risk.*

"That's the essence of my report, governor," Kate heard Drenda say.

The governor's voice said, "that's good, so why don't we have a drink and relax."

Lyle made two turns, the tires squealing. "Can you tell her to get out of there?"

"I think she knows. Shh. I want to listen."

"You really know your stuff," Gudgel said. "May I see

your report?" His image became larger as he approached Drenda. He unbuttoned his collar and took off his tie. He leaned so close that his face filled most of the screen.

Kate wished she could reach out and strangle him. "Can we go faster?"

Moderate traffic on the six-lane commercial street didn't care about their urgency. They swerved around a slow gardener's pickup truck and trailer but had to stop at a red light, their path blocked by streaming cross traffic. Kate could hardly keep still.

When the light changed, the Mustang's rear tires chirped and the car surged forward with a growl. Over the exhaust noise Kate heard, "Please governor, no. I should leave." The shaky video showed only the governor's arms and chest. "No, governor, no."

Kate's heart raced as if *she* were Gudgel's target. She dialed 911.

"Yes, I want to report a sexual assault, a rape—happening now." She identified herself and gave the address. "It's at the governor's condo. My friend is being attacked. No I'm not there. I can hear her over the phone. I'm on my way there."

"You didn't say the governor was the rapist," Lyle said."

"I know. I thought it would sound crazy or political and they might not take me seriously."

Kate searched the road looking for openings in traffic. Another red light ahead and Lyle slowed, but it turned green before they reached the intersection, and they sailed through.

"Did you bring a gun?"

"To see the US Attorney? Wish I had."

Kate looked again at the GPS to see how close they were, then she heard a siren wailing. A Phoenix PD cruiser raced past them, lights flashing. Ahead she could see the beginning of the sprawling, upscale condominium project. A decorative stone wall surrounded two-story, adobe-like buildings. Every hundred yards bronze cowboys, cattle, and other standards of western art sat in wall recesses.

Solid iron fencing marked the main entrance to the complex. Large electric gates, operated by remotes or cards, kept out the unwanted. Lyle started to swing the Mustang's nose up the drive, but Kate shouted, "No." Up ahead she saw the flash of red and blue lights coming from another opening in the wall.

Lyle spun the steering wheel and they lurched back on the road. A small sign on the wall said "private entrance." That had to be the governor's.

He turned in, then had to swerve to the left to avoid slamming into a police car in the drive. Although the iron gate stood wide open, an Arizona State Guard Humvee sprawled sideways in the lane. Two guardsmen in camo uniforms stood beside their vehicle, arms crossed on their chests.

Lyle pulled toward the exit lane near the Phoenix PD car. Its driver hit his siren for one short, piercing blast. Both cops in the car shouted and waved their arms. One of the guardsmen took his time to uncross his arms and beckon the cops forward. One uniformed officer jumped out and shouted at the guardsmen to get out of the way or they would be arrested. The beefy guys in camouflage seemed unmoved.

Kate bounded out of the Mustang and ran toward the driveway confrontation. "I'm the one who called 911," she yelled. "My friend is inside the governor's unit about to get raped. Get this vehicle the hell out of here."

The policeman looked from the guardsmen to Kate and back. "Hear that?" he said placing his hand on the butt of his pistol.

"Ma'am, relax," one of the guardsmen said. "The governor is in a business conference. You can't disturb them now."

Kate wanted to get her hands on the guy, her frustration turning to panic. Before she could think, she heard a loud car horn. Lyle honked and waved at her to come back. A car had just left the lot leaving the exit gate open. She hopped in and Lyle accelerated down the exit lane. The police car followed scraping against the gate as it swung shut. A sign pointed to the governor's address. "It's just ahead," Kate said.

She tried to reconnect to Drenda's video, but gave up as Lyle pulled to a stop in front of a low patio wall. Behind the wall, a solid-looking wood door. They ran to the door and heard Drenda shout 'help" over Kate's phone.

Lyle hammered on the door briefly, then stepped back and kicked the door latch. Nothing.

Two uniformed police officers reached the door. "She's yelling for help," Kate said holding up her phone.

"Please stand back," one of the officers told Kate and Lyle.

He yelled, "police. Open up." But a second later he took a half step from the door and kicked the latch with his cowboy boot. The door opened with the sound of splintering wood.

"Help."

Kate, Lyle and the two cops all heard it. The younger of the two officers dashed down a hallway first, Kate and Lyle right behind.

"Stop," shouted the officer as Kate followed him through the bedroom door.

Governor Gudgel, wearing only his dress shirt, crawled on hands and knees across a king-size bed and reached for a nightstand drawer. The officer grabbed his arm and wrestled him to the bed. Lyle grabbed Gudgel's other arm and pulled. Drenda moved off the bed to pick up the remains of her torn dress. Kate sighed with relief to see Drenda still wore her panties.

"I kicked him in the balls," Drenda said.

The second cop moved in, taking over for Lyle. The officers muscled the governor off the bed and ordered him to get his pants on.

"I'm the fucking governor, you asshole. You'll be fired for this."

"Yes sure, governor. But first you have to put your pants on."

Kate pulled a sheet around Drenda and hugged her. She helped her pull on her bra and torn dress. While the first officer handcuffed the governor, the second looked into the nightstand drawer and, using a corner of a pillowcase, lifted out a semi-automatic pistol.

"What do you suppose he planned to do with that?" said a man in a suit who walked up to the end of the bed. "I'm Lieutenant Decker," he said waving a badge.

"Officer, take the suspect downstairs while I find out who these folks are."

"Decker," Lyle said. He identified himself as a former PPD detective. "I'm Lyle Deming."

"Aren't you the detective who—" Decker said.

"Yup. Now could we see that our friend here gets any medical attention she needs."

"I'm okay, Lyle," Drenda said. "Now."

CHAPTER 74

The police lieutenant had responded to the call when the governor's name was mentioned on the air. Soon a captain showed up to organize the multitude of officers, crime scene techs, and EMTs who turned out. Lyle felt satisfaction seeing the two Arizona Guardsmen being questioned by detectives. They would soon be cuffed. Interfering with the police was a felony.

Drenda suffered only bruises on her left arm and a leg as the governor manhandled her into the bedroom. Lyle and Kate accompanied her to the police department.

She later told Lyle and Kate how the governor went from chief executive to a not-so-subtle seducer to an abuser in a matter of minutes after the last staffer left the condo. When she didn't respond to Gudgel's compliments and advances, he became more direct with suggestions how they could have fun sex, he being the governor and all. That Gudgel might have been reaching for a loaded gun at the time the officer confronted him, Lyle thought, might complicate his attorney's plea for immediate release.

Detectives questioned Lyle and Kate and their account of breaking into the governor's condo matched that of the responding officers. They waited for Drenda to tell her story to detectives. As they sat in a meeting area furnished with utilitarian tables, chairs, and a coffee machine, Kate reviewed the video on her phone.

"Look at this," she said. "Somehow Drenda put her glasses down in the right place. She showed Lyle the governor holding his small victim by her arm in the living room. Although upside down again, the governor was clearly visible.

"Son of a bitch," Lyle said. "How'd you like to have ten minutes in a room alone with him?"

"Five minutes would be enough." Kate was *tough*.

He guessed that Drenda's work as an undercover operative for the park might give Gudgel's attorneys courtroom ammunition, but attempted rape is attempted rape. Unfortunately Drenda would have to testify, unless Gudgel managed a plea deal. Even so, he would also face charges ranging from public corruption to blackmail to accessory to murder that could add up to a life sentence. Lyle remembered that Arizona Governor Evan Mecham was impeached and removed from office in the late 1980s for charges that didn't approach the level of Gudgel's criminality.

He phoned the US Attorney and explained why they were late.

"The governor's in jail?" the prosecutor said. "Now I really need to see your evidence."

"Then there's the Arizona State Guard, aka Gudgel's militia," Lyle said. "After today their star is going to take more polishing than they can muster." He summarized how guardsmen interfered with police to stop them from responding to a rape call and that other guardsmen were implicated in covering up murder in Fremont County. *With the guard's head cut off, maybe it will go away.*

The next day Lyle and Kate spent more than seven hours at the US attorney's office, followed by a talk with the Maricopa County district attorney. Both jurisdictions could have a piece of the governor. It would take time to investigate Gudgel, Ecoperi security, the Arizona State Guard, and other parties and to draft indictments.

In the meantime, the business of attracting and entertaining thousands of Nostalgia City tourists could proceed without governmental slander. Kate could plan an LGBTQ event at the park, and Drenda's 1970s socio-cultural milestones display could receive funding.

Driving back to Nostalgia City from the prosecutors, Lyle felt exhausted from the long day, from the long weeks, in all the ways life can exhaust you. Hate drains the spirit even if you think you're just an observer.

Close to home they passed through the freeway off-ramp at the San Navarro Highway, State Route 247. Traffic moved smoothly.

"Looks like this'll be finished soon," Lyle said. "Irwin Construction got the message. How did you get them to stop stalling and finish the road?"

"I had a copy of the contract," Kate said. "I knew Irwin wasn't telling the truth, so I needed to use just a little vamping."

Lyle steered down the offramp. *Maybe that was it.*

NOTE FROM THE AUTHOR

Thank you for reading my book. If you enjoyed this, please consider writing a brief review on your favorite book website. Reviews help readers (and writers) many ways. Ultimately, online reviews allow writers to continue to produce more books for you to read.

If you would like to find out about the other books in this Nostalgia City series, or would like to contact me, please visit my website at https://baconsmysteries.com

ACKNOWLEDGEMENTS

Writing this book required help. My thanks go to critique-group members and beta readers Linda Townsdin, Mary Adler, Ruth Myers, Barbara Ristine, Patricia Smith, Marilyn Sides, Karen Dunaway, Ottilia Schershel, Jonnie Richardson, and Emily Ross. Thanks to my line editor Christel Hall.

As with some past books, Washoe County, Nev., Chief Medical Examiner and Coroner Dr. Laura Knight, MD, helped me with details of death and dying. I'm grateful for her assistance. Any errors on these subjects are mine, not hers.

Some of the information on hate groups I obtained from the encyclopedic research of the Southern Poverty Law Center. The SPLC, mentioned by name herein, is to be congratulated—and financially supported—for its work exposing the hate that infests every state in the union.

Thanks to Lauri Wellington of Black Opal Books who helped launch this series a number of years ago.

Early in the writing of this book I suffered an arm injury and had to write and edit many chapters using voice software. Fortunately, I recovered. Not everyone is as lucky, and I dedicate this book to the patience, courage, and determination of people with disabilities.

ABOUT THE AUTHOR

Mark S. Bacon began his career as a Southern California newspaper police reporter, one of his crime stories becoming key evidence in a murder case that spanned decades.

After working for two newspapers, he moved to advertising and marketing when he became a copywriter for Knott's Berry Farm, the large theme park down the road from Disneyland. Experience working at Knott's formed part of the inspiration for his creation of Nostalgia City theme park. He later wrote commercials and ads for an LA advertising agency and was public relations manger for a financial trade association.

Before turning to fiction, Bacon wrote business books including *Do-It-Yourself Direct Marketing*, printed in four languages and three editions, and named best business book of the year by the *Library Journal*. His articles have appeared in the *Washington Post, Cleveland Plain Dealer, Denver Post, San Antonio Express News*, and many other publications. Most recently he was a correspondent for the *San Francisco Chronicle*.

Death in Nostalgia City, the first book in the mystery series, was recommended for book clubs by the American Library Association. *Desert Kill Switch*, the second series book, was the top fiction winner in the 2018 Great Southwest Book Festival.

Bacon taught journalism as a member of the adjunct faculty at the University of Nevada – Reno, Cal Poly University – Pomona, and the University of Redlands. He earned an MA in mass media from UNLV and a BA in journalism from Fresno State. He and his wife, Anne, live in Reno with their golden retriever.